THE DEMONS WITHIN

THE MAINGARD CHRONICLES, BOOK 2

CARL F NORTHWOOD

PUBLISHED BY CARL F NORTHWOOD AT INGRAMSPARK

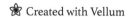

For Mark,
who blazed the trail for me.

AUTHOR'S NOTES

Continuing the saga of Bex and Ishtara, et al and expanding the world of Maingard (and beyond) has been an absolute joy. But continued thanks needs to be given to my long-suffering partner Nicci for all her support, but also for her dynamic design work. Once again, thanks to Pippa for the incredible cover art.

A big thanks to Mandi and the rest of the Act Two mob for support and motivation. Finally, a big shout out to all those from the Alameda and Redborne RPG groups that helped keep the love of Fantasy alive for me all those years ago.

PROLOGUE

With the Royal Pennant of the House of Barstt signifying it was on the business of the Red Throne flapping from the stern pole, the small ship had cast its moorings and had slipped from the Royal Harbour. The heavily armed guard ships had let it through the blockade that had been in force since the discovery of the kidnapping of the princesses, and the assassination of King Anjoan. The ship was *The Dagger*, a small brig owned by Count Eglebon Dutte. The aptly named brig cut through the early evening waters with ease, its sleek outline making it one of the fastest ships in Miangard.

The captain, Raust, looked out and nervously spied the black clouds ahead. He didn't like the look of the weather and spat to his side for good luck. He rubbed his shaven head as he looked over his crew. Four good men were on deck right now with another four resting in bunks below. The ship's cook would be cleaning the galley as the main meal had been taken early which was usual when passengers were on board.

Raust looked back at the cabin door and gave a slight chuckle. The passenger had annoyed him ever since he had come aboard but had retired after the evening meal looking worse for wear from the ship's movement. If the landlubber had thought that bit of the journey had been rough, then he would get a rude shock when that weather ahead hit.

He felt the rain on his weathered face and knew it was going to be a rough journey and not just because of the weather ahead. For ten years he had been in the employ of Count Dutte and never had he seen him like he had been that afternoon. The Count had been agitated beyond words, wringing his hands as he passed his orders on. The previous orders to sail to Marneheim had been succeeded by new ones to sail to the Isle of Winds. A passenger, a herald from the court, was to be transported to either Count Neechy or Lord Visney commanding the Third and Fourth Squadrons respectively.

The Count had returned later with the herald, a middle-aged man wearing the red livery of the palace and carrying a small bag containing his orders for Visney and Neechy. For a man who had just conveyed orders of utmost urgency, Eglebon Dutte had acted strangely after ushering the herald on board. He had held Raust in conversation for nigh on quarter of an hour, ignoring the herald's frantic attempts to interrupt. As he spoke had looked anxiously up and down the quay and had then finally acknowledged the herald's protestations and left Raust speaking midsentence.

Raust pulled himself back into the present and sighed. Nobles seemed to have nothing and everything to worry about. He looked across to the mainmast and saw that Grose had not reefed the sail yet.

"Grose! Hurry it up, you lazy bastard!" He couldn't see the young sailor and wondered whether he had gone overboard as the waves rose around the now struggling ship. He switched his gaze to the other side of the ship and called out to the crew.

"Ganner, Yorik! Where's Grose?" He shifted from his vantage point and made his way over to where the young boy had been working. The deck was wet from the rain but no worse than the area he had just left. Of the youngster there was no sign. Raust gripped the rail, his big fists clenched hard, as he leant out and peered into the darkness. He called out again, louder than before. It was then that he realised that there hadn't been a response from Ganner or Yorik.

"Tobe's Tits!" he exclaimed to no-one but himself. If they had all gone below, he would skin the lot of them. He stepped lithely of the deck of the rocking ship only to find the port side empty of life as well. He turned and looked back to the stern of 'The Dagger'.

His heart leapt into his mouth as a shadow rose out of the deck in front of him. The dark shape shifted into the figure of a man, taller but slenderer than the captain. The ghostly figure lunged forward and Raust staggered, finding it hard to focus as his eyes clouded over. The exclamation he was about to make died with him as the short sword penetrated his throat. The sword slowly withdrew, and he sagged forward to fall onto the deck. The last thing he saw were the black felt boots of his murderer turn and walk softly and silently to the cabin in the stern.

Modral the Assassin paused before the cabin door, his hand reaching for the latch. The banded leather armour, black as the shadows he worked from, flexed as he moved, neither stifling of hindering him at any point. He was grateful for the mask that covered the lower part of his face that added a little protection from the stinging wind. Sea spray dripped from the cowl of his hood as he hesitated at the door to the cabin.

He had already despatched the crew below silently and with ease. Not one had stirred in their bunks as he slit their throats with as much indifference as a man might cut bread. After all, that is why his services were as expensive as they were. His expertise and his ability to ply his trade of murder and subterfuge at a moment's notice carried a high price that almost merited the exorbitant fee that the Guild applied.

The client had given exact details regarding the layout of the ship and not only the number of crew and passengers but where they should be at certain points of the day. This was the second mission that Modral had carried out for the client, and he smiled, knowing that The Guild would be keeping notes for the possibility of extortion at a later date. In this line of business, you never knew when you would need to call in an extra favour. The Guild itself was shrouded in secrecy. It was well known within the other rogue guilds, such as the Thieves' Guild, that the authorities had agents within their ranks, but the Brotherhood of Karnast was small and highly secretive. Neither the Crown nor even the Phantom had managed to infiltrate its ranks, but even the occupants of the Red Throne, in its sordid past, had used the Guild for its own ends.

Modral now paused, mentally ticking off the crew in his head. 'One missing' he thought, and he realised that the last crew member would be at the stern of the ship, working on the spanker sail. He pulled himself up onto the cabin roof and crept towards the stern.

The old wizened sailor never stood a chance. The rolling of *The Dagger* didn't affect Modral as he leapt from the cabin roof, crashing into the last sailor. The wiry figure was propelled onto the gunwales of the ship and turned, half stunned, to face his attacker. The assassin landed with a roll, and had come up to meet the shocked sailor with the point of his sword. With little satisfaction showing on his stony face, Modral pushed the man away, the blade sliding from the sailor's stomach.

The assassin turned his attention to the focus of his contract and once again approached the cabin door. His breathing slow and controlled, he opened the door and stepped inside. The herald sat near the centre of the room in a high-backed chair, certainly the worse for wear due to the motion of the ship. A small table was at his side, covered in maps and charts. The two lanterns swung alarmingly from the cabin roof as the swells picked up and rocked the ship even more. The herald, dressed in the red robes of House Barstt looked up as he entered, whatever colour left in his face draining at the sight of death walking into his cabin. He snatched at the small satchel that was on top of the charts and tried to pull a small dirk from it.

Modral closed the distance between the two men swiftly and silently. His dark eyes seemed to bore into the scared, old man in front of him. His sword was already at guard, pointing unwaveringly at the herald.

"I am a herald of the Red Throne sent by Queen Sarsi herself. It is an offence punishable by death to interfere with my business!" the old man stammered as he held the dirk up between himself and Modral. His hand shook as he did so. Modral said nothing in reply and reached into a belt pouch with his free hand. He withdrew a large coin and flicked it from his fingers causing it to land in the herald's lap. It was an old copper crown from centuries past but the king's head that should have looked up at the herald as his gaze turned towards it, had been obliterated by a skull scratched into the soft metal.

"That coin was marked with death by the Grand Master Karnast in Tannaheim Hall." Modral's voice was neutral, his words spoken in a monotone. The Karnast he referred to was the Guild master of the Assassins' Guild in the Western Kingdoms. It was a nom de guerre, more a title than a name as it was in recognition of the first assassin and the founder of the first guild. He carried on.

"It is your death, a death from which there is no escape. Strike me down and another will take my place and you will be hunted until your last breath." It was the liturgy of the Assassins' Guild, an oath and warning given that the contract will be fulfilled.

The dark figure of Modral danced forward, the blade a perfect extension of his arm as his strike hit home. The herald's eyes had barely lifted from the coin that had landed in his lap as the tip of the blade sank into his chest. Modral made sure that the herald was dead by a coup de grace across his throat.

It was only at this point that he allowed himself a wry smile. The job was completed apart from a couple of loose ends. He hooked one of the lanterns down and opened the small glass door. Reaching into the small satchel that the herald clutched in his dead hands, he took out the orders for the commanders of the Third and Fourth Squadrons and set light to them with the flame. Satisfied that no trace of the orders survived, Modral then went back onto the deck.

Once the squall had settled down, maybe in the morning, he would lower one of the small boats on board and let himself drift away from the scene of the crime. On the morning tide, a ship would sail from Tannaheim with a similar course to The Dagger, looking for him. Once back in Tannaheim, he would once again disappear into the Maze under the city until the next time his services were called for.

Churt entered the room under the Inn of the Luckless Wench on Cheap Street. Its location was known to only a few in the city and even those drinking above in the bar and tap room weren't aware of it. This was one of the meeting places of Tikar Welk, the shadowy figure known as the Phantom.

The table that took centre place in the room was covered with exotic fruits and hams. Six of the seven seats were taken, the empty one stood with its back to the door and he sidled into it. The tall back stood high over his head as he reached forward and grabbed an apple from the array in front of him. He looked at the others around the table. Opposite him was Yanna, a girl of similar age to him with brown ragged hair and clothes to match. She smiled at him as he sat and grabbed an apple, mimicking his movements. As she bit into the fruit, the juices left streaks in the grime around her mouth.

On either side of Churt sat two adults. To his left was a beautiful woman with long, black hair styled in ringlets. She wore a long, purple dress that best displayed her slim figure whilst her white skin was adorned with several pieces of silver jewellery. The man to his right was obviously a soldier or had been one at some point. He turned to Churt as he crunched into the apple and acknowledged him with a slight nod. His face was worn, and the absence of hair gave him a slightly freakish look and made his age hard to distinguish. Churt noticed the familiar ridges of chainmail under the man's white tunic.

On the other side of the table, on one side of Yanna was an old man, his grey beard unkempt and straggly and his dark grey robes had obviously seen better days. A gnarled and twisted stick rested against his arm and his aged hands had the appearance of talons when he reached out for food from the table. On the other side of the young girl sat a male youth, older than Churt and Yanna, but he had not yet reached the need for shaving. He had a cocksure look about himself and his black hair was untidy and dirty. As Churt looked across at him, he smiled, revealing a blackened, crooked row of teeth.

"Always the apples, eh Churt?" The stern authoritative voice of the man who occupied the final seat at the head of the table brought him back to his immediate surroundings. His head was bowed forward slightly, and his face obscured by the voluminous hooded cape that covered his head and body.

"You get good ones, Tikar. You stop getting ones this good and I might change." His familiar tone drew a short intake of breath from the lady next to him.

"It is okay, Lady Theres. Churt and I go back a long way, despite his young years. He wouldn't be the same Churt without his cheek. But I have asked you all here to hear what I must say at a time of great peril and threat to our city, kingdom and world and to once again ask for your help.

"No doubt that you will have heard through your contacts that our King has been murdered. The information that we gave to the Palace was not heeded in the way that we thought it would be." There were some nervous looks around the table and the young man next to Yanna gave a wry smile.

"He wasn't the King of all of us. He didn't do a lot for the likes of Yanna, Churt and me." The young man blushed as he said it, now a little embarrassed for speaking his mind. The hooded man paused before answering.

"That may be so, Tobian. It has been noted by all in our organisation that there has been and may always be social differences between the classes. That will not change no matter who sits on the Red Throne. But Anjoan was the King of Danaria and he has kept the peace since the Orc Wars. Trade has flourished and on the whole his rule has been just."

"But now the Lord of the Inns will take the Throne? Will that improve things?" Tobian continued, his face now flushing with anger. The Lord of the Inns was how many people of the Maze referred to Prince Garlen.

"It appears not. My sources within the Palace have advised that Garlen has given up his right to the Red Throne and has requested that his mother take it instead." Tikar Welk, the hooded man, looked up before continuing. Deep within the folds of the hood, Tobian could make out two piercing blue eyes but the rest of the features were obscured by shadows and a leather faceplate that the man wore over the lower part of his face. Whilst the news of the assassination of Anjoan was known to them, the revelation that Queen Sarsi had been given the Throne was new to all. There was a slight murmur of surprise.

"The assassination of King Anjoan, for assassination it was, is only part of why I meet with you now. This is the third such meeting that I have had this night. Queen Sarsi and her son, Garlen, are about to lead Danaria to war." This proclamation resulted in sharp intakes of breath around the table.

"With who?" Lady Theres leant forward and asked the question that everyone wanted to ask.

"It must be against the Orcs again." The bald soldier next to Churt reasoned. Tikar Welk shook his head slowly and raised his hand.

"No, Ser Gavan. It is not the Orcs. What I am about to say may sound preposterous, but I am inclined to believe it. Maingard has been invaded by a foe from a world beyond our plane. Mystics have long thought that these worlds may exist but there is no knowledge of anyone travelling between them, that is, until now.

"A force has already taken Jacarna and Tarim. Both cities have fallen, and their populations are being enslaved as we speak. This happened barely a week ago. The murder of Anjoan is only the first part of their plan against Danaria. It is an obvious tactic to spread confusion and fear amongst the Houses of the West and to reduce the effectiveness of their leadership in the war ahead.

"The Royal Princesses, Moren and Ingren have also been abducted and their whereabouts is unknown, though the Palace has speculated that they are being taken to Jacarna to be held as hostages."

"Extra-planar travel is unheard of, Tikar. It can't be done." Lady Theres stated, still in a state of shock at the news.

"Magic is not truly embraced within the West, my Lady," replied Ser Gavan. "Just because we have not achieved the power to do this does not necessarily mean that others haven't."

"It can be done." Over the hubbub came a voice, at first quiet and then a little louder to gain everyone's interest. "It can be done," repeated Churt.

"And what do you know about magic?" said Theres almost disdainfully.

"Nothing, my lady. Except that it scares the pants off me." explained Churt.

"I asked Churt to address you all as he addressed the others at the other two meetings. Churt has been gathering information for me for the last few weeks on the slaver Yab M'Vil." Tikar announced. Tobian spat on the floor as he heard the name.

"That scum, I don't know why we don't just hit him. Take him out once and for all."

There were nods and murmurs of agreement from Ser Gavan and Yanna.

"There is no need. He is dead." Churt turned white as he revisited the horrific scenes from the night before. Tobian was gobsmacked, instead resorting to a hearty guffaw.

"Dead?" said Yanna. "Who killed him?"

"She did. The demoness." Churt almost shook as he relived the tale for the fourth time that day.

"Yab's men found something in the forest several days ago. They called it a Lampanyx, which I think, means 'fire demon' in their language. It escaped and killed them all."

"How?"

"What does it look like?"

"How did you escape?"

The questions came thick and fast and even though Churt had heard them all this evening already, he still struggled to find the right words. Thankfully Tikar intervened.

"Churt described this 'lampanyx' to me earlier today. A fire demon – or demoness, this one is a female – sounds apt. Human in form and covered in flames. How it escaped is conjecture at the moment, but other sources have advised it merged with a woman, a woman of Maingard, and is existing in a symbiotic relationship with her.

"I say other sources, because she has been at the Palace. She addressed the Throne to say she had travelled here to give warning of the invasion and then transformed into her demoness side to scare the court after Anjoan had been killed. Apparently, some of the Lords and Generals didn't believe about extra planar travel either."

"Well, if she killed that fat pervert M'Vil then she is a friend of mine!" exclaimed Tobian, a smile once more upon his lips.

"Yes, she is on our side for now. But I need your help now. Yanna," the hood turned towards the young girl, "the woman that is now part demoness is a native of Samak. Her name is Bex. Find out all there is to know about her and her past and report back by dawn. Take no more than two others. I can spare no more to help you." He turned and surveyed the room to look at Tobian and the bald knight.

"We have no option but to side with the Red Throne. If Tannaheim falls, then we will all face a fate worse than your social injustice, Tobian. The events of today were accomplished with the assistance of people from this city, either knowing or unwittingly. Find them. Turn over every rock and look in every nook in the city. Someone must know something. I want to know who the traitors are. Start with the scum who helped take the Princesses. Find out who they were and work through a list of their families, associates or whores.

"Yanna, when you are done with your part, you will become our liaison with the Throne. You have talked with the Hawk before; he may listen to you more now. Lady Theres and Churt, I have something special for you. I will speak to you both in a moment." He stood, his hands planted flat on the table before him and he addressed the party once more.

"I will not be able to be reached for the foreseeable future. When you have news, return and speak with The Brandyman." He indicated the old man who sat next to Yanna who, until now, had remained out of the proceedings. He nodded and his face broke into a toothless grin.

"I will compile the information and feed it to young Yanna here." His voice didn't sound as old as he looked.

"Where will you be, Tikar?" enquired Ser Gavan.

"Where will I be? I will be doing what I do best," answered the Phantom cryptically.

2

———

"Where are we?" whispered Moren. She clutched her sister tightly as they both sat huddled on the floor of the cabin. The room was no bigger than a cupboard, with barely enough room for either of the girls to lie flat out. The only light came from outside the door, a small grating slightly higher than eye level that allowed just enough light from the lantern beyond to break the darkness.

Ingren had regained consciousness after her little sister and had awoke to find Moren curled up next to her sobbing. She had felt shattered and ached, as if she had risen from a tumultuous night, and had lain still for a few moments listening painfully to Moren's sobs. The older girl had wrapped her arm around her sister and held her tight. Realising her elder sister was awake had quietened Moren's sobbing and had brought a brief smile to her face. The smile was dashed from her face as Ingren jumped up to investigate the room.

Princess Ingren moved slowly around the room poking at the walls and floor before standing tall in front of the door. She had to stand on tip toes to peer through the grating.

"What can you see, Ingren?" Moren stood and grabbed at

her elder sister's arm. Ingren shook her sister off and continued to look through the grating, angling her head to look as far left and right as she could along the corridor that was on the other side.

"Nothing!" she hissed, and her younger sister stomped away to the far corner of the small room. She instantly regretted her quick temper and turned to Moren. "It's only a corridor. And to be honest, I have no idea where we are." Ingren took a final look at what lay beyond the grating before lowering herself to stand flat footed. She rested her forehead against the wood of the door. Moren paused before answering. She looked up at her sister and stared wide eyed at her.

"Ingren, I am really scared. What those men did to Old Master Tarnal and Diri and Klush. It was horrible!" Ingren bent down and hugged her sister. The men who had abducted them had burst in on their lesson with Master Tarnal at the Palace. During the fracas, the frail Master had been killed along with their cousins, Dirian and Klush.

"I know, Mori. I know. But you have to stay strong. You are a Barstt and right now, Father and Garlen will be turning the city inside out trying to find us." She kissed Moren's forehead and held her tight, daring to believe her own words. They had the effect upon the younger girl that she hoped they would have. Moren stopped sobbing and relaxed her grip on Ingren.

"Do you think so, Ingren?"

"Of course, Mori. They will find us." Ingren smiled at her sister and drew Moren's head forward to rest upon her chest. They will be looking, she thought, completely unaware of her father's fate. The only problem was she didn't think they were still in Tannaheim.

3

Gneral Karchek, the Lord Commander of the Almighty Emperor's Host sat on King Renta's throne. He wore his customary armour except for his helm. His grey battle-scarred face bore the fresh wound given to him by the Princess Rothannir, a deep cut above his left eye making his visage even more terrifying. Narki had crudely sewn it shut though the wound was puffy and swollen.

He raised the silver goblet to his thin lips and sipped at the red wine, almost oblivious to the taste. If truth be told, he just wanted to return to his chambers and sleep. His head swam and he had been drifting in and out of the first stages of fever for most of the last few hours. Karchek though, hated his counterpart, General Margran, and he didn't want to appear weak in front of the small blue-skinned general.

The throne room had been cleared since the fall of Jacarna and King Renta's death. It still showed its scars of the vicious fighting that had seen the fall of the once proud city state. Smashed windows still gaped, and the ruined walls stood as a monument to the fate of the Jacarnan forces.

The four black armoured guards that were stationed at the

four corners of the throne slammed the steel shod butts of their halberds to the floor as the doors to the throne room swung open slowly. Dragging his left leg behind him, a short, black-robed man limped in. He made his way to the centre of the large room. His hair was cut short and dyed blue, the woad that coloured it also forming it into several uneven spikes. On his shoulder sat a small grey rat, its long tail curled around the back of the man's neck to the other shoulder. Karchek fixed his glare on the man, aware as always that the man and the rat shared many facial characteristics. The man's nose was long and his front teeth sat forward, protruding over the man's lower lip.

The blue haired man bowed slightly to the seated giant and clasped his hands together in front of his lowered head. The salutation was quick and short-lived, the rat like man stood again and announced with a loud voice.

"The Almighty Emperor's Lord Commander of the Host, His Excellency, General Margran." At the announcement he turned and spread his arms wide before repeating his bow, this time in the direction of the entrance. General Margran entered the throne room at the head of a considerable entourage. His guards were garbed in black armour like Karchek's guards, but whilst the guards standing next to the grey giant wore red cloaks, the newcomers wore green.

Margran himself was the complete opposite of Karchek. He was a dwarf in comparison, standing only five feet tall and wore a shirt of silver mail that ended at his knees and a dark green cloak thrown over his shoulders. His white hair was luxurious and long, tied back into a ponytail that almost reached the hem of his armour. Margran's skin was a shade of deep blue and his eyes were a soulless black. As he walked towards the throne in which Karchek sat, he stripped of his mail gloves revealing perfectly manicured nails adorning slender fingers. He handed the gloves to the blue haired man who now stood waiting.

"Wintel, fetch me some wine," the blue skinned warlord ordered the blue haired man who quickly beckoned one of the servant members of the entourage over. A young boy hobbled forward, naked except for leg irons that made his gait incredibly cumbersome. The young boy carried a wineskin and a tankard.

Wintel snatched the tankard from the boy whilst the rat that sat on his shoulder chattered constantly as the boy fumbled with the stopper to the wineskin. Nervously he poured the red liquid into the tankard, sloshing some over the rim.

"Careful, boy!" exclaimed Wintel. Once the tankard was filled, he handed it back to the young boy who slowly and apprehensively raised it to his lips and sipped from it. Satisfied that the wine was not poisoned, Wintel handed it to his Lord.

"One cannot be too careful," shuddered Margran as he gulped several mouthfuls down. "These youths serve their purpose well." He laughed sinisterly as he waved his free hand towards the wine bearing youth who hobbled back into line. As he withdrew, Karchek noticed the fresh scars on the boy's back, scars cut deep over the tanned skin.

"I am sure your youths serve you well, Margran," sneered Karchek, all too aware of his counterpart's desire of young males.

"They do, Karchek. They do indeed," laughed Margran. "But I make sure my bitches don't fight back." He nodded towards the pus-filled wound above Karchek's eye.

"A moment's carelessness, no more," countered the grey giant. "She won't be doing it again." He reached gingerly to the wound and could almost feel the yellow gunge inside ready to erupt like a volcano over the side of his face. Momentarily he faced two blue skinned generals as his eyes fought to focus properly.

"Let us discuss the next phase of the *knartevilder* in private."

"As you wish." Karchek took a second to make sure the

dizziness had passed before standing and leading the way to an antechamber behind the throne room. The small room was sparsely furnished with just a table and several chairs. Tapestries depicting a stag hunt adorned the walls. As the door to the small chamber closed behind them Karchek turned and faced the small blue skinned warlord.

"Why are you here, Margran?" The grey giant stood imposingly over the other general. Margran seemed to take no notice of the threatening behaviour of his large counterpart and gently sipped his flagon of wine.

"The Emperor has commanded that I give you assistance on your next phase of the *knartevilder*, the assault on Tannaheim and Danaria."

"I don't need your help, Margran." Karchek's head swam. "Why have you gone crawling to the Emperor, you perverted lick-spittle."

"Everything I do is in the Emperor's Name, Karchek. I am sure you understand that."

"Right now, you ignorant dwarf, Anjoan's whelps are on their way here! They are on their way here to be my hostages whilst I negotiate the surrender of their forces wholesale to our own. A relatively peaceful subjugation after the slaughter of Jacarna and Tarim. The defenders here were too stubborn for their own good. Too many now lay as food for the ravens instead of swelling our ranks and slave pens."

"Speak for yourself, Karchek. My forces are nearly at full strength and already we prepare for the subjugation of the Eastern Ports.

"Adept Sarwent has already reported back to the Emperor and informed him of the progress of the *knartevilder*. He seems pleased at the twenty slave hulks that I have despatched so far to Homeworld and has commanded me to give your forces whatever aid I can spare." The small General continued.

"If you get in my way, I will snap you like a stick, you

poisoned dwarf." Karchek knew that as soon as Margran had announced that the Emperor had sanctioned the change to the initial plan, then he wouldn't have any further recourse against Margran and would have to accept his help. Whilst the Host fought for the Emperor, the reward earned by the common troops was the looting, murder and rape of the native populous. The Generals however, demanded something else: respect. Every city taken, every slave sent back to Homeworld only enhanced their reputation amongst the Host. That was all they lived for, to serve the Emperor and to have their deeds written down in the annals of the Host. The despatch of twenty slave hulks was a good prize for the conquest of one city. Nearly two thousand prisoners could be crammed shoulder to shoulder into each one. Forty thousand souls for the Almighty Emperor. Margran had certainly worked fast with the clearing of Tarim. Blessed with a bit of luck, Karchek sneered to himself. Trust Margran to have been handed the least defended city. A week into his subjugation of Jacarna and only six slave hulks had left for Homeworld.

"The Almighty Emperor wills it, Karchek. I am sure I will be able to give you the necessary aid – after, of course, I have finished with the Eastern Ports."

"Stay out of my way, Margran. That is a warning – your only warning. I hope you catch some sort of cock-rot from one of your boy whores." The grey giant downed his wine and stared back at the smaller man. The old scars on his face seemed to throb as if they were alive and he bared his teeth in a vicious snarl. If Margran was intimidated, then he didn't show it.

"Very well, Karchek. Don't come shouting for me when you are up against it then. Now, I have work to get back to. Tarim is nearly empty – nearly but not quite." He smiled falsely and turned to leave. Karchek clenched his fists, fighting back the urge to send a rebuke or, even worse, a physical attack after him. The doors opened as if by magic for Margran and he strode through, his dark green cloak flapping about his legs.

Karchek bellowed with rage as the doors closed. He took his anger out on the sturdy table, flipping it over as he bellowed again. His head swam and his stomach churned, the fever taking hold again in his moment of ire and stress.

"Darnag!" he called for his steward before the cramps hit his stomach and brought him to his knees.

4

Jerone Witchguardian ran. He ran like the wind and had been running for what seemed an eternity. In reality, it had only been an hour or so since he had left the burning tower and his mentor and companion Janda. As he ran, he felt the leaves and branches of the trees whip against the bare skin of his arms and chest. The whooping of the pursuers echoed about the forest and he had to focus as he ran to make sure the sounds were still behind him. His lungs heaved and his chest was almost bursting with the strain and adrenalin.

The bleeding from the cut that Janda had given him to confirm his passage to manhood had subsided despite his exertions and the ache had dulled slightly. His bare chest was a dirty, mottled mess of blood and soot that seeped down to the top of his fur trousers. His knife was held tightly in one hand and in the other he held a small branch that he had grabbed as he ran and that he hoped he could use as a cudgel if he needed to. His small satchel containing the herbs and roots that he had picked for Janda bounced at his hip, with the charm that Janda had made stored safely inside.

Something niggled inside his head. He sensed that his chasers were spread out in an arc behind him. His pursuers were warriors, the young men of the tribe who were used to hunting and skirmishing with the neighbouring peoples of the forest. Even though he was running for his life, they should have caught him by now. It was as if they were herding him towards something or someone. If that were so, he knew that he didn't have much choice. He would be unable to fight his way past them and go back the way he had come. That meant going on to meet whatever or whoever was waiting for him.

Up ahead of him was the Bridge, the bridge that crossed the White River and led to the lands that lay to the south of the forest. Little more than twisted vines and ropes over the river, it was the point of safety he sought. If he could make it to the Bridge with enough of a gap between him and the pursuers behind, then he might be safe. He hoped they wouldn't dare to follow and track him through the Border-lands into the lands of the 'Others' as those not of the Forest were called. He also prayed to Herne that he would be far enough across the Bridge so as to be out of range of their spears.

He hurdled a fallen tree trunk and stumbled as he landed, sprawling headfirst into the undergrowth. His crude cudgel flew from his hands. As he scrambled to all fours, he looked over his shoulder and spotted movement some hundred yards behind him. 'Damn them,' he thought, 'damn every last one of the bastards. They were too close.' He had failed Janda. Herne only knows why she had put any faith in him. Hadn't he failed the Test of Manhood twice? She should have known he would fail her.

The self-preservation that drives most men spurred him on and he broke back into a sprint. There were loud calls behind him and whoops as the chasing braves caught sight of him and realised how close they were to their quarry. He blundered on, throwing nervous glances over his shoulder at the howling wolves behind.

His heart hammered like a drum as he burst out of the undergrowth onto the scrubland that ran alongside the White River. The river was wide and long, winding through the forest and forming a natural barrier to the world of the forest people and the wildness of the Borderlands beyond. It was fordable in a few places but those crossing points were two or three days travel in either direction. At this point the White River ran through a canyon formed over millions of years. The Bridge was his only hope now of evading capture and death.

Two steps into the openness of the scrubland and his fragile hopes were smashed into pieces. A figure was seated at the start of the rude rope bridge that stretched across the river, a figure that lifted his head as he heard Jerone leave the forest and stared at him through his long, white hair. Jerone slowed to halt and finally stopped halfway between the forest edge and Anders Whitehair. He bent double to try to catch his breath as the first of the chasers broke the forest edge.

Anders Whitehair rose and drew himself up to his full height. He rolled his head in a circular motion and stretched as he stood. All the time he kept his glare on Jerone. Jerone could see every muscle and every sinew twitch as Anders shook the inactivity from his body. He saw the scars etched into the skin of Anders' cheeks. Scars that counted the lives he had taken. Eight on each cheek. Sixteen lives violently ended.

One of the following braves suddenly charged forward, his spear raised above his head with the long blade pointed downwards, aiming at the oblivious Jerone's heart. There was a shrill scream, not from Jerone but from Anders.

"Nooo! Leave him! He is mine to kill and mine alone!"

The scream alerted Jerone who turned to face his attacker. The charging brave, in mid leap, tried to check his attack and left himself unprotected as Jerone swung his knife in a wide arc. The blade caught the warrior across his stomach leaving a wide, red gash. Jerone staggered back and the brave fell to the ground holding his stomach and wincing in silent agony. There was a loud holler from the rest of the warriors, and they shook their spears angrily as they closed the distance between Jerone and themselves.

Jerone turned to the Bridge, only to find the tall frame of Whitehair bearing down on him. Still winded from the exertion of running and the attack from the fallen warrior, Jerone held out a hand in desperation, trying to ward Whitehair off.

Anders Whitehair lashed out with the shaft of his short spear, landing a vicious blow on the arm of Jerone. The tall, whitehaired warrior danced around his opponent waving his spear.

"I am going to gut you like a pig, Witchboy." He lashed out with the spear again, hitting Jerone on the head and knocking him to the floor.

"I have killed your witch, burnt her alive in her tower and now I will end your miserable life!" He lashed out again but this time Jerone was able to roll away and scrabbled backwards on his backside away from the killer that stood before him. Anders' chest heaved, the black scars of heroism rising and dipping as if nodding in agreement. At the mention of Janda, Jerone remembered the charm she had made. His fingers fumbled to get inside his satchel, and he grasped the little figure with the white feathers for hair and thrust it out for all to see. The noise from the watching braves faltered slightly as they recognized the witch charm.

"Let me pass, Anders Whitehair. . . . or else!"

The tall warrior laughed in front of him.

"I have killed Janda, boy! Do you think I fear her trinkets?" He stepped forward, raising his spear above his shoulder. Jerone remembered her words, 'When you confront Whitehair, this will protect you if you still believe in me.' He muttered to himself as he staggered to his feet, "I'll always believe in you, Janda."

"What's that, Witchboy? Speak up before I send you to meet your witch."

"It is not just her trinket. That is my magic as well, Anders Whitehair. I am no longer Jerone Witchboy but Jerone Witchguardian. Now let me pass!" His words shocked even himself. Never before had he been able to stand up to Anders Whitehair, his chief tormentor.

With all the speed of a cobra striking its prey, Anders lashed out again with the shaft of his spear. The wood connected with Jerone's knuckles with a crack and the charm flew from his hand in a high loop and Whitehair deftly caught it.

"Witchguardian? You don't seem to be doing a good job of it, boy!" Anders spat out at the stricken youth. He rested his spear against his chest and raised the charm in both hands. He deliberately snapped it in two and Jerone could hear the twigs and bones crack. Anders threw the broken charm down at his feet and slowly trod on it. The warriors howled even more and closed in, hoping that their leader would allow them to strike the quarry that they had so successfully driven into the trap.

"Fuck you, Anders!" was all Jerone could reply. The tall warrior leaped forward with a snarl. Caught in two minds which way to dodge, Jerone ended up slipping on the ground and rolled backwards, propelling his attacker over his head with his feet. There was a shout of surprise from Whitehair as he was sent flying over the edge of the canyon and then Jerone felt the blows and kicks as the other warriors grabbed him. He was pulled roughly to his feet with two braves holding each arm. Another hit him hard in the face and he noticed one further warrior peer over the edge to look for Anders.

"Wait!" that warrior called, turning from the sight below. "The Witch's words were correct!"

The warrior pulled back from the canyon edge and shouted

to his compatriots, pointing to the ground and then to the sight he had seen on the riverbank below. Jerone sank to his knees as they let go. They scooted over to the cliff edge. As they followed their companion's gaze, they all melted back from the edge and spat at him, muttering all the time.

He stood and walked gingerly to the edge. The body of Anders Whitehair lay in a crumpled heap at the river edge below, the spine bent at an impossible angle and a pool of blood seeping from his head, staining the once bright white hair.

Jerone turned to face his attackers who found it hard to face him. If they lifted their gazes from the ground, it was to mutter insults at him or spit. He noticed the charm that Janda had said would protect him, crushed and thrown to the ground by Whitehair. The twig that made the spine of the little figurine was bent double in a cruel parody of Whitehair's body below. The skull that the witch had thrust onto the main twig for the totem's head had split in Ander's attack on it, and the white feathers that Janda had used to represent the hair of Anders were streaked with the crimson juice of a berry that had lain at the exact spot that Whitehair had thrown it to the ground. He praised Janda under his breath and lifted his arms wide as he addressed the scared warriors.

"Behold! This is my magic. Whitehair didn't believe and now he has paid for the murder of Janda." There were mutterings from the watching braves.

"I am going to cross the Bridge. I have a job and duty to do. Yours is finished. Take Whitehair's body back to his father and tell him that Jerone Witchguardian is sorry. I have no anger with Veng Stonefist but his son disrespected the power of Janda and had to pay for his crime.

"If you follow me, I will kill you. You have seen my power. Now go!" The last words were screamed at the braves who turned tail almost as one and ran. Jerone Witchguardian turned and staggered out onto the rough planks of the Bridge, one hand holding the coarse hemp rope.

FREED FROM HER BODY, she had risen into the sky, the thermals from the fire that engulfed her home (both the wooden tower and the empty vessel of Shoola Brighteyes) carrying her high. She was intangible and formless, invisible to even the most eagle-eyed of watchers. She had looked down upon the village that had been her home for many summers and watched as the warriors had surrounded her tower. From her vantage point, she had watched as Jerone had made his escape and for a few seconds had contemplated following him.

Two things had made her say no. Firstly, if Anders had caught him, there was nothing that she could do to assist him whilst she was in this state. Secondly, if he needed her assistance now, then he didn't really deserve his given name, Witchguardian. Whilst that seemed harsh, she did have faith in him, even if it was a small piece. She had seen something in him, all those seasons ago, a desire to try and to keep on trying. Some might have called it perseverance; others might have said obstinate or stubbornness. No matter what it was called, it caused her to give the young boy shelter and to give him a little protection from the other members of the tribe.

Judging by how Jerone had acted that morning, she was sure that the faith she had shown him wasn't misguided. If he had acted like that in his Test of Manhood, then he would have passed either time. All in all, she was quite proud of him. He had shown decisiveness, bravery and concern only for her. Maybe it had been fate that he had failed the Tests; karma that she had discovered him that morning many moons ago under her tower.

She floated in the wind, heading north across the forests of her people, heading for the wild and desolate tundra beyond.

Before long, she saw what she had come to see. On the shores of an icy river that meandered through the wildness to the ocean far to the north, lay a rocky outcrop. Upon the rock that jutted out from the sparse woodland, out over the riverbank, were a myriad of flat pieces of rock. Some were still piled up on top of each other forming crude walls that had once been the outline of a homestead. The mud that had clad the walls and filled the gaps were long gone, the wooden beams and roof, rotted and decayed over the hundreds of years that had passed since the homestead had been a home.

This is where it had started, this was where she had discovered her first Channeler. Nearly fifty lifetimes had passed since then. Nearly fifty bodies left and nearly fifty searches for the next Channeler. Each time, she had travelled here, to see where she had begun her journey. She usually spent some time here before moving on, not just for a sense of nostalgia, though. Sometimes her new body wasn't ready, wasn't aware of its new vocation.

This was one of those time. She couldn't sense anything. Her consciousness couldn't detect the usual tremor in the ether that indicated her new host was ready. Normally she wouldn't have worried, but these were troubling times.

5

Radnak awoke with a start and tried to sit up. He instantly regretted it as the wave of nausea washed over him, causing him to twist his torso and vomit over the floor. He coughed hard, rasping his throat and he wiped the drool from his lips with his hand. The half-orc looked around and his addled mind tried to make sense of his blurred vision.

"Mother, he is awake!" he heard a voice near to him and then felt the warm hand upon his bare arm as someone tried to ease him upwards. He suddenly became aware of a stinging sensation on his forearm and he went to grasp it with his good hand. As he did so, gentle hands took his hand and lifted them away from the pain.

"Now, *Sverd* Radnak, try not to touch the wound no matter how it stings." His eyes started to focus, and his gaze shifted from the slender fingers that held his hand along the green arms to the beautiful face of Iga.

"Lady Iga, is that you? Thank Crom Crade that I have not lost you." He tried to sit up again, but the feeling of sickness stormed over him and he forced himself to keep hold of the contents of his stomach.

"Calm yourself and hold still. You have been very close to death these last few days. It has taken all my skill as an herbalist to bring you back from Crom Teder's grasp. I thought many a time that you were gone from me," the soothing voice paused before correcting herself and continuing "from us, I mean, forever." Crom Teder was a god of the goblins who seized the souls of the dying and kept them as his servants in the underworld.

"What happened?" Radnak closed his eyes and lay back. He tried to concentrate and focus his mind on what had happened to him.

"Don't you remember anything?" It was as if a dense fog was obscuring his thoughts and memories and he shook his head slowly, a pained expression covering his face.

"We are in Jacarna. There was a battle, an invasion." The fog started to clear with each word that Lady Iga spoke. Images of the flying ships and the explosions rocking the palace came back to him. He remembered the silhouette of Lady Iga as she stood in the doorway of the small cellar room as he struggled with his opponent. He saw the desperation in the cat man's eyes as he wrapped his arm around his neck and squeezed. He felt once again the bite of the cat man and then the sensation of falling to the floor. And finally, he saw the two young goblin lords standing behind his beloved Lady Iga, a scared look on the face of the younger brother.

"Crom Crade! The young lords! Are they okay?" He thrust himself upwards with his arms and sat bolt upright. The sudden movement brought on a fresh bout of coughing and he was sick again. Lady Iga's voice was as soothing as her cold hands that gently took hold of his face.

"They are fine, *Sverd* Radnak, and they have been as

worried about you as I have." His vision started to clear, and he saw Igant hurry over to his mother as she beckoned him. He carried a small bowl of water and a cloth. Gently Lady Iga dabbed the specks of vomit from his face and cleaned him up. Radnak allowed himself to slowly sink back to the bed and clenched his fists. He had never felt this weak.

As he lay still and stared at the ceiling, he felt that something was amiss. Slowly he turned his head and took in his surroundings.

"This room, it is not the one that we chose. We have moved?" It was more of a statement than a question. The silence hung in the room until Lady Iga spoke out.

"Yes, we did move. The first chamber was not suitable with you in that condition, Radnak."

"Your wound stank, *Sverd* Radnak," added Igant helpfully. Radnak blushed, more with anger at himself for being so helpless rather than embarrassment.

"This chamber is secure? Who chose it and how safe is it?"

"It is safe and secure, Radnak. Now please rest."

The half-orc propped himself up on one arm as he looked about, his eyes flitting about the room trying to gauge entry points and defensive positions. Igant smiled.

"It is okay, *Sverd* Radnak. There is no way into this room."

The fog seemed to fall over Radnak's mind again. What did the young goblin mean? Were they trapped in here? Igant answered his confusion.

"Janis. Janis is a *Jordskaever!*" He stopped abruptly, unsure as to whether his mother had wanted him to divulge what had happened. Radnak turned back to face the tall goblin woman.

"A *Jordskaever?*" His incredulousness was hard to disguise, and he shook his head as if to clear away some of the fog that had settled again. "A *Jordskaever?* Is it true?" There were stories of times long gone, of myths and legends that told of such beings. The sort of stories that were told around the feasting halls in caves deep underground. A *jordskaever*, a rock warper. A goblin able to affect the molecular structure of rocks and earth, passing through as if it wasn't there. He had once doubted that any Goblinkind alive had met one and now he was a bodyguard to one. He shook his head again as he tried to get to grips with the fact that Janis, the mute son of Lady Iga was a powerful creature of legend.

"Yes, it is, Radnak. I didn't know, we didn't know. I doubt he knew himself until it happened." She blanched, remembering how she had asked her two sons to hide the bodies of the two invaders that Radnak had killed. Janis had stood still, clenching his fists continually as Igant tried to drag the dead away. She had presumed that it was fear that had paralyzed her younger son, but she was wrong. It was anger. His large eyes flitted from the fallen Radnak to his mother and then to his brother struggling to pull the dead invader away. Janis seethed within, silent as always. Finally, he snapped and strode to his brother. He leant down; his face contorted as he gripped the cat man by his shoulders. With a grim, determined look he pushed downwards. The body slowly started to sink into the stone flagstones until the head and torso was buried along with his fists. He recoiled in horror and fell to the floor staring at the obscene spectacle of a body half submerged into the stone.

His brother was paralyzed in terror at what Janis had done, yet when he turned to his mother, all he could see in her face was pride. After he had regained his composure he had experimented until he could control his power properly. The two bodies were disposed of properly as if they had never existed.

Later that next night, Igant and Janis had found another chamber whilst their mother stood vigil over the stricken bodyguard. The new chamber suited their position better with the corridor outside the only door to the room blocked by rubble from the fallen ceiling. Janis' power had allowed them all to enter the chamber and sealed them away safely from the invaders.

"Where is he now?" Radnak had noticed that the young lord wasn't present.

"He has taken it upon himself to patrol the corridors at night. He will be back soon. Now rest, *Sverd* Radnak."

6

Bex woke with a start, grabbing the hand that rested on her shoulder before she opened her eyes. The subtle twist of her wrist left the owner of the hand in discomfort and his 'Eeeek!' of pain showed it. She recognized the voice straight away and squeezed the hand a little harder.

"Landa! What in Tomnar's name are you doing here?" The blond barman gritted his teeth as she applied more pressure and waved his free hand in an attempt to ask her to stop. She saw he was unarmed and relaxed her grip slightly. She repeated her question.

"What are you doing in my room?"

Landa held his wrist in his other hand and grimaced as he tried to rub the pain away.

"I have come to warn you, Bex. They have come for you!"

"What? Who have? I mean.... what time is it?" Her head pounded from the wine last night. 'Drinking' and 'early mornings the day after' were never her friends.

"It's a little after the third cat. Not quite dawn." Bex groaned long and loudly. She must have only had an hour or two of sleep. No wonder she felt like she did.

"Shhhh!" Landa put his finger to his lips, beckoning her into silence. "They'll hear you. Mon is talking to them now, but I think you might still be able to get away."

Bex leapt out of bed oblivious of her nakedness in front of Landa and started to dress.

"Who is here? Get away? What are you talking about?"

"Soldiers! Lots of them!" He moved to the door and opened it slightly, peering out. Closing it, he turned and carried on. "Soldiers, all in black, Bex. And they asked for you!"

"What exactly did they say, Landa?"

"They asked whether they had the right place for you. Bex of Samak they asked."

"Did they say exactly what they wanted me for?" Bex finished lacing her bodice up and pulled her boots on.

"No,"

"All in black?" Sudden realisation jumped into Bex's head. "Is their commander short and blond?"

Landa nodded. Bex sighed and grabbed Landa by the arm. Ushering him to the door, she opened it and pushed him out onto the landing.

"Tell Garlen I'll be down shortly. And get me some coffee!"

Slamming the door, she sat back down on the bed and continued to dress.

'*Please don't drink again, Bex. I feel awful.*'

'*Welcome to the morning after, Ishtara.*' She responded with a droll smile on her lips. Ishtara felt the effects of wine as well. At least she had one pleasure in life that would annoy her symbiotic friend.

'*Garlen is here?*'

'*I think so. He is going to ask me – us - to help him rescue his sisters.*'

'*And will you do so?*'

'*Yes, if you don't mind.*' Bex added as an afterthought.

'*Let's get ready.*'

She donned the same black outfit that she had worn for the infiltration of Yab M'Vil's villa. Reaching under the simple cot that was her bed, she withdrew her 'spider', and arrangement of webbing and buckles that carried her equipment and spread it out on the bed. Bex opened the chest that sat at the foot of her bed and pulled out several pouches and tools which she clipped to the arrangement of belts and buckles. Satisfied she had what she thought would come in useful, she folded the spider and rolled it in a blanket. Next, her pair of grecks followed, the blades slipping into her soft leather boots.

From a chest under her bed she pulled out a heavy coat of mail. Despite the weight, it did not make a sound as she lifted it. Each link had been individually wrapped in a dark cloth. She folded it neatly and placed it onto a blanket, wrapping it into a roll like the spider. Next came two small coin purses, her entire wealth apart from her equipment, which she slipped into a small belt satchel.

Finally, she retrieved a scabbarded blade from under her pillow and slowly drew the sword from the ornate sheath. The steel flashed in the candlelight and along the blade was an inscription in the black runes of a long-forgotten language, runes that spelt out the name of the sword, '*Caladmorr*'. She had acquired it some time ago, when she had been adventuring with her first love, a mentor after she had left the Guild, called Hawkenlacen. She gently raised the blade to her lips and brushed the steel in a soft kiss.

"I'll need your protection now, my love."

'*Did you love him?*' As she thought about him an image flashed into her mind. '*He is very handsome.*' Ishtara continued.

'*Yes. Yes, I did.*' She stared at the sword for a second longer then thrust it back into the sheath and fastened it to her belt. As she left her room, she picked her full, black cloak from the bed, swept it into place and left.

From the landing at the top of the stairs, she could see

Garlen sitting in a booth with his feet raised up on the table, and a flagon of wine in his hand. He still wore the same clothes as yesterday but had a leather cuirass over his shirt. A long sword hung from his belt and he looked even more dangerous than before. Around him were twenty or so soldiers all wearing an assortment of blackened armour.

"Isn't it too early for wine, Garlen?" she asked as she descended the stairs. The soldiers turned their eyes to her tall, lithe figure as she stepped off the bottom stair and into the bar. Several of the soldiers whistled at her.

"Is she going to entertain us on the mission, Captain?" one asked and there were several guffaws of laughter. Garlen waved down the intrusion.

"No, Rica. Lady Bex will be our guide. She does have a particular set of skills that I wager that none of you have seen before." Several of the soldiers laughed.

"I wouldn't bet on that, Garlen!"

"She doesn't look like a lady, Garlen."

Bex simmered inside at the soldier's comments. She was well aware of how coarse barrack room banter could be but there was something about these soldiers that unnerved her. The army in Tannaheim was a standing army, its units wore uniforms and the men in each unit carried similar weapons. With the men who stood around her now, their only uniformity was their *non* uniformity. They wore a wide range of styles of armour mainly leather and chainmail, though one or two wore steel breast plates in the style of the southern states. Their weapons were even more varied. The one called Rica wore a bow over his back; others carried swords, spears or maces. One even had two rows of throwing knives strapped across his chest. All wore black and all had the look of killers.

'*Shall we show them?*' Ishtara said. A picture of Bex transforming into a blazing inferno sending the soldiers scattering to hide formed in her mind.

'*Not yet,*' Bex smiled inside.

'*But you feel insulted, why?*'

'*Because of what they think they see in front of them.*' She could feel Ishtara forming another question and carried on, blushing inside and out. '*Because of what I once was. I was once what they think I am now. I just thought I had left all that behind when I escaped from the guilds.*'

'*Well, shall we show them what you are now?*' It was more a statement than a question and Bex could feel her body become hotter as Ishtara startrd to squeeze her from her mind.

'*No! Let's play for a bit.*'

'*Play?*'

'*We'll string them along for a while*'

'*Bex, you confuse me sometimes*'.

Garlen held up his hand to quieten his soldiers. As rough and unruly as they looked, they all instantly fell quiet.

"No, you are right. She doesn't. But you will all address her as one and treat her like one. It would be unwise for any of you to antagonize her."

"We don't have room for passengers on this mission, Garlen," a tall soldier spoke out gruffly. He was older than most of them, bearded but balding and his arms crossed in front of him.

"You are right, Mathor, as you are always right. But she won't be a passenger. She can handle herself." Garlen raised his flagon to his lips, flitting his glance from Mathor to Bex.

"So, what skills does she bring to this party?" Mathor spoke again. He seemed to have enough authority to question the Prince.

Garlen swung his legs down from the table and stood up. At that moment Kilde walked in from the kitchen with a large cup of coffee in her hands. Bryn and Mon Baxt followed her. The tall guardsmam had obviously refreshed himself at the palace the night before and now appeared as a new man. He was clean shaven and the blood and grime from his last few days of fighting and riding was washed away. His mousy brown hair was no longer lank and unkempt but fell to his shoulders and he continuously brushed it away from his face. As Bex took the coffee from Kilde, her eyes lifted to meet the Earl's. He smiled at her and she felt her body react.

'Cute'

'Will you stop that!'

"Lady Bex does have powers unseen to all of you at the moment, but in addition to that she can pass through areas quieter than any of you," he paused and looked at the small wiry man with the throwing knives across his chest, "and that includes you, Kardanth. Locks won't stop her, and she can climb like a mountain goat," he turned to Bex and bowed slowly, "I apologise for the comparison."

"You mean she's a thief," one of the soldiers spoke out.

"I prefer the term appropriator of valuables, but yes – I am a thief, and at other times I have even been a Sword – amongst other professions." Bex used the term that applied to many forms of the word mercenary. It could mean a soldier hired by a Lord for a campaign, a thug employed by a businessman for protection or simply, an adventurer for hire. She sipped her coffee and raised her eyes at Bryn, giving an apologetic smile. His gaze shifted away to a point over her shoulder and he stared past her. Smarting, Bex turned to Garlen.

"How did you know?" she asked.

"Your tattoo – a guild mark if I am not mistaken." He nodded towards her hand and the moon tattoo. "You should cover it up."

"A thief she may be, Garlen, but can she handle herself." Mathor asked once more.

"Yes, she can. Take my word for it. She could possibly be the most dangerous of us all." He drained his flagon and placed it back on the table, nodding to Bex's packs. "You are ready?"

"Yes, I just need to say my goodbyes."

"You don't have long, we leave in five minutes."

She turned to Mon and hugged her, whispering goodbye to her. She could have sworn she felt a tear on her cheek from the older woman.

"You'll be back, Bex," was all she said.

"Here, Mon. Take this; it should cover the cost of the rent of the room, hopefully until I come back." She pressed the larger of the two coin-purses into Mon's hand. The innkeeper shook her head and passed it back.

"Already taken care of, Bex. Prince Garlen paid everything. More than everything. Your room will be here for you . . . as long as Ol' One Eye stands."

Bex turned to the other members of staff and hugged each one, even Landa. He froze at her touch, his hands hovering over her back for a second before realising that this could be the last that he saw of her. He finally held her and kissed her cheek.

"Bye, Bex. Hurry back."

Lastly Bex turned to Kilde and handed her the other coin purse.

"For you, Kilde. Don't refuse and take care." Before the younger girl could say anything, Bex turned and walked away.

7

L ady Theres looked completely different now than she had the previous night in the cellars of the Inn of the Luckless Wench. Gone were the jewellery and the finery, replaced with a faded black dress and a discoloured apron. The luxurious ringlets in her hair were gone too, her hair cut short so that it barely reached the collar of her dress. The Lady was gone, replaced by a plain but still fairly striking house servant.

The young boy who stood behind her though, was still unmistakeably Churt. His mousy brown hair was a mess and he was dressed in the same patched and worn trousers and shirt as he had worn to the meeting with the Phantom.

They stood at the gate of the townhouse of Count Eglebon Dutte, nobleman of Danaria. Though the House Dutte kept ancestral lands to the north east of Tannaheim, at Marneheim, Count Dutte preferred to stay mainly in the capital. Four storeys high and with views over the bay and harbour, the house had cost a small fortune when his father had purchased it a decade ago.

A man garbed in the heraldry of the House Dutte

approached at a slow pace. He was middle-aged and completely bald. His features reminded Churt of a pig and he suppressed a faint grunt under his breath.

Theres seemed to sense what Churt was thinking and surreptitiously knocked his foot with hers. The man paused a few yards from the pair as if afraid to get too close. Theres could feel his eyes undressing her from top to toe and back again. She knew his sort and smiled inwardly. It wouldn't take too long to get the information that the Phantom needed, if indeed his suspicions were correct. Though, she thought, it wasn't often that Tikar Welk was wrong.

"I take it you are the new maid. I am Under Steward Harte." His eyes moved from her to rest on Churt and his face broke into a sneer as he took in the young lad. "Your references from House Galon seem in order. You start right away. If you present yourself at the side door and ask for Ira, she will show you to your room and set you to your duties. I will see you this evening to see that you have settled in and whether there is anything I can help you with." He subconsciously licked his lips as he spoke, and he pointed towards the side of the large house.

Theres walked past him without another glance and Churt hurried to keep up with her. At the servant's entrance they asked for Ira as directed and found themselves faced by a short, large, middle-aged woman. Her grey hair hung in curls on either side of her chubby face. She cackled as Theres introduced herself and Churt and she beckoned over another servant, this time a tall Theshian.

"Doma, take these two to Bharack's old room. They can stay there for now. I hope you stay longer than she did." She broke out into a cackle again and then turned her attention to another servant, this time a young man dressed in the hose of a page.

"Tegpor! Under Steward Harte wants the fires building up

in the master's study and the guest suite." The young man nodded and turned back in the direction he had come.

Doma led the pair down a small windy staircase to the servants' quarters below. She was tall and had to duck through the low doorways on their route. She was dressed in a black dress which was common amongst the servant class of the city and wore a white apron with the blue star of House Dutte upon it. The dark-skinned girl paused outside a small door and pushed it open, indicating that they should enter.

Theres stood in the doorway and looked upon their quarters for the next few days. The room was about eight foot square with a single wooden cot along one wall. A small grating in the ceiling let a little sunlight into the room, otherwise the only light source was a small oil lamp on the table in the corner. She looked back at Doma.

"What happened to Bharack? Why did she leave?" she asked. The tall Theshian looked back, a sad look in her dark eyes as she looked back at Theres. Theres was about to ask again when the girl opened her mouth. The Phantom's agent expected a reply but was taken aback to see the mutilation that the young girl had endured at some point in her short life. What remained of her tongue was scarred and swollen.

"What happened to you, you poor girl!" It was more of a statement than a question, Doma unable to reply. She reached down and took the Theshian's hands, inspecting the wrists as she raised them up. The scars and marks on her skin from shackles were unmistakeable.

"You were a slave. And that is when they did that..." she paused for the right word, "horror to you?" Doma nodded twice and her eyes fell to the floor. She gave Doma's hands a little squeeze and added, "Thank you for showing myself and Churt to our room. You had better get back to your duties. I will be right along." Doma trotted back along the corridor with a little glance back at the older woman. Theres ushered in the younger boy and closed the door behind them.

Part one of the Phantom's plan had been successful. With the resources that the Phantom had at his disposal, they had been implanted into House Dutte and now had to search for the evidence that Tikar Welk was sure to be found. After the secret meeting with the Phantom had ended the night before he had taken them to one side to explain his plan and suspicions.

"There is something awry at House Dutte. Something I cannot put my finger on. They have something to do with the murder of Anjoan or the abduction of the two Princesses – or maybe both. I have arranged for you to fill a vacancy there as of tomorrow. Don't ask me how," he raised his hand to ward off any interruptions. "The Hand of the Phantom has a long reach. Find out what you can but be careful. This is probably the most dangerous situation I have asked you to enter for me."

"How can you let them look at you like that, Theres?" Churt's voice brought her out of her reverie.

"Like how?" Churt threw himself on the cot before he answered.

"Like that pig of an under steward did. He looked at you like you were a piece of meat. He had better not touch you!"

"Oh Churt, you are adorable." She perched herself at the end of the cot and reached out to stroke his cheek. He shook his head away from her hand, annoyed at the patronising tone of her voice.

"It's not right."

"No, it's not. But you see Doma and she has endured?" Her voice was quiet but authorative. Churt nodded, his anger subdued slightly.

"Both my sister and myself were taken by slavers from our homelands to the north of the Wolf Mountains. Yab M'Vil's men took us both along with others from our town. Froen was far more beautiful than me, two years younger and the stars shone from her eyes. You should have seen her, Churt." She gazed wistfully at the small stream of light coming through the grating in the corner of the ceiling.

"One night, as the ship made its way along the river to the sea, the men got drunk. They needed entertainment and what all men want." She looked up at him, seeing the look in his eyes that seemed to implore her to stop.

"That's right, Churt. All men want the same. However, the good men earn it whilst the bad ones take it. They chose Froen as she was the most beautiful." Her voice broke as she recounted her past.

"She didn't last the night. Yab M'Vil was upset with his men. Not for the deed, but because they cost him a few gold crowns. Tikar rescued me, like he rescued almost everyone else that carries on his work." She wiped a tear from her eye and turned away from Churt. "See, you made me cry now. I promised I wouldn't cry for her anymore but that anything I do, it would be to work against the injustices of the world. That is what she would have wanted." She stood up and turned to face the young boy.

"See, Churt. That is why I let them, because I have the choice, the knowledge that I am working against them. Letting them think they have the power over me helps me get what I need, what Tikar Welk needs. Knowledge to stop them." She spread her arms and he shot up to run to her embrace.

"And besides, it always feels better when I know that Tikar has plans to end their miserable existences."

8

Outside, Garlen, Bryn and the soldiers were all mounted and waiting. A few more soldiers had been waiting outside bringing the number to forty. Bex recognized the scarred face of Gordin, who had accompanied Garlen, Bryn and Bex in their pursuit of the kidnapped princesses. All the horses were as black as night. Bryn held the reins to the only horse that was without a rider and she walked over and fixed one of her packs to the saddle and swung up on to the horse.

"Thank you," she said to the guardsman who ignored her and turned away, coaxing his mount down the line of soldiers.

'*What is up with him?*' Ishtara asked.

'*He seems upset with me, ever since he found out that I am a thief.*'

'*Well, I do find it unnerving myself,*' her demon responded. '*As I say, on my world....*'

'*Yes, I know! There wasn't any crime!*'

The retinue moved through the city to the North Gate. The streets were emptier than normal. Usually at this time in the morning the streets would have been a hive of activity and Bex guessed that the news of the assassination had become common knowledge.

They rode in two files and she found herself next to the young soldier called Rica who had spoken first. She sized him up. He was her height and bigger built. He looked the youngest in the company, but he was still several years older than her. His closely cropped hair was receding slightly at the sides and his eyes, although bright with life, showed a type of darkness only seen in those who walked hand in hand with death.

His leather armour was adorned with blackened steel discs. A longbow was strapped across his back and a sword hung from his belt. As he rode alongside her, Bex couldn't help noticing that he was missing two fingers from his left hand. She wondered who these mysterious men were.

'*Ask him.*'

'*What?*'

'*Ask him, Bex. I'll go mad with just you to talk to.*' Bex smiled to herself and leant across towards Rica.

"Who are you? I haven't seen soldiers like you in Tanna-heim before."

Rica turned towards her and was silent whilst he contemplated what to say.

"And you won't," when he finally spoke his voice was quiet. "We don't exist. Garlen calls us his Ghosts." He paused for a while longer before speaking again.

"You see Mathor ahead, riding with Garlen?" he nodded towards the stocky older man who rode next to the Prince. Mathor rode with authority, his back straight and his eyes surveying the street ahead as if he expected an ambush at any time.

'*Well, we are at war.*' Ishtara spoke inside.

'*Yes,*' mused Bex. '*I suppose being careful is why he is an old warrior as opposed to a dead one.*'

Grey hair surrounded his bald pate and his beard was

braided into three forks. He was one of the troops that wore a steel breast plate, its metal gouged in places from many battles and skirmishes. A great two-handed sword sat in a scabbard across his back and as he rode, he chatted to the Prince. Bex nodded.

"When he was younger, he was a sergeant serving under King Drajen, Anjoan's father. The young Prince Anjoan was sent to do his Service and became one of Mathor's troops. Drajen thought it would cure Anjoan of his brashness and cockiness." Rica laughed. "Anjoan ended up saving Mathor's life at the Battle of Long Ridge. Mathor never forgot that, neither did Anjoan. When Garlen reached the age for Service there was only one unit that Anjoan would think of sending him to." He laughed again. "Mathor said that Garlen was even cockier than Anjoan had been. He was a snotty nosed prince who had spent his time bedding maids and courtesans in the palace and fighting duels with other Lords and Earls. But he changed. War changes a man – or kills him.

"We fought four years in the south against Vadar's Orcs and Garlen showed us he could not only fight but had managed to take all that military history the Masters filled his head with at the palace and mix it up with all the experience that Mathor had and turn himself into a master tactician. We became an irregular force, carrying the war to Vadar, hitting his supply chains, targeting his officers and more." Rica tailed off, his stare showing his mind was back in the Orc Wars, remembering those he had left behind.

"What then?" Bex prompted. The young soldier shrugged.

"When the Wars were over, Garlen left the army and returned to Tannaheim. He bought out our contract and took us into his service. We work for him now."

"What do you do?"

"We...." Rica paused again, unsure whether he should

continue. He was saved by Mathor who had turned back and rode slowly along the line to their position.

"Garlen requests your presence at the head of the column, my Lady."

"Thank you, Mathor." She spurred her horse on and trotted towards the front of the column. She reined her horse in next to the Prince's.

"A fine day for it." He kept his eyes ahead as he spoke.

"For what, exactly?" Bex answered.

"Riding to certain death, the end of the kingdom, death and glory. Take your pick." He turned to look at Bex and saw her expression. "Or neither," he added slightly more jovially. She tried not to rise to his nonchalant attitude.

"Where are we going?"

"Jacarna." That one word shocked Bex, Garlen might as well have said the moon.

"Jacarna is in ruins and probably the biggest military encampment in Maingard. You are aware of that, my Prince?"

"And it is where my sisters are probably being held, Bex."

"Probably?"

"Yes, more than likely. I spoke further with Earl Kar last night. Before he left Jacarna, the enemy had taken the palace complex and was using it to hold certain captives together with being some kind of command area. It is my belief that it is where Moren and Ingren are. I will return them to my mother. And if I can do damage to the Cassalian command at the same time, all the better."

'*Sounds good to me.*' Ishtara said.

"Do you have a plan? Your men believe you to be a master tactician, I think the term was."

"The plan is fluid at the moment, Bex. As all good plans are. The basics of the plan are we use Earl Kar's knowledge to get into the city and palace, your skills to get to my sisters, and then we get out."

"Quite simple, when you put it that way," she retorted sarcastically.

"I am glad you see it that way, Bex." Garlen annoyingly ignored the sarcasm in her voice. "I just hope we are in time."

'I hope so too. But I am certain the Cassalians are going to use the princesses in order to force the Queen to surrender.' Ishtara butted in.

"It shouldn't take too long to get there, Garlen. I am sure we will be in time. And Ishtara is certain that they will use your sisters as bargaining tools." Bex spoke out instantly regretting doing so as she saw the pained look on the Prince's face.

"And when my mother doesn't surrender, Bex? How long will they last then?"

They rode in silence until they reached the North Gate.

9

Karchek, The Almighty Emperor's Lord Commander of the Host, sat ramrod straight on the throne in the empty palace. Most of the rubble had been cleared away now, though the cold air blew in through the smashed and shattered windows. Fatigued from lack of sleep, his eyes sitting deep in dark pits, he was glad of the cold breeze as it cooled his fever.

The gash over his left eye had crusted over with a tacky yellow scab that was still wet to the touch. The crude stitching formed black bridges that crossed the scab, joining the two coasts of swollen purple skin. His head swam, his vision blurring intermittently whilst the wound in his groin made it uncomfortable to sit or stand for any long periods.

The main door to the throne room opened and the small wizened figure of Narki entered, waving away the door guards as she passed. The black armoured guards wisely disappeared, relieved not to have to be in the same room as the mysterious shamanic figure.

"What do you want, Hag?" Karchek's voice wasn't as aggressive as he normally was when he spoke to Narki. She ignored the tone of his comment and moved closer to the throne, mounting the steps to stand before him. Narki held her clasped hand out in front of her and slowly unfurled her fingers to reveal what was hidden.

"What have you got there?" Karchek didn't move his head but could see her movements from the corner of his eye. Narki laughed, her cackle was loud and reverberated around the throne room.

"Oh! The mighty warlord, conqueror of a hundred worlds – laid low by a little princess. Open your eyes, General Karchek." He smarted, his pale face flushed, and his wound throbbed visibly. He slowly looked down at Narki and what she held out on her palm.

It was a shard of crystal, the stem of a wine goblet. Just for a second, Karchek started, a very slight recoil at the impromptu weapon that Rothannir had attempted to assassinate him with.

"This is what your whore stabbed you with, Karchek. I found it on the floor of your chamber." He closed his eyes and sat back.

"I know what it is, Hag. What use is it?"

"Your whore poisoned the shard with her own excrement and foulness. The very discharge from the wound that you dealt her, mixed with her own shit has entered your bloodstream and is slowly killing you. Quite an ignoble end for such a great warrior don't you think, General Karchek? Ignoble and ironic. The warriors of a hundred worlds couldn't kill you but a mere girl does."

"Begone, Narki. I don't need this." He focused and settled his manic glare on her. "I could still crush you like a bug."

"Do it then, Karchek, and seal your doom. Within an hour my herbalists will return with a plant that will complete a poultice that I have been working on. It will drive out the infection and heal you. The mixture has to be just right though. Too much and the poultice will kill the infection but will also damage both your nervous system and your immune system. Too little and it will be ineffective."

Karchek grunted in reply, knowing that Narki would heal him if she had the opportunity. She had the knowledge, being the best herbalist and alchemist in the Host. She had a hundred worlds worth of experience in harvesting and using plants as medicines and poisons.

"I will return in an hour, General Karchek. Try not to die in the meantime." Her laugh once again split the silence and echoed about the great hall as she withdrew.

She was as good as her word and returned within the hour. Not that Karchek had taken any notice of the time, the pain in his head causing him to wave away his commanders and their reports of the progress in the subjugation of the city. Narki found him slumped in the throne, his massive frame crammed uncomfortably within its confines. A flagon, empty of the wine it once held, dangled from his hand. He opened one eye as she approached and his feverish mind at first tried to tell him that there were two Narkis climbing the steps of the dais carrying her small alchemist's satchel.

"Well?"

"Do not despair, Great Karchek. I have the poultice here. Old Narki will see to it that your whore won't be responsible for your death." She didn't break step and pushed her hood back, revealing her graying hair.

Karchek grunted in reply and Narki placed her bag upon the small side table next to the throne, brushing away two empty wine bottles as she did so. Muttering to herself she emptied her bag, one item at a time and placed them almost reverently on the table. First came a knife, the blade of which was of polished black stone. Then came some scraps of cloths and a small bottle of water. Lastly, she removed a bleached white skull and placed it next to the other objects. The skull was slightly smaller than that of a human and the features were a different too, with the eye orbits larger and the nasal cavity at the end of a slight protuberance. The top of the skull had been cut round, forming a lid, and a small handle had been fitted to the top, complete with a red gem.

"Let me prepare the wound." She reached up and held her hand across his wounded eye, guiding his head towards the back of the throne. Her grip was surprisingly strong and authoritative.

With her free hand she took the knife and in one movement sliced into the wound. A flow of pus and detritus flowed from the cut which she wiped up with some of the cloth before washing the area with water. Once satisfied that the wound was ready, she lifted the lid from the skull, revealing a soft, gritty, grey salve. Digging into the poultice with her fingers, she scooped up some of the pungent smelling material and applied it liberally over the open wound, making sure the whole area was covered.

Karchek sat impassive through the operation, his teeth gritted. Narki paused her muttering and took a step back to examine her work.

"Are we done, Hag?" Karchek asked, his eye under the covered gash closed to a thin slit. Narki gave a little chuckle.

"You know we aren't finished, Karchek. You have another wound. Stand and lower your trousers." Groggily he stood and glared at her. Impatiently she reached out for his laces at the front of his waist only to find her hands swatted away by his.

"Leave it." Teetering slightly, he started to unlace his trousers and then pulled them down. He had to grab the arm of the throne as he did so to balance himself properly. Without even glancing at his groin area, Narki grunted.

"Further. I need the wound area clear to work." Karchek snarled and pushed his trousers down further, freeing himself completely and he sat back down, his buttocks on the very edge of Renta's throne, trying to lay as flat as possible. The old woman reached out to the table again and lifted the knife. As she turned back to him, she chuckled again.

"Shall we begin?"

The wound was close to the root of his member and had only been rudely treated. It was even more sore and infected than the wound above his eye. The skin was discoloured around it and the edges of the wound were black.

"You are an idiot, Karchek. This should have been dealt with before this." She carried on and treated the wound as she had done the first one. When she had finished her hand brushed against his shaft.

"Is this what your whore saw, Karchek? Before she tried to kill you?"

"Away, Hag!" He pushed her hand away and reached for the top of his trousers, ready to pull them up. Narki chuckled before grabbing him again, firmer this time.

"Perhaps I could use it, Karchek. It has been a few years since I have enjoyed a man. It could be a thank you for me saving your life. . . ." She looked up at him and chuckled again. The chuckle rolled into a huge peel of laughter as she stood and collected her equipment together and walked away.

'A few years since she had enjoyed a man? In the name of the Emperor! I would rather . . .' Karchek muttered to himself as he redressed himself and sat back, closing his eyes.

10

T he Ghosts and Bex rode on during the day. Once Tannaheim had passed into the distance and had disappeared out of sight the mood had changed in the troop of soldiers. It seemed to Bex that the city walls and towers symbolised normality for the Ghosts. Once they were out of view the soldiers were once again behind enemy lines, as they had been in the Orc Wars. Gone were the idle chatter and the immature jokes about their companions, replaced with a more sombre and professional attitude.

For much of the day she rode at the front of the column with Garlen punctuated with short periods on her own or riding next to Rica. Garlen was busy as they rode, riding forward to liaise with the soldiers riding point and then back to the end of the line to speak to those riding there.

"He was like this in the Orc Wars, when we first met him." Mathor said, shaking his head slowly. "Totally unprofessional." Bex turned to look at the old soldier riding next to her. His bald head shone in the bright morning sun as he reached up with one hand and twisted one of the braided forks of his beard.

"Why is that?"

"He is in command; he should be at the head of the column. We'll know where he is then, if we need him. He will change when we get closer to danger, of course. When we tell him." He smiled.

"He is somewhat different than I imagined him." She looked ahead at the Prince as he rode next to Kardanth, the small soldier with the collection of throwing knives. Kardanth was riding second point, a position two hundred yards ahead of the main troop, a half-way mark between the scout further ahead and the column.

"Really, how did you imagine him?" Mathor enquired, looking dead ahead. Bex looked flustered and several images crashed through her mind. Finally, one settled, Garlen standing tall adorned with a crown and a flowing red cloak. In one hand he carried a sceptre and in the other a flagon. About his feet were strewn empty barrels and beer corpses of his companions. Several near naked women knelt and clawed at his legs.

'*Really?*' asked Ishtara, almost incredulously.

'*The name Lord of the Inns doesn't just come from nowhere, Ishtara.*' Bex answered her inner demon and then turned back to Mathor.

"He does have this reputation as a ....." she struggled for a word that was less insulting than drunkard. She realised Mathor was straining not to laugh and when he noticed her realisation, he gave out a mighty bellow of laughter.

"Another one falls for the stories!" He looked extremely pleased but then realised that Bex was blushing. "Forgive me, you are only one of many that have been taken in by the gossip and tales. It is surprising how quickly rumour spreads when you bad mouth a high born. It spreads like wildfire, embellished at every turn – and the wonderful thing is, many of those who pass it on wouldn't know if Garlen was pissing next to them in a privy!" He gave another guffaw, almost as loud as the first one.

'*I told you so!*'

'*Be quiet!*' retorted the thief. Mathor reined his horse in and turned to canter back down to the rear of the column leaving Bex riding alone.

'*It seems that there is more to your Prince than meets the eye, Bex*'

'*It does, but just what is he hiding?*'

11

J erone Witchguardian had felt compelled to walk south. At first, when he had crossed the bridge after the death of Anders, he was still in flight mode. With each step he took on the wooden rope bridge, he had expected his one-time pursuers to not heed his warning and to resume their chase. Nervously he had made his way to the opposite side before glancing over his shoulder. The far side of the gorge was deserted, and he breathed easily. He entered the treeline and walked for another hour or so before stopping to take stock of his situation.

"Janda, what would you have me do?" he asked. He wasn't sure whether he expected an answer. He sank down to the forest floor amongst the bracken and sobbed. Since he had woke that morning, shaken awake by the now dead Janda, his entire life had been turned upside down. His only real friend and ally gone, his nemesis dead and a self-imposed exile that he was sure would result in his death should he break it. Add to that, a quest thrust upon him by his mentor just before she expired, coupled with his passing of the rite of manhood trial at last with his attempt to save Janda had left him in emotional turmoil.

He wiped his tears away with his hands and sat back against the wide trunk of one of the massive oaks. A breeze rustled the leaves and ferns, and the wildlife of the forest chattered about him. Staring as the sun cascaded through the leaf canopy, a glint of light brought his attention to something partially obscured by ferns at the base of the next oak.

Carefully he parted the curly leaves of the ferns. What he saw was metal, shinier than the dull steel of his own knife but the object was larger. It was club shaped with a long, curved flange of metal at the centre of each side. A thick shaft wound with leather stretched away into the undergrowth. Excitedly he grabbed the head of the mace, lifting it up. He hadn't raised it very far before he dropped it again, throwing himself back with shock and grasping for his knife from his belt. Attached to the base of the hilt was a parched, brown hand and wrist, partially mummified with part of the ulna bone protruding from the end. Once over the initial shock, he reached out for the mace again, gingerly taking it by the top of the haft and dislodging the hand with his knife. Standing, he hefted the weapon up, admiring the heavy but perfectly balanced hammer. It was about two and a half feet in length and seemed constructed to be used either in one or both hands. Feeling brave again, he used it to brush away the bracken where he had found it. As he thought, the previous owner of both the mace and the hand was still there. The skeletal remains of a warrior clad in mail with what was left of a blue tabard lay face up with the dark, empty eye sockets staring up at Jerone, perhaps seemingly to accuse the young man of complicity in his death. About his neck was a gold chain with a locket attached inlaid with a rampant horse in silver.

Gold and silver were not things that were cherished by the people of the forest but Jerone had seen precious metals before.

He therefore knew its worth to the people who lived outside the forest and decided to take it. Unlocking it from around the neck of its previous owner, he took it and raised it to his own neck. As his fingers started to work the clasp he paused, looking down at the corpse he had just looted twice. The accusatory look was still there, and he thought better of wearing it and placed it into the small bag he carried.

As he dropped the small locket into his satchel his hand glanced against the small drawstring pouch of black powder that had belonged to Janda. He knew he had something else to do before he moved on. He covered the corpse with bracken again and carried the mace back to the tree where he had sat when he had first glimpsed the weapon.

Sitting down with his back against the trunk, he placed the mace between his feet and withdrew his knife from his belt. His hands sought a stick from the forest floor, and he placed it between his teeth. He slowly and deliberately placed the tip of his knife against his cheekbone close to his nose and pushed the point in until he could feel the flow of blood. He then drew the knife across his face towards his ear, feeling the tip drag through his skin. Once the cut was made, he noticed the flow of blood down the crease of his nose and cheek. At first, he mistook it for a tear, the sensation of warmth as it crept across his skin. It wasn't until it reached his lip that he realised it was blood, the metallic taste catching him by surprise.

He moved the knife to the other side of his face and made another cut. He cut himself once for the life of the brave who had attacked him in Janda's house, and once for the life of Anders Whitehair. He had contemplated not cutting his face for Anders, just as Anders had goaded him. But the chief's son had been a great warrior and Jerone felt he should wear the mark of his kill proudly.

Taking up the drawstring bag, he tipped the black powder into the palm of his hand. He took a minute and stared at the pile of coarse grains. He used his fingers to push the pile over his palm, watching as the mound changed into different shapes. When he was ready, he scooped some up between his fingertips and rubbed it into the open wounds. It smarted as much as the ritual scarring on his chest had when Janda had rubbed the coarse grains of soot into his cuts. At the thought of his old mentor and friend, he sat back and closed his eyes as the tears finally came. The salty drops mixed with the blood and soot leaving streams on his cheeks.

It was several hours before he felt composed enough to move. Slowly he pulled himself to his feet, grasping the trunk of the oak that he had rested against. What to do, where to go? The quest given to him by Janda was immense, almost impossible. How could he find one person on this world? To find one person in the Forest was a hard enough task, even if he knew who the person was. One that was unknown to him was impossible.

Then why had Janda tasked him with it. Why give him an impossible task? To make him fail again as he had done so with the Test of Manhood? His hand strayed to the matted and dried blood that was crusting on his chest. He had passed the Test! Janda's last act was to cut his chest and confirm his passage to manhood. Why had she done that just to throw him to the wolves with a quest that wasn't possible?

She had enough faith in him to have kept him safe all these years. Faith enough to elevate him to Manhood and to give him the epithet 'Witchguardian'. A poor witchguardian he would be if he couldn't find the witch. So, the quest must be possible, he reasoned. Difficult, but not impossible.

"Give me a sign, Janda. I beg of you." He turned his face towards the sky, as if expecting the Channeler to be there. Instead, he saw the late afternoon sun disappear behind gathering clouds. Here, on the south of the river, the forest was broken, the trees less dense. Nature had filled the gaps with bracken and thorns, and young saplings pierced the under-growth like swords, pointing skywards.

No answer came from his Channeler. That's because she was dead – the thought flashed across his mind. He had seen her frail body smashed and he had closed her unseeing eyes before leaving her body to burn as the flames engulfed her house. Dead.

Then the shame hit him. Hadn't she asked him to believe in her? The charm that she had woven to protect him from Anders Whitehair had worked after all. Her faith in him needed to be repaid. This was another test, almost as difficult as finding her. He now needed to show faith in Janda.

He clenched his fists and looked up. At that moment, the clouds broke, and the sun managed to stab a faint ray through the canopy above that seemed directed straight at him. There! That was his sign. He smiled, hefting the warhammer to his shoulder.

"Janda isn't here," he laughed to himself, his own spirits lifted. "So, she must be somewhere else – which means I must move on." He chose eastwards, one direction as good as another.

It was only a short while before he came back to the river, its path turning south to meet his. He heard it before he saw it. Here the river ran fast, crashing against the rocks that broke its surface. Jerone could see that the river's course dropped here. He looked up and downriver, he could see a few hundred yards in each direction before the river disappeared round bends in its meandering course. Droplets sprayed into the air forming rainbows as the sun caught them.

He knelt in the shallows, quenching his thirst with the ice-cold water. Taking the opportunity to splash his face and wash away the blood and grime, he grimaced as the cold slapped him. He rubbed his hands clean again before thinking that another sign from Janda would be helpful. This was only the second time that he had seen the river this close, the first being one of his failed Tests. He stared at the marvel of it, how it had been here since the start of time. The power of it and how it sustained life, both within and around it. It was a thing of beauty just like the Forest he called home.

What had Janda said about the river? He thought back to one of her many stories that she told each evening as they ate. They were more lesson than story, though. He could visualise it now, the memory of her voice bringing a tear to his eye.

'A drop of water forms at the spring and joins the many others. They all flow along the river but take different routes, some getting caught in still waters, others in rapids or eddies. In the end, they all arrive at the same point but at different times.' Having seen the river, he had asked about the start and the end, wanting to know more but she had scolded him for missing the point of the story.

'The river is life. The drops of water are the many men and women of this world. The still waters, rapids and eddies are all events in one's life that defines how long they live. But ultimately, we all arrive at the same point.'

He stood and turned downriver, staring at the white foam as the current carried it out of sight along the course.

"We all arrive at the same point." He whispered.

"Death." Now he knew his way. He would follow the river as it wound its way to wherever it went. And when he found Janda, as he was now sure he would do, he would ask again about the beginning and end.

12

"We make camp here for the night." It wasn't an order, more of a statement from Garlen as they approached the point rider who was waiting patiently near a small copse of trees.

"We have at least another hour or so before dark, Garlen. We should ride on." It was Bryn who answered him as he rode next to the Prince with Mathor on the other side. The tall, balding soldier didn't even wait for Garlen to reply to Bryn but whirled his horse around and cantered down the line of the troop passing orders.

"Here there is shelter for the horses. Besides, I need the men to see something." He pulled his horse to the side of the column and raised his voice to address Bex who was riding some ranks behind.

"Lady Bex, a moment of your time, if you please." She kicked her horse into a trot and fell in beside him.

"Whatever my Prince requests," she simpered falsely with a knowing smirk on her face. She saw the effect addressing him with his title had and was able to add before he commented, "If you insist upon being titleless amongst your men including Bryn and myself, then I insist upon the same. I am after all, no lady." She could feel Ishtara snigger inside.

"Whilst I trust my men with my life, Bex, I am not sure I could trust them to withhold all urges whilst travelling with someone as beautiful as you. Especially with your chequered past. I would rather they think of you as a Lady rather than. . ." he paused to find the correct word.

"As a whore?" Bex completed his sentence for him. He blushed slightly and nodded.

"The man who did this to me," she gently caressed the scar that run down her forehead and cheek, "when I find him, will pay very, very slowly. One of his men paid very dearly for being my pimp, Garlen. I gutted him when I was fifteen. I have fed the crows with quite a few more since then. I think I am able to handle myself."

"Bex, my men aren't common guild scum. They are killers, every one of them."

'You have a little help now.' Ishtara spoke within her head.

"And besides," Bex tapped her forehead, "I have a little help now."

"And that leads me on to what I have to ask you." He pondered for a while as his men passed by. He tapped his forehead as Bex had done.

"Your friend, I need my men to see her in all her glory. When we fight for real, I want them to know what to expect when Ishtara appears. I don't want them to drop their guard if caught unawares. That is why we need to camp now. I want you and Ishtara to demonstrate what you can do."

'It is a good point.' Ishtara put forward.

'Yes, I believe you can be a bit frightening, my friend.' Bex joked back.

'Tell him, yes.'

"We agree. On one condition."

"Oh?" Garlen looked a bit puzzled.

"I want some answers afterwards, Garlen. I want to know what the Ghosts do for you and what you aren't telling me."

"Agreed." Garlen sighed.

The troops bustled about with preparing the camp. Several men peeled off to care for the horses, feeding and watering them, whilst more made fires ready for cooking.

"Feed well, men. No more fires after tonight. From here in we make do with dry rations."

"We could always roast Konar, he would feed us for a week or two!"

A portly soldier who was stirring gruel in a pot over one of the fires stood up and faced the warrior who had made the jest, snatching a knife from his belt and waving it threateningly.

"And do you know why I am so fat, Luset?"

Luset skipped back away from the knife and laughed. The Ghosts who sat near the fire looked up from cleaning their equipment and hooted along with Luset.

"Every time I slept with your mother, she cooked me a big breakfast, you young whelp! That's why!"

The soldiers hooted louder and roared with laughter as Luset snarled back at the older chef.

"Enough!" Garlen's voice cut through the hullabaloo and the Ghosts fell silent. They ate in near silence a meal of hot gruel and warmed roast meat washed down with ale. Once they had finished eating, Garlen called them to order.

"My Ghosts! We ride once again on a perilous mission and I am proud and glad once again to have you by my side. The man you pledged allegiance to when you enlisted, my father, lies dead – killed in a cowardly act by the invaders. Our kingdom lies threatened no matter how successful our mission is now. Even if we rescue my sisters, the invaders will still attack Tannaheim and the Western Kingdoms. It will then be the turn of your families to be threatened but I promise you this, I will do everything in my power that as many of you return to fight for our homelands."

A sombre silence fell over the men as they realised that some of them may not return from the trip.

"On our missions before it was us alone who faced the swords of our enemies. Now today as we face our greatest test, we have two – no, three more to our number. Bryn Kar, a warrior of Jacarna will give us knowledge of its layout and can guide us to where we must go. I wager now that not many of you have travelled to Jacarna, let alone have the same knowledge." Garlen motioned to Bryn who stood and acknowledged the ranks of soldiers.

A blond soldier raised his hand, his blue eyes burning with energy.

"I have visited the Jewels of the East."

"Well, I am sure if this warlord Karchek has made his command centre in the brothels and taverns of the waterfront, Vertes, then maybe Bryn Kar will pass to you the responsibility for leading us there." A ripple of laughter broke from the ranks of the men as they gathered around, some seated, some standing.

"And we have Bex, who will introduce you all to Ishtara, our third companion now." As Bex stood up, she let her cloak fall to the ground and strode out in front of Garlen. She could feel the gaze of all the men on her.

"Mathor? Do you have the staves?" Garlen turned to Mathor who nodded and stood, passing him four staves cut in the Samakan tradition – just short of the height of Bex and as thick as the woman's wrist. Garlen handed one to Bex who spun it in front of her.

'*What sort of demonstration does Garlen want?*' Ishtara asked.

'I have sort of a notion, but just how much control do you have when you take over my body?'

'I have enough, why?'

'You will see.' Bex answered, happy to leave Ishtara seeking a proper answer for once.

"Bex, you mentioned earlier you could handle yourself against my men. Would two make it fairer?" Again, the men laughed and chattered amongst themselves. "Or maybe three?"

Kardanth stood up and shouted, his hands going for the hilts of one of his throwing knives on his chest. The small man was angry at his Prince as much as at Bex.

"I'll show her, Garlen. She can keep that fancy sword of hers and I'll take her with these!" He gestured at Caladmorr that hung at her belt.

"No knives! I need every one of you." Garlen held out a stave to Kardanth who reluctantly took it.

"Who else? Rica? Luset?" Garlen played to the crowd. Bex was pleased to see the young Rica shake his head and turn down the offer. Luset, however stood up and grabbed the stave from Garlen.

"With pleasure, Garlen. Will there be any looting of the body afterwards?" he turned to the watching soldiers and smiled, winking at them and encouraging them to roar with amusement. Garlen looked apologetically at Bex who shrugged her shoulders. She could feel Ishtara simmering inside.

'Easy, Ishtara, easy.' After soothing her inner demon, she turned her attention back to Luset. He held his staff outstretched pointing at her.

"That depends, Luset. Do you have anything worth taking after I put you down?"

Her comment brought a crow of laughter from many of the men, glad that she was giving back as much as she had been given. Several of the men started cheering her name.

"Anyone else?"

A scarred soldier stood up and gestured to Garlen. The man was bald with several scars across his face.

"Callar, good to see you stand!" Garlen announced, handing over his last staff. Bryn walked over to her and held her arm, leaning forward to speak into her ear.

"Take care!"

Bex nodded and undid her sword belt, handing it over to him. She stepped out into the circle and raised her staff. The three men took up their positions and warily spread out in front of her.

'Ah, I see what demonstration he needs now. I take it you don't want to kill them?'

'Er, no! That isn't the desired result, but let's just get out of this as best we can, eh? I was hoping for better odds, though.'

'We have faced worse together and come through it.'

Bex smiled to herself. Garlen held his hand up to bring the crowd to silence.

"Ready?" he dropped his hand to start the duel. His hand had barely begun to move before Luset swung his staff at Bex, catching her off guard. It was as much as she could do to sway her head backwards and even then, the edge of the staff crashed against her forehead. She flew backwards, landing heavily but rolling over to her knees and hands. Callar came rushing in, staff held overhead in two hands, ready to deal a terrible blow.

'Now?' She could feel Ishtara start to rage and expand within her.

'Not yet.'

She lunged forward with her staff held above her head in a classic block, with the point angled down to one side. Callar's staff met it with a resounding crack and her own weapon was nearly thrown from her grasp. She barely had time to acknowledge the look of surprise on Callar's face to be met with a block of such brute force from a woman before Kardanth darted forward with a jab. Bex twisted her body to one side to avoid it and swung a lazy attack to ward him off. She noted, that despite the early attack from Luset, he was not eager to join the attack.

Callar and Kardanth attacked together and it took all Bex's skill and Ishtara's extra energy and reflexes to avoid them. She blocked from Callar again before kicking out with a side kick at Kardanth. Her boot connected with the wiry man's chest and he staggered back winded.

Bex's respite was short lived though. As Kardanth crumpled backwards, Callar swung again, catching Bex with a glancing blow across her upper arm. She warded off another attack and moved back to catch her breath. As she heard the calls and jeers of the watching soldiers, she noticed Garlen watching pensively whilst Bryn watched with a disgusted look on his face.

"Come on, you bitch! I am going to break every bone in your fucking body!" roared Luset as he marched menacingly into the fray. Kardanth was also back on his feet and had regained his composure.

'How about now?'

'Let them get a little closer'

'They are quite close already, Bex.'

'Just a little closer!'

It was then that one of the onlookers threw a small coin purse into the makeshift arena.

"10 crowns on Lady Bex!" It was Rica. His shout brought a fresh chorus of cheers and jeers but Bex was pleased that the young soldier had first turned down the offer from Garlen to fight her and then was willing to bet his gold behind her. Several others took him up on his offer, throwing their own coin purses into the ring and shouting their wagers. Luset was not amused and rounded on Rica.

"Backing that bitch, eh Rica? I saw you talking with her on the ride out, are you looking for something from her tonight?"

The answer came, however, not from Rica or Bex but from Ishtara. Both Garlen and Bryn had heard the booming voice before, back in the throne room at the events after Anjoan's murder. However, most of the watching soldiers had not. The hooting and cheering that had accompanied the fight stopped abruptly and an uneasy silence fell over the arena.

"The answer is no, Luset. No, he isn't. Though he would stand more chance than you." Luset turned his attention away from Rica and slowly faced Bex/Ishtara.

"Conjuration tricks won't save you, bitch! I am going to break you!" He snarled viciously at Bex; his stave held out in front of him pointing at the Samakan woman. Callar, however, dropped his staff and stumbled backwards, falling to his backside with his arms splayed out behind him.

"She's smoking, Luset, smoking!" Kardanth yelled. Luset was about to admonish the small wiry fighter but then noticed what Kardanth and Callar had seen. Smoke rose from Bex's form, spilling from the gaps in her clothing in plumes. Both Kardanth and Luset could feel the heat radiating from the black-haired woman and they involuntarily took a step backwards. A large crack rent the air that caused several of the onlookers to dive for cover. Those that kept upright would have the memory of the young Samakan woman erupting into a pillar of flame etched deep into their minds.

From the column of fire strode forward Ishtara in all her glory. Tall and striking, the form of the fire demon advanced upon Luset, her skin a swirling pattern of red and orange lava. Flames blazed along the top of her skull, in between the twisted horns that pointed towards the heavens.

Whilst Callar scrambled backwards, Luset swung his staff, a horrified look drawn upon his face. Ishtara blocked the blow easily and swept her staff down against Luset's legs. The boastful soldier was knocked from his feet and crashed heavily to the ground. Or would have crashed heavily to the ground if Ishtara had not dropped her staff and reached out to snatch a grip on his trailing ponytail. She hauled him up, lifting him high so he had to stretch to keep his toes on the ground.

"Do you want more?" she asked.

"Enough!" Garlen broke into the ring, his voice broke the silence and brought the stunned crowd to life. Bickering erupted along the ringside with some men collecting winnings and others protesting that it had been unfair for Garlen to pitch his three men against a demon.

'I think you can let him go now, Ishtara.' Bex spoke, suddenly aware that she was now the invader in someone's mind.

'Ahh, Bex, I think he wants to play more.'

Ishtara turned to Garlen, a solitary yellow flame burning deep in the black coal pits that were her eyes. She was slightly shocked to see a small element of fear in his eyes, something that had not shown on the young prince even with the news of the Cassalian invasion and the attacks upon his family. She turned her attention back to her struggling captive, leaning in so her face was closer to his.

"Do you want to rape me now, Luset?" she asked, her lips curling into a grin. He could feel the heat from her face and tried to shy away. "Well, I am feeling, how do you say it? I am feeling in heat right now. Is that right?"

"I said enough!" Garlen squared up to Ishtara who tutted and dropped Luset to the ground. She turned and walked away.

'I think we showed them, Bex.'

'We sure did. I hoped it served its purpose.'

'I'll let you have your body back now.' Ishtara smiled. Bex felt the gut-wrenching pain again and collapsed to her knees, exhausted by the exertion of the fight and the transmogrification.

"Luset! No!" Bex heard the shout from Garlen and turned to look over her shoulder. Luset had sprung from his crumpled heap on the floor and was lunging at Bex with a short dagger in his grip.

'*Bex, look out!*' Ishtara exclaimed. Bex felt the demon's power build up as if to change again but it was too late. As the blade pierced her shirt and entered her shoulder, she opened her mouth to scream but only a breath escaped. She flung herself backwards and her gaze lifted to the dark sky above. The last thing she saw was Luset's head spring from his shoulders.

13

The skyship approached the city of Jacarna. Its dragon head was made of steel with details picked out in gold, the eyes bright purple stones. From the corner of the jaws of the dragon, blood stained the wooden hull carmine in streaks, giving it an appearance as if the dragon had just devoured its prey. Instead the prey stood on its deck, two young girls, their long dresses torn and dirty. Their demeanour betrayed their noble upbringing as they stood straight and upright, facing the prow of the skyship. Their faces however, betrayed their young years as their frightened eyes stared at the vast panoramic view that opened in front of them, illuminated by the rising sun.

Many of the larger buildings of the once great city were in ruins, shattered shells that had once housed the opulence of one of the Eastern Cities. Smoke billowed from many fires and the two young princesses could see great sections of the walls that had offered no protection from the alien onslaught, reduced to rubble. Great pieces of stone lay over the once peaceful meadows that surrounded the city and had also spilled into the city itself, a giant wave of destruction sweeping away many of the small homes inside the great walls. In the distance they could see a forest of tents set as an overspill of the city and a hundred or more skyships laid to rest on the green pastures. The tents were raised in straight, regimented lines.

"You won't win, you know. It will be easier for all if your ruler submits to our Emperor," a rasping voice spoke from behind them. Ingren, the older of the two, turned around and saw it was the commander of the skyship. Lord Carmig was taller than most inhabitants of Maingard and his armour made his shoulders and chest even more imposing. He wore black plate emblazoned with a relief of a dragon demon in silver. His black hair was long on one side of his head but a horrid mash of burns and scars on the other side prevented any growth, giving him an insane, lop-sided look.

"My father will search high and low for us and when he finds us, he will kill you and his armies will turn your men, no matter how many, into carrion feed," the words came easily to Ingren even though her tone faltered.

"Your father is dead; I am afraid to say." Carmig turned away. "Killed by one of your own kind who knew that we offer the only choice for you."

"You bastard!" the tall skinny girl flung herself at him only to find herself knocked to the deck by his blow. She lay on the deck sobbing as her sister stood immobile and cried.

"It was done to reduce the capability of your forces. You will become the bargaining tools to bring your mother to her knees," he rasped. "Get her to her feet. And stop her crying!" he walked away, annoyed at himself for letting the feelings of the two youngsters get to him. Two guards rushed forward; the upper parts of their faces obscured by grill like visors. They grabbed her under her armpits and lifted her to her feet, struggling. Another walked forward and moved Moren, her younger sister, towards the gunwale of the skyship. They were approaching the city fast now, and just in front of the main gate into Jacarna was a huge bonfire, the flames roaring high and the smoke rising tall like an immense tower. The skyship started to pass within metres of the smoke when the two girls became plagued by a sickly, sweet smell. Both clasped hands over their nose and mouth in order to stop the smell penetrating and Moren took a step forward to peer over the side of the skyship.

Ingren knew what the smell was. A year or two ago whilst riding with her tutor and squires they had come across a dead rider and his horse. He had fell on hard ground, both horse and rider breaking their leg and, unable to move, had died a slow lingering death. Nature had taken its course and by the time the young princess's retinue had discovered them, the rider and horse had both turned bloated and decayed, food for carrion and flies. The smell coming from the bonfire and the heaps around it were the same as then, only this time stronger, more pungent.

Moren collapsed back, bile and vomit pulsing from her mouth as her stomach heaved at the sight below. Ingren fell to her knees to hold her younger sister and couldn't help but look over the side as well. They were burning corpses, piles of dead waiting to be thrown on to the large pyre already blazing. The crematory was already three times the height of a man and giant human figures were scooping up armfuls of limp bodies and tossing them like broken dolls into the flames.

The skyship closed in on the fortress like palace and came to a rest on the flat roof alongside several other ships. Boarding steps were wheeled up to the side of the ship allowing the passengers to disembark. Guards held onto the arms of the princesses and escorted them off the ship behind Lord Carmig.

14

Jerone walked south. He had spent the rest of the night sleeping soundly and was refreshed in body and mind when he had awoken. He had eaten a quick breakfast of fruit along with a small piece of salted meat that he had brought with him from Janda's home. Ever more confident that there would be no further pursuit he walked on the banks of the White River as it wound its way south. Travelling downstream, he walked along the wide river with his hammer propped casually on his shoulder, on the path worn into the grassland that bordered the water's edge.

"Ahoy!" He jumped at the shout from behind him and spun about. He hadn't heard anyone approaching and was kicking himself for being surprised. As he looked up, he saw why. The voice came from a man standing in the bow of a small sailed barge. The boat rode low in the water with the surface of the great White River no more than a foot below the gunwales. A solitary mast held two triangular sails, the aft one secured by a wooden boom at the lower edge and the head sail stretched down the bow, close to where the newcomer stood.

Like Jerone, he was bare chested despite the cold and wore

red breeches. His barrel chest had a smattering of orangey red hair, but he was completely bald upon his head. His beard was large and unkempt, and had been dyed to a deep red that was not dissimilar to the carmine of his trousers.

"Ahoy, Friend!" His voice boomed out over the river. "Can I interest you in some fine food and accompaniment on this fine morn?" Jerone pondered the offer. He had eaten enough this morning already, but the boat offered rest and possibly would make his travel safer should Veng Stonefist renew any pursuit of his son's killer. The forest people would not think of looking for him in the company of the outsiders. He nodded enthusiastically and beckoned the boat over towards the bank.

Red Beard turned to the slight figure who sat at the stern of the boat next to the tiller and motioned that they should steer for the shore. As the boat neared the riverbank, Red Beard held out his hand to Jerone and they clasped forearms as the forest man jumped lithely aboard. The boatman was slightly taller than Jerone but a heavier build. The young forest man was well aware of the power in the newcomer's grip.

Now as they stood face to face the two men sized each other up. Red Beard wore silver rings in his ears, four on each, and now that Jerone was up close, he could see a number of small scars on the man's arms and chest. A thick bladed sword sat in a buckskin scabbard hanging from Red Beard's belt. His dark eyes stared at the younger man causing the youth to flinch slightly.

"Risas-tu" he shook Jerone's hand vigorously and carried on. "From Nordal. I take it from those," he pointed to Jerone's scars, "that you are from the forest." He nodded in the direction of the great wood. Jerone nodded.

"You won't need that here." He pointed to the hammer that Jerome carried on his shoulder. Grabbing a pole from the deck of the boat, he pushed off from the bank. Jerone watched Risas-tu as he strained against the weight of the boat, his back a powerful wall of muscle.

"Jerone and yes, I am from the forest. How do you know about us and the way of the forest people?"

Risas-tu turned back and moved to the centre of the boat, taking a seat on a low bench in front of the mast. He indicated to Jerone to sit near him and the dark-haired youth did so, sitting with his back against the low side of the boat. Behind the mast, the deck was cut away to form a small open hold for cargo and a black and white striped canvas formed a low tent over it.

"I trade with them, some of the tribes that live on the slopes of the Nordal Mountains and the riverbanks to the north." Risas-tu glanced at Jerone. He sensed that the man from the forest was about to contradict him.

"Not all of your people are as secretive as you think. Many of the northern elders will trade anything for gold and silver. And I mean anything. There is even a trading enclave on the north bank of the White River about a hundred miles upstream."

"My elder warned us against the outsiders, their greed and their ways. He said that Herne feared that our way would be worn down, eroded and replaced." Jerone finally spoke, upset and bewildered that some of his people had been swayed by the outsider's gold.

"Your way is safe enough for now, purely because the kings of Maingard couldn't be fucked interfering with a load of tree huggers." He gave a hearty chuckle, completely ignorant of the fact that he may have insulted his guest. They sat in an uneasy silence for a minute or two.

"Where are you headed, boy?" Risas-tu finally broke the silence.

"Anywhere." Jerone turned his head to face the forest that

had once been his home. "Anywhere away from here." He sighed and closed his eyes.

"I'm heading to Jacarna. I have someone waiting for my cargo as soon as I can get there. You have heard of Jacarna, haven't you? One of the Jewels of the East." The black eyes stared out at the forest man again and the bushy red beard split as the boatman grinned, displaying immaculate, white teeth. Jerone looked back, perplexed. Risas-tu's grin broke into a roaring laugh at the forest man's confusion.

"Jacarna, City of the Silver Horse!" Risas-tu threw his head back and laughed again.

His words brought Jerone bolt upright and scrabbling inside his satchel with a start. His fingers wrapped around the chain and locket and he took the piece of jewellery out.

"A silver horse like this?" he held his hand high, the locket dangling in the morning sun. The reflected rays dazzled both men as they looked upon the beautiful craftsmanship.

"Aye, lad. That is the Silver Horse of Jacarna. A mighty fine example of the skills of Jacarna's goldsmiths. I thought you followed your elder's advice and stayed clear of us outsiders and our greed?" His eyes narrowed as he questioned the young man.

"I did…. I mean, I do." Jerone spluttered, clasping the locket back against his chest. "I found it." Risas-tu's eyes narrowed even more.

"You found it? Or stole it?"

"I found it!" Jerone snapped back. Did taking a locket from a corpse still count as stealing? He did not know, having not come across the problem before but felt offended by Risas-tu's tone.

"Whoa, lad. I told you that you had no need of that here." Jerone looked at the bearded man, puzzled. Then he noticed that he had brought the warhammer up to the ready in his right hand whilst his left still clutched the chain and locket. Risas-tu held out his left hand as if to calm the forest man but his right hand had slipped down to the hilt of the menacing looking sword at his side. Jerone blinked and then let the warhammer slide back down through his grasp to the deck. The boatman from Nordal laughed again and clapped his hands in front of him.

"You found it. That's what we will agree on. Now how about a bite to eat?" He stood and reached for a wooden crate that was about a foot square. Opening the lid, he took out a small loaf of bread and split it in two, holding out one half for Jerone. The young man gingerly took it almost apologetically.

"Thank you. And I will go with you all the way to Jacarna, if you will take me."

"Aye, lad. Just don't go getting any little mad moments again, eh?" They ate in silence, listening only to the sounds of the forest that passed by a bowshot away.

Jerone carefully placed the locket back into his satchel and put the strap over his shoulder.

A faint grunt, or was it a groan, came from under the canvas tent behind Risas-tu. Jerone listened intently should the noise come again. When it was evident that silence had fallen again, he looked up at Risas-tu. The bald man sat quietly chewing his bread, his eyes nearly closed.

"What is your cargo, friend?"

"Livestock," came the simple reply. Jerone looked across at the black and white striped canvas stretched over a taut rope that run from the mast to the stern of the boat. There wasn't much of a gap between the edges and the deck.

"And don't you be looking under that canvas, friend." Risas-tu hadn't moved, his jaw movement almost imperceptible under the bushiness of that untidy beard. Jerone tensed slightly at his tone, the word 'friend' not being in a friendly tone at all.

15

Bex dreamt that she was at sea. The small boat that she was in, no bigger than a ship's dinghy, was rocking in a haphazard but mesmerising fashion. The sun beat down on her bare face and she was aware that her lips were dry and cracked. Her eyelids fluttered opened allowing the sun's rays to burn the insides of her eyes. She felt a dull ache in her left shoulder and tried to reach out to it with her good hand.

'*Bex, can you hear me? Are you okay?*' The voice seemed to materialise in the air next to her and she twisted her head to search for the speaker.

'*Bex, I am here. It is Ishtara, inside you. Don't struggle, you took a nasty wound.*'

'*Where am I? What happened?*'

'*Take your time, let me explain.*'

The sun disappeared and she found herself able to look about. The ache persisted in her shoulder, an ache that turned to a shooting pain every time she moved or put pressure on that shoulder. She wasn't on a boat but on a bier suspended between two horses. One was her own whilst the other had a rider. Her eyes focused on the shadowy form and she realised it was Rica.

'*Well, that means that I am still with the Ghosts.*'

'*Do you remember anything?*'

She thought hard, remembering the arena, Callar, Kardanth and Luset approaching with staves. Scenes from the fast and furious fight flashed past her eyes, kicking out at Kardanth after blocking and dodging attacks from the three men. And then, the feeling of heat and pain as Ishtara pushed her way from her mind to replace Bex's body with her own fiery, demonic form. The terrified look on Luset's face as she held him up by his hair and the sharp shout of Garlen to end the fight all came back. But the fight hadn't ended there. After reverting back to Bex came the flash of Luset's blade as he lunged towards her, the dagger cruelly piercing her shirt and shoulder.

'*You remember everything, Bex.*'

And then the realisation that she had been stabbed, falling instinctively backwards to reduce the blow. That had only been part of the reason that she hadn't taken a more serious wound. The impetus of Luset had been weakened by a sword blow, a blow that had decapitated the enraged attacker. She remembered clearly now, the swing of the steel, her hands rising at first to fend off Luset's attack and then to deflect his tumbling head. A blow from a sword that had possibly saved her life, a blow that had been savagely dealt by... the fog of war cleared to reveal the determined face and blond hair of Garlen.

'*That's right, Bex. Garlen reacted before anyone else. Lucky for you,*' Ishtara paused, '*well, lucky for us really.*'

'*How long?*'

'*Don't worry, you were only out for the night. We have been travelling an hour or so.*'

"Luset?" she spoke out, mumbling her words and wincing as she tried to lift her head up.

'Dead, obviously Bex. Not even the Qoi can survive that!'

"Ah, now that is a shame," Rica had noticed that she was awake and looked down upon her. "Your waking thought is about him, just after he loses his head. He will be upset."

Bex groaned and lay back.

"Don't you worry about him; few tears were shed for him last night. A few ales were drank to him but not many tears." Rica lifted his voice to a shout and bellowed forward to Garlen that Bex was awake.

"Besides, I have to thank you. I won a tidy sum on you last night." Rica grinned as he looked back down, his teeth as messy and crooked as his hair.

"I should be thanking you, you turned Garlen down when he offered you the staff."

"To be fair, Gordin told me about you when you followed the kidnappers in the palace." Rica mentioned the older soldier who had accompanied Garlen, Bryn and Bex into the sewers.

"He told me how you lit the way with your hand. You unnerved him. I figured if you could do that with your hand then I didn't want to find out what you could do with the rest of you."

Before Bex could answer, Garlen and Bryn rode up, swinging into line with Rica and Bex's riderless horse.

"Lady Bex, you are back with us. My apologies for last night. I didn't expect it to end like that."

'Well, how did you expect it to end?' snorted Ishtara, luckily only to Bex.

'Shhh!'

"My thanks though, to you for saving my life. And my apologies that it cost the life of one of your men."

"Luset was not the most popular in the Ghosts. At best he was an annoyance to the others, at worst – a bully. At one point, at the time of the Orc Wars, he was a fine soldier but since we returned, he was different. A good fighter but not a good soldier. That he proved last night when he disobeyed an order. Unfortunately for him, it cost him his life. But you have no blame attached to you for his death. It was my fault entirely. I should have retired him years ago." Garlen seemed to look at no one when he spoke but Bex could see he was affected slightly by the death of Luset. He paused and then looked down over Bex's empty horse at her as she lay on the bier.

"Can you ride, Lady Bex. I have my side of the bargain to keep. I think it is time I explained myself and the reason for the Ghosts to you and Earl Kar here."

Bex nodded and lifted herself to a sitting position. Garlen called for the column to halt whilst Rica and Bryn helped her to her feet and then removed the wooden stretcher from between the two horses. As she wrapped herself in her cloak and fastened it about her neck, Bex felt a whole lot better.

'Thanks to you, Ishtara.'

'What for?'

'Your power accelerates my healing. That wound should have put me down for a lot longer. I owe you my life.'

'Tish, my dear Bex. Without you I would be dead, cold and alone on this dying world. At least we can try to bring some healing to it.'

Rica handed her the reins to her horse and she clambered onto the black steed in a slightly inelegant fashion. She nodded to Rica in acknowledgement and manoeuvred her horse next to Garlen's. The Prince sat relaxed in the small light saddle whereas Bryn, his horse next to Garlen, was slightly stiff on the unfamiliar saddle. The cavalry saddle favoured by Jacarna was substantial and heavy.

Bex was surprised to see the dark-haired soldier's face break into a slight smile as he handed her the sword belt and scabbard that she had asked him to hold before she had fought in Garlen's duel the night before.

"Thank you, Earl Kar."

"It is a fine blade. I took the liberty to examine it closer whilst you were recuperating last night. It seems perfectly balanced."

"It's one of the fabled *weirdswords*. The runes inscribed on the blade spell out..."

"*Caladmorr.*" Bryn Kar interrupted her.

"That's right." She sounded a little annoyed that her thunder had been stolen by the Earl knowing what the ancient runes said.

"*Caladmorr*, the sword once wielded by Rhag-ar-Sinbel, the demon thief. It was reputed to be able to take him into the shadow world to protect him and in battle, no armour could stand before it."

"The *weirdswords* are just a myth. A story bards tell to wile away the winter hours and earn a few miserly crowns." Garlen harrumphed.

"Who knows what the difference between myth or reality is unless they meet it, Garlen. The stories of the *weirdswords* have been passed down for fifty generations or more." Bryn turned his head to address Bex, "I would be interested how it came to be in your possession."

"I was with a friend, a very good friend. And we found it in a barrow in the sandy wastes south of the Eastern Ports." She smiled demurely.

"Enough about my sword, let us talk about you and your Ghosts."

The blond Prince stood up on his stirrups and shouted out to the front of the column, giving the signal for Mathor to ride on. The three joined the column and rode together, the Prince in the middle flanked by Bex on the left and Bryn on the right.

"As you know, I was sent by my father to fight in the Orc Wars in the hope that it would cure my rebellious attitude after..." he paused, staring ahead with an air of melancholy. "After my sister's death."

"I arrived in the south as a snotty youth of sixteen summers.

Mathor was my demanding and relentless sergeant and we were part of the main line of arms facing Mayak's forces. When the orcs fought like orcs, they were successful. Small warbands no more than a hundred swords strong. Their raiding parties roamed far and wide behind our lines and our supply lines were threatened more often than not." He gave an ironic laugh and carried on.

"But when Mayak's generals mobilised his forces in numbers equal to ours, the fighting came to a deadlock. Shield wall clashed upon shield wall and the earth was soaked with blood – human and orc alike.

"For five long months the lines of battle hardly moved. What gains were made one day were lost the next. And then, one day in Eostremonath, it all changed. An orc war party raided deep behind our lines and assassinated several our army commanders. A major offensive by Mayak's forces tried to capitalize on the confusion and nearly succeeded. It was chaos and disarray until Lord Shales, the Queen's brother stemmed the flow."

His voice had changed slightly, some of the authority had slipped from his tone but there was still the grim, steely determination that Bex and Bryn had got used to.

"Our lines held, just. Then Shales ordered the formation of a similar unit of our own. A party to raid and disrupt the enemy. I volunteered along with Mathor and Kardanth from my own unit. All in all, a hundred men chose to join, and we left that night under the command of Lord Haldred the White. I was surprised that Shales let me go but he never said a word. He did however get a few choice words from my father when he found out." He gave a hearty chuckle.

"The next night we were several miles deep into orc territory when Haldred lost it. He sent me and about thirty others to reconnoitre a forest ahead prior to camping for the night. Whilst we were about our business, an orc cavalry unit, boar riders, hit the others. They didn't stand a chance and with half a mile of open countryside between us and them, we couldn't aid them." His voice trailed off and he was silent for a moment.

"But that is war, Garlen. I understand how you feel though. My unit died one by one through the streets of my own city." Bryn spoke quietly, hoping to reassure the Prince. Garlen turned to Bryn, staring directly into his eyes.

"They fed our wounded to their boars, Bryn." His voice was raw, and for a second, Bex noticed his eyes glaze over as the memories of those who were long dead haunted him "We heard them even from that distance. The grunting and roaring, a hideous sound but that wasn't as bad as the crunch of bone and armour." Bex winced, the unimaginable now vivid in her thoughts. Most orc cavalry rode horses like their human counterparts, but the elite units rode huge boars, big enough to carry a fully armoured orc and its own armour over its thick skin, and do so at a charge. They made for a terrifying opponent.

'Ew! I am glad this war thing did not exist on our world, Bex.'

'It is evil, I will grant you that, Ishtara. But a necessary evil.'

'Agreed, Bex. Without this warlike nature of yours, your world would be as dead as mine.' Bex didn't reply, knowing that Ishtara was correct.

'It still doesn't mean that I should like it.'

"What did you do?" Bryn asked, eager to break the silence.

"We melted away and hid like rats. The survivors all looked to me for leadership – after all I was a Lord, a son of the King. Most wanted me to lead them back home to safety but there was something that was unfinished for me, the way that Haldred and the others had died. I wanted vengeance." Garlen's fist clenched momentarily and the steely determination flooded back, returning the prince to the Garlen that Bex and Bryn had become used to over the last few days.

"We made our way south and chanced upon two hunters.

They were hunting orcs as well, their own village ransacked and pillaged by the orcs. We learnt a lot from them over the next few weeks, how to move, hide and kill without being unseen. We wreaked our vengeance for several weeks before making our way home." A wry smile broke upon his face that turned to a mixture of a sneer and a stifled laugh. "We even found the boar riders that had killed our men when they had camped for the night. We left their heads stuck on spikes as a warning for others and we poisoned their boars with a mixture of wortwyrm and stoneblood. It was good to watch the beasts bleed out from their insides. Well, it did for a minute or two."

"Once back with our forces we found Shales extremely excited. It seems that prisoners were telling tales of an army of ghosts that would appear from nowhere and kill before disappearing once more. We decided to carry on, taking reinforcements from the army of men who displayed the character that we needed, training them and working them hard.

"And then the war ended. Mayak and his generals just turned and marched away. I didn't want to see my men just thrown out of the army or worse, sent to garrison some far away post in lethargic boredom. They had skills that would be wasted when not in war and it was from one war that we came to another. Tannaheim had started to collapse into anarchy. With civic funds diverted to the war effort, crime had become rampant at home. Using my Ghosts was father's idea, a scalpel to cut away the dead and rotten flesh in our society. Now all we needed was something or someone to direct the cut." Garlen took a breath after the mention of his father. He looked at Bex and Bryn in turn and knew that they hadn't realised the secret.

"It was at my father's behest that I took on two identities. The first was…" he looked across at Bex and smiled.

"The first was 'The Lord of the Inns', Prince Garlen the womanizer, drunkard and fucker. A disreputable rogue who was no use whatsoever. To all intents an identity to ensure that all thought the Crown Prince was a fool."

"And the second identity?" Bex asked.

'I knew he was covering something, Bex!'

'Hush!'

Garlen turned to Bex and stared at her. His piercing blue eyes blazed with a degree of indignance at her question.

"Tikar Welk of course!"

"Anjoan's Phantom?" Bex exclaimed.

"Yes," Garlen looked ahead, focusing on the back of the rider in front rather than look into Bex's eyes.

"Tikar was my idea. I told father that I had no desire to reign and at first, he was furious; furious and disappointed. Gradually he came around to the idea that I would only grudgingly take the crown and ascend the Red Throne if there were no other alternative. And so Tikar Welk was born, a phantom who stalked the shadows of Tannaheim and the kingdom of Danaria, excising criminals and traitors. I recruited my own agents who gathered information of threats against the Throne and the City, and then my Ghosts would take action." He looked up at Bryn who just stared at the Prince in an understanding and admiring way.

"Criminals? Is that how you recognized my guild tattoo?" Bex asked. Garlen noted the not too understanding tone and quickly faced Bex.

"Criminals, yes." Then he noted the scowl across Bex's face. "No, Bex. Not your common criminal but..." Bex's scowl widened and Garlen actually blushed.

"I'm sorry, that didn't come out right."

Bex guffawed with laughter at his embarrassment which lightened the moment but did nothing to lighten the colour of Garlen's face. Within the confines of Bex's mind, Ishtara roared also.

"I meant those that prey on the misery of others; like rapists, traffickers and slavers. Just like Yab M'Vil."

At the mention of the corpulent, bald slaver, Bex shot an inquisitive glance at the Prince.

"Why mention him?"

"I had wanted to take him out for several months. A thousand or more youths from all over Maingard are brought into Tannaheim every year on his say so alone. I have had agents in his organisation for some time, feeding me information and waiting to strike."

"And then you fed me in turn, getting me to do your dirty work?" Bex scowled again. Being used was one of her pet hates.

"Not really, no. Believe me please, Bex. You were never meant to do our work for us. When I found out that you were interested in M'Vil, I had you followed. I would have warned you away, but I had a feeling that wouldn't have worked."

"I did plan on unleashing my Ghosts upon M'Vil, but you beat me to it. We would have been, how would you say? A little cleaner than you. I was told of your handiwork in the morning."

'I am glad he didn't interfere at the bastard's villa. We didn't need any help.' Ishtara added indignantly.

"Ishtara had a hand in it as well." Something clicked with Bex. "Ahh, so that's why you weren't as shocked as the others when Ishtara showed herself in the throne room? You already knew."

"Yes, Bex, and now you know. But we have a long way to go now." He nodded left and right to Bex and Bryn and kicked his horse onwards to the front of the column, ordering his troops to pick the pace up.

16

Moren cried, tears pouring down her face as she sobbed. To the younger girl's credit, Ingren thought to herself, she hadn't cried as they had been taken from the ship and had been half dragged, half carried down to the cell where they now found themselves. The ship had landed on the roof of the palace, a large flat stone area that had little in the way of battlements at the edges. After all, they weren't normally needed at the height of forty storeys.

From there, the Cassalian known as Silda had led the way as the soldiers had carried the princesses down. Once the soldiers had left the ship, either they had removed their leather face masks or unclasped them so they fell to one side. The exit from the roof was little more than a storm hatch, set at an angle to the floor and the stairs below had seen little use before the invasion. As they progressed downwards, the stairways improved, opening out wider and less steep. And then, for a while, they left behind the bare stone walls for walls that had plaster and ornate decorations, even though some were showing damage and signs of battle. Ingren saw several stains on the flagstones and walls that she guessed were bloody evidence of the demise of the defending soldiers.

Soon the stairways turned back to bare stone again and the lamps gave way to less frequent torches. The grotesque armour of their captors seemed to come alive in the flickering torchlight and the demonic faces appeared to mock and snap at the two girls. Ingren guessed that the palace had been built on many levels and that they had passed through the service levels onto those that the Royal family had occupied and then back into the lower service areas. Yet still they carried on.

For the first time, the sight of the odd door gave way to sets of thick steel bars blocking their way, guarded by troops that were different to the Cassalians. Some had blue skin, others were cat-like yet stood on their back two legs like humans. The young girl recoiled when she saw them but then realised that they weren't as terrifying as the men that held her. As they passed through the doorways of bars, the stairs changed again. The soldiers carrying them slowed as the walls narrowed, squeezing them. The light faltered and Silda took a flaming torch from the wall to light their way. They took another few flights of stairs, steps that circled tightly. The air changed, becoming damper and the stench of death and misery became stronger, invading not only her nostrils but seemingly seeping into her very skin. Ingren felt as if she was being squeezed down the gullet of some foul leviathan, heading straight for its stomach.

The steps opened out to a wide corridor with narrow, iron bound, wooden doors every six feet or so. This corridor in turn opened out to a large circular room with a dozen blackened doors fitted with barred windows set against the wall. In the centre of the room stood a brazier with red hot coals caged within. She grimaced when she noticed several brands and tools resting on the coals.

Silda opened one of the doors and Ingren saw that beyond it was a small cell, just big enough for a grown man to lay upon the cold stone floor. The girls were unceremoniously pushed through the doorway, sprawling on the floor. The imposing form of Silda blocked the door. He grinned as he spoke for the first time since they had left the ship.

"His Excellency, Lord Commander of the Almighty Emperor's Host, General Karchek will see you at his leisure." He hawked and spat at the two prisoners, the globule of phlegm hitting Moren's dress. He turned and motioned to his men that it was time for them to leave, slamming the door shut behind him and turned the key.

"Whores!" he muttered under his breath as they left.

It was then that Moren had started crying, huge sobs interspersed with her calling out for her father. At first, Ingren held her sister and tried to reassure her.

"Mori, please. It will be alright, you'll see. Garlen will rescue us. Right now, the biggest army the West has ever seen will be marching here to rescue us."

"Remember when we were younger and got lost in the forest outside the city. Mother had taken all of us on a picnic and we had strayed, running off with Dirian and Klush...." She broke off, realising that she had just said the names of her cousins, the two boys cruelly murdered during their own kidnapping. As her sister erupted in a further bout of huge sobs she ploughed on.

"You do remember, Mori, you do. We were scared and cold as the evening was drawing in. Who found us? That's right, Garlen. And who kept you safe until he came? Yes, me! I won't let anything happen to you, Mori, I won't!"

It did little to help as doubt was even starting to creep into her own tone. She waited patiently for what seemed like hours but was, in fact, just a few minutes listening to her sister. She knew that comforting her sister wasn't going to help. They both had to be thinking clearly to escape from this mess. Ingren stood and paced about the small cell. It was small with no furniture and only a small slit in the wall about eight foot up, just as the wall met the vaulted ceiling. A gutter ran central across the room, disappearing through a small gap in the wall, presumably she thought into the next cell.

"Shhh! Moren, Stop it now! I need to think, and you need to act like a Princess. Like a Barstt."

"Oh Ingen, I am only eleven! I am scared!"

"You are nearly twelve, and a Princess. Act like one!"

The words seemed to break through her sister's terror and brought her slightly nearer to a calm state of mind. Taking her chance during the calm, she examined the cell closely. She decided that every stone had been cut by a master mason as there was hardly a gap to be seen. The bars in the door, set about face height so captors could keep an eye on the unlucky wretches who found themselves incarcerated within, were set solid. An adult male in good health would not have been able to budge them, let alone a teenage girl. The light from the slit in the wall gave little illumination and indeed, the ceiling of the cell was hidden in shadows.

Ingen sighed and sat down next to her sister, reaching around her with her arm and hugging her tight.

"It will be alright, Mori. I promise you." Somehow there was less conviction in her voice than before.

They had sat without moving for several hours when they heard someone approaching. Ingren jumped up as someone fumbled with a key in the lock, placing herself between Moren and the door. The heavy door swung open and the figure of Silda was once again silhouetted in the doorway. He beckoned the two girls out of the cell.

Slowly Ingren stepped forward and turned to Moren, motioning that she should stand. She could feel the cold hand of her sister slip into hers and she gripped it tight. Princess Ingren of Danaria took a deep breath and stepped forward.

Apart from Silda, there were five others that had come to see the two princesses. Two were soldiers, dressed in black plate armour that covered their chests and arms. The carried halberds, long spears with axe heads mounted on the shafts as an additional blade. Unlike Silda, their helms covered their eyes and noses apart from small slits to see through. Their mouths and chins were visible, a deathly grey.

The third figure was a crooked man, his arms and legs akimbo, as if they had all been broken. His back was bent, and his features reminded Ingren of a rat, eyes beady and piercing and a nose that was long and pointed. His blond hair was matted and unkempt. It was hard for the young girl to see where the dark leather straps that criss-crossed his torso ended and his dark skin began.

The fourth was a small figure, clothed in a dirty brown robe that hid her true form. The hood was pulled over her face shrouding her features. Ingren could see a wizened brown hand clasp the top of the stick that tapped out a steady beat as she walked across the chamber.

The final man, if he was a man, was the most terrifying. A giant, nearly nine-foot-tall, stood in the centre of the room. His grey, pallid skin matched the grey of his quilted jerkin. He wasn't only immense in height but stature as well, his chest almost as wide as Ingren was tall. He took a step forward and Ingren saw the personification of evil in all its glory. His face was not only a mash of old scars, trophies from battles long ended, but there was also a fresh scar, crudely treated. An island of dried scab and matted plant material sat in a swollen purple sea above the giant's left eye. The light that the brazier cast to illuminate the grim tableau licked across his armour, giving life to the demonic features carved into it. She gripped her sister's hand tighter and could feel

Mori shrink away under the fiercesome stare of the newcomer.

General Karchek, Lord Commander of the Emperor's Host stared down at the two girls. So, this is the start of the next phase of the *knartevilder*, he thought. He grimaced as he moved, pain throbbing in his head and his groin. It had now been a day since the Hag had put the grim smelling poultice on his wound and it hadn't healed yet. To be fair to Narki, she had said it would get worse before it got better, the alchemical effects of the reagents within the plants that she had used would draw out the poison back to the wound where it would be absorbed by the poultice itself. The result was that he felt awful, his head pounded, and his vision blurred in waves, waves that came more frequently and pain that increased and increased.

"So, these are the Crown Princesses of Danaria. Anjoan's whelps? They look pretty pathetic to me."

His voice was harsh and grating, exactly as Ingren had imagined it would be. Yet she knew that he was right. They looked dishevelled, their hair in disarray and their dresses torn and filthy. Moren's eyes were red from crying and Ingren was sure that she looked the same. Still she bristled with indignance at the giant's words and pulled herself up straight.

"I am Princess Ingren of the House Barstt, daughter of Anjoan, King of the Red Throne of Tannaheim and Danaria, granddaughter to...."

The giant raised his hand and she stammered to a halt, the fire dying out inside her.

"I know who you are. Royalty or commoner, it makes no difference to me. The only importance that you have at the moment, is that of a hostage, a bargaining tool. Whilst I have no regard for the pathetic life that exists in the plane, I do have some regard for my soldiers. War costs lives and I do not want them to lose theirs unnecessarily. I would rather your mother surrender to me. That's right," he paused seeing their confusion. "Your mother has taken the throne instead of your drunken sot of a brother."

"No! That's a lie! Right now, my brother will be coming to save us. Coming at the head of the biggest army you have ever seen!" Ingren was red with anger but she also knew that it was possible that her brother had disintegrated at the loss of father, after all she had learnt that he had struggled with the death of Antht, his twin sister. That had been when Ingren was very young. The memories of her older sister were distant for her. She wasn't sure how much of Antht that Moren really remembered, being two years younger than her, rather than just the stories that her mother had told them.

Karchek roared with laughter. He leant forward, crouching so his face drew level with Ingren's and laughed again. She could smell the rank decay of his wound and saw the glare of evil in his eyes.

"If he is, he may think differently when I start to carve you up and send him the pieces. He has already lost his father. I am sure he would not want to lose his sisters as well."

He stayed crouched, his huge face staring at the two girls. He would have to have a fresh girl to replace the Princess Rothannir. Not that he would stop using her, death was no escape from his brutal lust, but he missed the fight and spirit that she had shown. Perhaps he might return later and use one of them – or both. If his head stood up to it. He blinked as a bout of double vision flashed before his eyes and it was a couple of seconds before that cleared. Then it was the blinding pain, like a dagger had pierced his temple, sinking deep into his brain. And then it was gone, He looked at the younger sister hiding behind and to the right of Ingren, then turned to stare at the older girl and then smiled, his tongue licking his lip as he did so.

It was then that Moren stood forward, fists clenched tightly at her side and her face puffy and red from crying.

"I hate you! You killed father and... and...." She was lost for words and tears streamed down her grimy cheeks. Karchek looked at her and she cowered. He laughed again, laughed at her pathetic appearance, at her attempt at bravery and how she shrank away. He turned back to face Ingren.

"She has a little fight. I wonder how much you have. It will be a joy to break her in. Maybe you as well. She is innocent whereas you might not be." He cocked his head at her, eyes looking her up and down, mentally stripping her until her young pre-pubescent body stood before him. She was thin, her body not yet entering the realms of womanhood. Karchek noticed her flush slightly and he chuckled again.

"A little fumble with a young Lord, or a stable boy perhaps? I wonder if your father knew he had raised such a whelp?" It wasn't the elder sister who responded though, but Moren. With Karchek still facing Ingren, Moren raised her hand and struck downwards at the face of the crouching Karchek.

"I hate you! I never want to see you again! I want to go home!" Her hand caught the swollen wound on Karchek's eye, ripping the sutures open and dislodging a large chunk of poultice, scab and flesh. Blackened blood ran from the wound and Karchek yelped with pain through gritted teeth as he sank further to the floor.

Silda steeped forward and grabbed the frightened princess by her arm before she could strike again and held her up high, so she struggled to keep her feet on the floor. Ingren stood dumbstruck at the actions of her little sister. The two guards stepped forward but Karchek waved them back.

He struggled to stand. The pain shook through his head as Rothannir's poison coursed through his veins. The room seemed to rock as if he stood on the deck of a ship at sea and he could hear the cackle of Narki the Hag as she stooped to his aid.

"No! Away, damn hag!" He stood tall and turned to face his

young attacker. He blinked twice as his vision refused to clear and he staggered as if he was drunk.

"You can't kill her, Karchek. You need her to force Sarsi to kneel to you." Narki the Hag cackled as Karchek seethed with anger. The giant general nodded slowly.

"But she doesn't want to see me again, eh?" He turned and beckoned to the crooked man. "Nevinoo, make it so. Take her eyes." Everything then seemed to move in slow motion for Moren.

She saw Karchek turn and walk away, staggering as he did so. One of the black armoured guards grabbed Moren from behind, wrapping one arm around her binding her arms tight against her torso and grabbed her hair with his other hand, holding her head still and tight.

Ingren screamed as Silda dragged her back and threw her viciously into their cell, slamming the door behind him. She held onto the bars of the little window in the cell door and screamed out for Moren.

Moren watched as the crooked man pulled one of the tools from the brazier, a long thin needle that now glowed red hot. The guard held her tight, but even so, she was paralysed with fear as Nevinoo, the crooked man, limped towards her.

Mesmerised by the glowing tip of the needle as it approached, Moren hardly blinked. She could see the cold air around the tip shimmer with the heat and then, as it neared her face, she could feel the heat prickle her skin.

The young girl screamed as the point of the needle entered her eyeball and she was suddenly awoken from her reverie. She could do nothing though, as the guard tightened his grip and she felt her eye burst, the soft innards of her eyeball flooding over her cheek. Moren, the eleven-year-old Princess of Danaria screamed, a long piercing scream of fear, pain and terror as she lost her primary sense. The last thing she saw, as Nevinoo started to plunge the needle into her other eye was the cackling form of Narki the Hag and the slavering face of the crooked man who had mutilated her.

Ingren echoed her sister's scream and hammered her fists on the door until her knuckles bled. Finally, she sank down and cried for the first time since they had been taken.

17

K archek had made for a terrible sight as he staggered up the winding flights of stone steps away from the dungeons below. Blood and pus caked the left side of his face and a loose piece of skin flapped over his eye. His wound was no better than the second that Rothannir had carved her mark upon his face.

His sudden appearance, stumbling half blinded and raging with anger, startled the two guards at the barred gate on the stairway. As soon as they had recovered their senses, they both moved to help him only for the giant to wave them aside.

"Away, get me Lord Remoh!" And, as if to underline his urgency, he grabbed one by the arm, his huge hand closing around the mail clad bicep. Staring straight at the hapless soldier's face he bellowed, spraying saliva and blood over his subordinate. One of the guards turned and sprinted off, his armour clanging as he ran.

"Now!"

He felt awful, the flickering flame from the torch that was pinned to the bare stone wall hurt his eyes and his head swam. The Emperor only knew what shit that hag had mixed into his bloodstream in her effort to cure him. Poisoned by that bitch of a princess in the first instance and then brought closer to death by Narki the Hag, and now brought to his knees almost by a little girl. By all that the Emperor holds dear, this shitty planet will feel his anger now.

He almost gave the order for his forces to move against the Tannaheim immediately but knew Jacarna needed to be completely subdued and emptied before he did that. He managed another couple of flights before he heard the footsteps of people approaching. The first guard had returned along with others. Karchek was glad to see the younger figure of Lord Remoh, one of his deputies.

Remoh was younger and slighter than the immense figure of Karchek. Still tall at just a little over six and a half feet, he was dwarfed by Karchek's height and girth. His short black hair merged seamlessly into a beard. When he spoke, his voice was calm and strong.

"Your Excellency, what has happened?" He motioned to two of the guards that followed him to pass by and secure the stairwell should there be any danger, but Karchek spoke to stop them in their tracks.

"Don't worry, it is nothing. Just one of those little bitches opened up my wound." He held a hand to his head and took it away, surprised at the amount of blood that now coated his thick fingers.

"Get me to the throne room right away and then get me that wrinkled hag. She'll be patching one of the bitches up in the dungeon below." As he spoke, he looked at the four Lord Remohs ahead of him and they all started to blur and shift in his vision. Karchek clenched his eyes shut for a second and opened them again. That was better, he thought. He could focus again but the pain in his head was as if the princess had stabbed him in his wound with a dagger. A dagger pushed to the hilt into his head. And with the angry, blind princess holding on to the hilt, causing it to wriggle with every movement of his. Karchek was suddenly aware of feeling hot and feverish with his undershirt clinging to his sodden back.

"Not the throne room," he added as Remoh ordered the guards to hold him upright. "My chambers. And get me that fucking hag!"

As Remoh started off, Karchek called him back. His legs buckled and his vision blurred again.

"Not you, Remoh. Take a skyship and fly to the Tannaheim. Liaise with Brant and tell him I want him back here. Then tell their queen that she has a week to surrender her throne to the Emperor and kneel before me. Tell her she will rule her land as my vassal and wife and her daughters will be returned to her unharmed. If she doesn't surrender, then her city will fall and the last thing she will see will be me raping her spawn as she dies....slowly."

Karchek started to sag in the grip of the two guards that held him, and it was all they could do to hold his immense frame upright. Lord Remoh snapped to attention and nodded to his commander.

"At once, your Excellency." He snarled at the two guards. "Get him to his chambers. At once!"

18

Morga scooped the dice back into the small leather cup and shook them vigorously. Turning his head, he spat on the floor and then rolled the dice onto the small table. He and Koopler were stationed at one of the huge towers that rose above the imposing wall of Tannaheim. Right now, the other two members of their squad were standing guard on the parapets of the tower above in the cold night air. Morga and Koopler were due to relieve them in an hour.

The fire roared in the tiny fireplace and Koopler sent sparks flying as he prodded the coals and wood with the tip of his sword. He was young, having not yet seen seventeen summers and the city guard armour looked big and loose on him. His gaunt face was framed by blond shoulder length hair. Morga on the other hand, was older, maybe by ten years. His dark hair was cropped short and his face twitched when he spoke.

"Three sixes! That's another copper crown you owe me, Koopler. That makes ten already tonight."

"Fuck you, Morga! I said I wasn't playing five minutes ago!"

"Bolam's Balls, Koopler. We don't go top side for another hour. What are we going to do for a whole hour?"

"If you shut up for a minute, I might get some sleep."

Morga was quiet for a minute as his companion settled down onto the bed of straw and furs. It seemed though he was counting the sixty seconds off in his head because he soon resumed talking, reaching for his dice and following the ritual shaking and spitting at the same time.

"You think Sarsi will take Anjoan's death sitting down? No way, Koopler! We will all bleed away so that she can have her revenge." He spat again and rolled. "We all have seats reserved in Kani's Hall, lad." Koopler rolled his eyes, there was little chance of him getting any further sleep before his shift started. He propped himself up on his elbow and looked at his older companion.

"You think so? Won't Sarsi just burn the bastards who did it? She is a witch after all."

"Witch, my arse, boy. She is no more a witch than your little cock is."

"She is, Morga, she is. My girl is a maid in the palace. She says that Sarsi is up to some weird magic in her tower."

"Like what, lad?" Morga chuckled.

"There hasn't been a funeral pyre yet, Morga."

"What do you mean?"

"No funeral pyre, Morga! What do you think I mean!" It was common practice in Danaria for the dead to be buried or burnt within twenty-four hours. For centuries, Royal corpses had been consumed by fire on a pyre.

"That doesn't mean anything weird is going on."

"That's not all. Another maid told her that the Queen slept with Anjoan's corpse last night."

"They were together for over twenty years, Koopler. Maybe she just wanted the security of being near him. Love does that sometimes I suppose."

"No, Morga! Not slept with - she *slept* with him!" He placed the emphasis on the second 'slept'. When he was rewarded with a blank stare from his companion he carried on. "Tobes Tits, Morga! Do I have to spell it out for you?" He made a crude gesture of pushing his extended forefinger through a ring made of his thumb and forefinger on his other hand.

"By the Gods! That is weird." Morga stared into the fire for a few seconds and then scooped the dice back into the leather cup. Shaking them energetically, he asked Koopler again. "Another throw? A copper crown says I beat you."

Koopler groaned and covered his head with his arms.

19

J anis moved silently down the corridor until he came to within feet of its end. From where he stood, he could hear the guard that stood watch in the circular room ahead. He noticed how the flames from the brazier that stood in that room cast eerie shadows on the stone walls.

He was close; above the scraping of the guard's chair and the occasional jangle of his keys, he could hear her. The young goblin Lord had first heard her in the early evening, her voice carrying above the sobs of her sister. Princess Ingren's voice sang a haunting melody that tried to soothe the many ghosts that languished in the dark dungeons.

"THROUGH FOREST AND VALE, *over river and dale,*
    They marched under the red and gold.
    Through forest and vale, over river and dale,
    Our fathers, brave, courageous and bold.

THE COLD SUN *of winter kissed their steel*

And hastened them to Kani's embrace.
To the Bloody King, they swore ne'er to kneel,
Our fathers, the brave men of Heor Grace.

THROUGH FOREST AND VALE, *over river and dale,*
They marched under the red and gold.
Through forest and vale, over river and dale,
Our fathers, brave, courageous and bold."

THE MELODY SANG of the bravery of the men of Heor Grace, a town of Danaria that had been put to the sword by the Bloody King, Tarn Norrick for refusing to bow to the constantly increasing taxation during his reign. Heor Grace had been condemned by Norrick and sentenced to be razed to the ground, to the last man, woman and child. That final winter's day, the brave men of Heor Grace marched under the red and gold banner of their Lord.

Although Janis knew nothing of the tune or the story behind the words, he was mesmerised by the intricacies of the tone and tempo of the piece. At first, he thought that the other girl was singing as well but after careful consideration realised that she was at best silent, or at worst, crying.

He turned and motioned to his brother to keep still. Igant was several feet behind him, his face tense and his knuckles white as they gripped the hilt of his sword. Since becoming unveiled as a *jordskaever* Janis had grown in confidence and was no longer the shy, sensitive brother. Igant looked on at him in awe and, Janis had noted, fear. He wasn't surprised at that. Whilst he thought highly of his slightly older brother, he was also aware of how strange and terrifying his new power must be to others. It even terrified himself.

Earlier that night, Janis had scouted the area. He knew the

young girls were held captive in the cell opposite the corridor that opened into the large circular antechamber. They were the only inhabitants of the dungeon levels. All others had been removed after the invasion; unfortunate wretches herded off at spear point to meet another doom. He knew also that there would be one guard. The enemy obviously felt safe within the walls of the fortress that they had taken. After all, they had stamped out hard on the opposition. He smiled wryly and thought to himself, 'or so they had thought!'

He turned to face the left-hand side of the corridor and closed his eyes, reaching out for the cold stone of the wall. Igant stared at his younger brother who inhaled deeply, and then the older brother looked away, knowing what was coming.

Janis exhaled slowly and leant forward, his long green fingers piercing the stonework as if it was water. He readied himself, his fingers gauging the density and consistency of the rock and then, when he was satisfied, he took a step forwards disappearing into the wall of the corridor.

He was sure that he would never get used to the feeling of the rock passing through him as he made his way forward. The rock left a taste in his mouth and his eyes smarted from the passing of small particles. The young Lord hoped that once home in the Kingdom of Moond, one of the shaman there would help him understand what his power was.

On his third step he passed through into air again and found himself gulping down the relative freshness of clear air again. He was in an empty cell, big enough for a grown orc to lay flat and with a door on his right. A small barred window sat at eye height in the door and the flickering flames of the brazier in the central room danced beams of light onto the upper parts of the wall of the cell.

Without breaking step Janis crossed the cell and pushed himself through the wall on the opposite side. This time the wall was not as thick and he was soon into the next cell. He slowly approached the door, crouching to minimise his form should the guard outside stand and look into the cell. He shook as he stood to glance out of the cell door window, afraid of what he had to do, but also aware that he had no choice.

The haunting voice of the girl in the cell buoyed his spirits and he breathed deeply to keep himself calm. She had started to repeat the long sad lament of the distant part of her family, their bodies long gone but the sacrifices they made immortalised in poetry and song for evermore.

His momentary glance out of the barred window showed him the guard had not moved. Seated on an old rickety stool with his back leaning against the dank stone, he seemed in light slumber, innocuous to the danger he was in.

Janis felt his stomach churn as he estimated the height of the man's head, thankful that the soldier had kept his battered helm on so that Janis would only feel the coldness of steel as he took his life. He took note of the depth of the wall and took two paces forward, turning to the wall, placing his hands wide apart onto the stone. He sighed and slowly pushed his hands into the wall until his forearms were buried deep and he could sense that his fingertips were clear on the other side. It would have been easier if he had pushed his head through the wall as well, but he didn't want to see the guard's demise.

Bringing his hands together quickly he felt his fingers connect with the guard's helmet. He grabbed the conical helm on either side of the temple and yanked backwards. The guard dropped his sword and brought his hands up to his head but it was too late. Janis had taken him completely by surprise and off balance and the guard was not prepared for the solid wall behind him to turn to a puddle and suck him into it.

As abruptly as he had grabbed him, Janis let him go, drawing his hands out of the wall where he stood. As the *jord-skaever* moved away, the wall returned to its original state, trapping the guard's head within the solid stone and killing him instantly.

Janis moved to the other side of the cell and leant against the wall with his head in his hands. His stomach somersaulted once again, and he finally retched. It was some moments before he composed himself enough to push himself through the wall and out into the circular room. He felt sick again as he saw the body of the guard jutting obscenely from the wall, his head buried deep in the stone.

He moved to the corridor and called for his brother who appeared a moment later. By that time, Janis had steeled himself to pull the ring of keys from the dead man's belt and to open the wall again so he could push him through and dispose of him.

Igant grabbed the keys from his brother and ran for the cell that held the singing girl. As he fumbled with the lock the singing stopped and he could hear scurrying inside the cell. Pulling the door open he stood and stared down at the two girls. The older of the two sat cross legged on the floor, her eyes staring defiantly at him from under her dark hair. Her face was grimy, and she was red around the eyes. Igant guessed that the human was about his age. The other girl lay with her face buried in the older girl's lap, her hair wild and urchin like.

Igant spoke, a nervous tone to his voice.

"We are here to help you, please don't be afraid." The older of the two girls tightened her grip on her younger sibling who raised her head towards the newcomer. The young goblin Lord blanched at the dirty, scarlet-stained bandages that were wrapped about her eyes and the blood and grime encrusted cheeks below. He gulped before adding, "Come with us, we have to hurry!"

20

B ex hugged the ground as close as she could as she shifted forward next to Mathor at the edge of the tree line. The old warrior had pulled a coif, a hood of blackened chain mail over his baldness and any joviality that Bex had seen since they had left 'Ol One Eye' was gone. His left hand, fingers adorned with steel and silver rings, was raised to his face, subconsciously rubbing the greying braids of his beard. His right hand gripped the blade of a short sword, his great two-handed blade still in the scabbard that crossed his back.

As with Mathor, Bex preferred her shorter grecks to the longer blade of *Caladmorr*. The confines of fighting in the undergrowth and betwixt the trees and saplings of the forest was only one factor in her choice. The magical blade was said to extract a heavy price from its wielder for every soul taken.

The tall Samakan woman now wore her heavy mail shirt that reached down to her thighs. Each link had been wrapped in a dark grey cloth, dulling the sound to an absolute minimum. The leather straps and pouches of the spider crisscrossed her torso.

'*A grim sight, Bex.*' Bex could almost feel Ishtara shiver inside her at the scene below.

'*Yes, Ishtara.*' It was a grim sight. The forest cleared from where they lay down to a narrow river some two hundred yards away. The water was obviously shallow as the worn path on their side disappeared into it and re-emerged the other side. About the ford, on either side of the water was a small settlement. About a dozen homes surrounded a larger tavern in a haphazard manner.

In the centre of a small field lay a great ship. A simple dragon head was carved into the prow of the ship, jutting forwards and a simple mast rose from the deck. Bex had seen ships like these in Ishtara's visions but seeing the real thing in front of her was another matter. The ship was broad across its beam and the upper deck was at least three times the height of a man above the ground.

To one side of the ship, kneeling in front of the tavern were, Bex assumed, the inhabitants of the hamlet. Some thirty unfortunates knelt in the mud, their hands tied behind them, as the rain drizzled down. Two men stood nearby, their weapons in their hands, guarding the prisoners.

Whilst that scene was distressing, the image of the poor wretch that had been tied to one of the supports of the covered porch on the inn was harrowing to Bex and Ishtara's core. His hands had been tied above his head and his knees sagged, his weight dead against his bonds. About his feet was a bloody red mess that a large wolf like hound was snuffling in. It had taken a few seconds for Bex to realise that part of that mess stretched upwards to the man's naked stomach and was indeed from a small wound in his abdomen. Every now and again the man twitched but Bex couldn't be sure whether he was alive or whether it was the effect of the dog animating him as it ate his insides.

"Tobes Tits! They are demons incarnate!"

"Aye, Lady Bex. You better pray to Kani and every one of his brothers that you don't find yourself falling into their hands." Mathor wriggled backwards and then when he was away from the edge of the tree line rose to a low crouch. Bex was impressed that a bulky man could move with so much agility, even more so whilst wearing the heavy plate armour.

"Wait and watch for Garlen's signal. Once he is in place, we will all move together. Rica's troop and you will cover the prisoners and take those guards out. My men will take out the ship and Garlen will rush the tavern." With that, the aging Mathor moved off.

The little wiry Kardanth had approached the inn earlier to reconnoitre the area. Following the sacking of the hamlet, the Cassalian troops had decided to loot the tavern and Kardanth had reported back to Garlen that fourteen enemy soldiers now occupied the tavern in various states of drunkenness.

Bex looked about at the men that waited with her. She knew two by name quite well. There was the quiet Rica, young yet with wearisome eyes. He knelt just back from the edge of the forest with his long bow out and an arrow notched ready. And there was Callar, the bald, scarred veteran who had chosen to fight her in Ishtara's demonstration. The other three men also had longbows and it suddenly hit her that Garlen was trying to keep her away from the fighting.

She cursed silently but then a movement from the settlement caught her eye. Two more soldiers had appeared from the inn. As they passed the bound corpse – Bex had decided that the unfortunate was long gone from this world – one of them launched a kick at the hound that snarled and loped off. Grinning, he took his helmet off to reveal a heavily tattooed face and a shaven skull. He said something to his compatriot, a shorter warrior that had the appearance of a cat walking upright. The cat man laughed long and loud, and finally pointed to a young woman amongst the prisoners.

The first soldier nodded, and he walked into the kneeling prisoners, viciously kicking several away. The young woman tried to scramble backwards but was unsuccessful. From where Bex was standing, she could see the woman was younger than her, slight and skinny. The rest of the prisoners seemed to be oblivious to the girl's fate and stayed with their heads bowed, some making nervous glances to the corpse tied at the tavern veranda.

The girl screamed and shouted as she was dragged away, her headscarf came loose spilling her long red hair as the tattooed monster strode away, his grip strong on the back of her collar. The two men returned to the tavern with their captive.

'What will they do to her?'

'You don't want to know, Ishtara.' But already the Qoi was flicking through Bex's memories and imagination. Vile images popped up in Bex's mind as she did so.

'Oh, Bex. We have to stop them.'

'I know, but easier said than done.' She looked down at the hamlet below and realised that if she came out of the forest some yards to her right, then she would be out of sight of the two sentries until the last few moments.

"Rica, can you and your men cover us?" She stood and moved down the path to her new starting point.

"Mathor told you to wait for the signal." The short haired soldier followed her; his arrow still notched to his bow string.

"Rica! You know what they are doing to her now. You've seen enough of this in war." Bex hardly raised her voice but every one of the five men felt the authority in her tone. "If I don't do this now, if we don't do this, she will be dead. And her death will be every bit as unpleasant as that man there." She flung her arm outwards, the curved steel of the greck pointing to the sagging body below.

"Bex! Don't you take another step. She is dead already. She died as soon as that skyship landed! We wait for Garlen's signal." He turned so his bow was pointing at the ground at Bex's feet and he tensed his fingers that held the arrow against the string.

'Bex! We have to go now!'

Bex's mind raced like a horse in full gallop. She hadn't expected Rica to take this stance, but he was obviously a warrior to the bone. She tried once more.

"She may be dead, Rica. But in a week or two, that could be your mother, your wife, your sister. Bolam's Balls, Rica – it could be your daughter. Yes, she could be dead – but that is not how I work. If you want to use that bow on me, you better be prepared to face Ishtara. Believe me, she is itching to get down there right now – so I wouldn't get in her way!"

Callar, the strong silent fighter stepped forward and put his hand on Rica's shoulder. He looked directly at Bex and then nodded to the hamlet below. Rica looked at him and the mute nodded again. The young bowman turned back to Bex.

"When you get to the last house, we will take out the two sentries. You'll be on your own after that unless they come out. Kani be with you."

"I've got Ishtara, I think that is enough!" and with that she flashed him a smile and took off down the slope in a low crouch. Rica turned back to Callar.

"She'll be the death of me, Callar. Either her or Garlen when he sees her on her way." The five bowmen moved to the forest edge and they knelt slowly and deliberately notched and readied their bows.

Bex ran on. Keeping low, she managed to keep one of the small homesteads between her and the two guards. She tried to compose herself and force herself to cover the distance between herself and the inn at a steady pace. Deep down, she knew that the girl would still be alive by the time she hit the tavern – it was obvious what the men had wanted her for. But her heart was ruling her body in this instance. Not only did she see herself within the young girl, a young Bex orphaned and alone on the streets of Samak at the age of ten, but the similarities between the girl and the slave that Yab M'Vil had assaulted was striking. Bex had been helpless several days ago but now, with Ishtara's help, she felt the need to redeem herself now.

She quickened her pace but then felt the wind knocked out of her as she was smashed facedown to the ground. Her left arm was pinned beneath her and the greck from the other hand had flown from her grasp as she landed. Dazed, she tried to look around and buck the heavyweight from her back. Her assailant growled, a long rattling sound that warned her not to move. She felt the dog's breath on the nape of her neck as she recovered herself. The great hound snarled again, drool spilling onto her bare skin. It bared its teeth, huge yellowing canines, as it leant forward. Bex could feel Ishtara start to push from inside and she knew that allowing the fire demoness to take control would be the only way to escape.

She heard a shrill whistle and then the hound yelped as if it had been kicked. She felt Ishtara threaten to burst out but then the dog was bowled over from her allowing her to roll and twist, thrusting upwards with her left hand as it came free from underneath her. The blade point stabbed into the soft skin under the lower jaw and carried on upwards through the roof of the mouth into the dog's brain. As she did so, another grey fletched arrow struck it in the flanks, joining the one that had knocked the hound from Bex's back.

Bex staggered back to her feet and looked over her shoulder at the trees where she could just make out Rica and Callar as they hid within the undergrowth. She bowed her head slightly to acknowledge their help and turned back to the task at hand. Steeling herself, she bent and retrieved her second blade and then strode purposefully from the cover of the cottages. She was twenty yards from the prisoners when the first guard noticed her. He raised his spear so that the tip of the serrated blade pointed at the figure that marched upon him.

A guttural expletive was cut short as Bex heard the now familiar whistle of Rica's arrow. Death was steel tipped as the arrows thudded against and through the leather jack of the soldier. He looked down at his chest in amazement at the two thirds of the arrow that hadn't penetrated his armour. As he sank to his knees, the second arrow hit his face throwing him onto his back.

Several of the prisoners let out a low moan as they took in the death of one of their captors and the sight of their would-be saviour. They scattered as best they could on knees or like floundering fish as they flopped onto their backs and wriggled and rolled. A few noticed that Bex was a woman, only one against the numerous enemies inside but most saw salvation in the dark striding figure that passed through them towards the inn beyond.

Once again, the tune of flying arrows sung past her and the remaining guard was flung to the floor like a rag doll as five arrows punched through him. Bex neither looked down at the prisoners no spoke to them, even as some begged her to untie them. She steeled herself as she passed by the hanging corpse and slowly pushed open the door to the inn. She could feel Ishtara tense as she took in the scene inside.

As with most inns and taverns throughout Maingard, there was one large open area for patrons with a long bar along the far wall. Bex guessed that beyond that would be the living area and kitchen for the owner. Unlike 'Ol' One Eye' in Tannaheim there was only a ground floor.

Bex and Ishtara quickly took stock of the situation. Three of the men were gathered about a central table where the girl they had dragged in was now laying on. Her clothes had been torn off and her face was bloodied. The man with the tattooed face who had chosen her outside now stood between her legs as the other two held a wrist and leg each. She was screaming and kicking but to no avail. The body of another girl lay crumpled on the floor. It was evident that Bex was just in time to stop the girl's rape.

The other eleven men in the room were a motley crew of different races – some were human, but others were blue skinned and tall. Two were feline and there was also a reptilian creature who stood as tall as Bex but was covered in dark scales that shimmered slightly in the light of the fire that roared in the hearth on the west wall. All the men stopped, stunned and surprised by the intruder. It took the girl a full second before she realised that something was amiss. She looked at the face of each soldier who held her and then followed their gaze to Bex, tilting her head back to look at the tall, graceful figure that stood silhouetted in the doorway.

'*Fourteen to one. Nice odds.*' Ishtara grinned inside Bex's head.

'*I know, hardly seems fair.*'

'*Yes, the poor unfortunate souls.*'

'*I am not sure if they have souls, Ishtara. They are nothing but evil bastards.*'

Abruptly the spell of surprise was broken and several of the men moved slowly forward and Bex caught a further glimpse of movement out of the corner of her eye. One soldier had been standing in the corner of the room and was now lunging at Bex. Her long arm flicked upwards and outwards, the muffled chain-mail of her hauberk hardly making a sound. The curved blade of her greck sank deep into the throat of her hapless assailant, his own momentum propelling him onto her sword and hastening him to his doom. She pulled her arm back and stepped forward, the deep wound made a slight sucking sound as the blade was withdrawn and the Cassalian fell forward.

Bex lightly advanced, noticing how several of the soldiers now started to surround her. She stood silently, tapping the blade of her second greck against her tall black boot menacingly. She could feel her skin start to blister and darken to a deep red. Wisps of smoke started to seep from her collar and from under her sleeves. The soldier who had been about to rape the girl drew a heavy sabre from a back scabbard and a short-bladed dagger from his belt.

"I'm going to put you down, Bitch! And then you will beg me to kill you as we all use you." His thin lips twisted into a macabre smile as he marched out towards Bex. As he passed the table that the young girl lay on, her head still angled backwards so she could see the form of her rescuer, the tattooed man struck. His arm lifted and plunged downwards with a speed and ferocity that Bex had not seen for some time. The girl's body jumped grotesquely as the dagger thudded into her heart. Her head snapped forward as if to see the cause of the piercing pain that momentarily poured through her being and then fell back, her dead gaze staring accusingly at Bex.

Before she could take in that cruel act, several soldiers lunged forward to attack but she nimbly blocked and evaded their swords before thrusting back thrice in quick succession to despatch three foes with ease.

'*Four down, ten to go,*' announced Ishtara.

'*Feel free to join in.*' replied Bex as she eyed up the enemy captain.

'*Thought you would never ask!*'

The metamorphosis couldn't have happened at a better time. The lunge from the tattooed soldier went wide as he started, his eyes showing fear and awe. Flames erupted from Bex as she sidestepped his clumsy attack and swung one of her own swords down upon his unarmoured wrist. The sabre thudded onto the floor with his hand still gripping the hilt.

Bex's other hand lashed out in a wicked punch, catching him on the jaw and knocking him to the ground.

Then the room exploded into bedlam. The attacks came thick and fast and Bex felt several blades catch her causing small cuts. In return, Bex struck several times and noticed with satisfaction that fewer swords were against her with every second of the action. She thrust deep into an opponent and grimaced as the body reeled away wrenching the blade from her grasp.

The flat of a blade caught her across the side of the head and threw her to the floor. Acrobatically she rolled and came up fighting, punching her sword into the stomach of a blue skinned soldier. She grabbed one of the cat men by the throat and watched as he struggled in her grasp, his fur singeing and catching light from her flaming hands.

As she choked the hapless cat man there was a lull in the mayhem. The remaining soldiers took a step back as the tall, red demoness held aloft his body as he shook and kicked in agony. His hands clawed at Ishtara's grip and the smell of burning hair pervaded the nostrils of those still living. Her trophy twitched once more and then sagged in her grasp. She dropped him with a dull thud to the floor and then turned to face the remaining four Cassalians.

They glanced nervously at each other as Ishtara advanced towards them, their fingers white with fear as they gripped their swords tightly. Finally, a wild-eyed dark-skinned warrior charged at Ishtara, sword raised menacingly above his head. Before he had taken two steps, however, he seemed to catapult himself into the air and, arms flailing madly, crashed to the floor with a thump. It took Ishtara a second to realise he had been struck with an arrow. Less than a foot of the yard-long missile protruded from his chest.

"Bex! Keep out of the way!" Rica called from the doorway. His hands reached behind him as he drew another arrow from his quiver. Callar and his three colleagues were behind Rica and were already aiming at the hapless invaders.

Fear was evident in the faces of two of the soldiers, a blue skinned warrior with hair thick with woad, and a black-haired human who could have come from anyone of a number of cities here on Maingard. Black Hair dropped his sword and sank to his knees, muttering what Ishtara and Bex took as some sort of prayer or litany. The blue skin just stared whilst the third, a larger version of the cat man that Ishtara had choked looked at each in turn.

"Cowards!" He snarled through gritted teeth as he twirled his heavy sword as if it were a dagger. He had hardly started to march down on Ishtara before the five archers let fly, three grey fletched projectiles thudding into the advancing soldier whilst one each struck the other two warriors. The cat man flinched and staggered, taking a final step forward before slowly dropping to his knees and falling backwards.

Rica, Callar and the other archers slowly advanced into the inn to stand behind Ishtara. Aghast they surveyed the scene of carnage. Here and there, a fallen man twitched, coughing up his last breaths. Rica motioned two of his men forward and they handed him their bows before drawing long sharp daggers from their boots. They moved amongst the dead and dying, and slowly pushed the misericords into those who still breathed.

Ishtara's flames slowly extinguished and she returned to Bex's form albeit with red skin. As one of the soldiers raised the tattooed arm of the enemy captain to administer the coup de grace Bex called out.

"No! He is mine to deal with." She strode over, her face a terrible visage that added weight to her authority and stopped the Ghost from his duty. She grabbed the outstretched arm at the wrist and dragged the captain away. He tried to strike here with the stump of his free arm, but his blows were too feeble to distract Bex. She made her way to the table were the dead girl still lay, her naked body spread-eagled upon it. Bex paused and looked down at the staring eyes of the corpse.

"I'm sorry." Bex reached out and grabbed the dagger that protruded from the dead girl's chest. The bone handle felt cold to her touch, more so probably due to the closeness she had felt with its unfortunate victim. She steeled herself and slowly drew the blade from the unmoving flesh.

The enemy captain renewed his attempts to escape her grasp, knowing that his hours were numbered but she twisted his arm painfully and impatiently dragged her captor from the inn.

The fresh air hit her like a punch, but she was glad to be out from inside the charnel house that she had created. Garlen's men were already helping the villagers that had been held captive and many of the once prisoners gasped at the red-skinned woman who walked from their inn.

"Lady Bex! A word if you please!" The voice cut through the silence and Bex turned to see Garlen himself striding to meet her, with Mathor and Bryn desperately trying to catch up. The Prince's hair was matted to his face with sweat and streaks of blood caked his right cheek. There was purpose in his voice and anger in his eyes as he mounted the steps of the wooden veranda of the inn.

Bex had turned back to the dead man who hung by his wrists from a large nail driven into the supporting post of the veranda. Pain was etched into the mask of death that he wore upon his face and Bex knew that the cowards who had strung him up had made his last hours as horrific as possible. Ignoring Garlen she bent down to the stricken soldier that she had dragged out. His eyes rolled in his head as she pulled his arm up.

"Why him?" She whispered at first, her voice barely audible to Garlen and Bryn who were closest. She repeated it louder when she got no reply. "Why him? What did he do to deserve this fate?"

"Bex! What you did was irresponsible!" Garlen reached out and touched Bex's shoulder, wincing from the heat of the armour. The tall woman looked round, at first at the hand on her shoulder and then straight into the eyes of the blond Prince who snatched his hand away as if it had been stung by her disdainful glance. Fire burned in her eyes as she could feel Ishtara start to surge through her again. When she spoke, it was with the Qoi's voice.

"Not now, Garlen."

He shrank back, visibly shaken at the venom in the glare and voice of Bex and her symbiotic demoness. It was only a momentary lapse and he quickly composed himself. He pulled his leather gauntlet off and raised his hand, running his fingers through his blond locks.

"See it doesn't happen again," with that he went to stride past her, motioning for Bryn and Mathor to follow him into the inn. He was interrupted though by a dry chuckle from the dying enemy commander that ended in a rattling cough.

"Why him? You ask why him?" He coughed again. Bex, Garlen and the immediate vicinity fell quiet as they struggled to hear. The dying man grinned up at Bex as he continued.

"He dared to stand up to us when we took turns with his daughter. The rest of those cowards," his eyes glanced at the villagers, "they never said a word after that." He coughed again, a little blood splattering from his smashed lip.

"That is what happens when you stand up to the Emperor. He will rape your land just as we will rape you as we put your cities to the sword. Before we finish you will wish that you were him..." He glanced again at the hanging man and nodded, before coughing again. He looked Bex straight in the eye, his gaze as black as hers.

"Get it done, Bitch. Kill me quick else my shade will walk

amongst the living until you die. And on that day, I will whisper in your killer's ear to make your soul linger a little more before you take your last breath." With that he started to whisper, with words so soft that not even Bex could hear, a prayer to whatever God he served.

Bex raged and Ishtara burst forth again, almost instantaneously. The fire demoness raised the dagger that had killed the young girl in the inn and swept it across the rope holding the tortured man aloft. His body fell in a crumpled heap among its own entrails. She yanked the stricken Cassalian high by his uninjured arm and drove the blade viciously through his forearm into the wooden support of the veranda, impaling him so his feet kicked as he struggled to reach the floor.

"I already died when you ravaged my land and took my people!" she snarled. She raised Bex's greck and cut through the lacing of his armour, letting the front of his cuirass fall to one side. Her hand tore his undershirt away from his bare skin and Ishtara drove the thin point of the greck slowly into his stomach, careful to inflict a non-fatal wound. As she withdrew it, she hooked a small part of gut out through the hole, pulling it until it reached the ground in a sick imitation of the torture that her victim had inflicted on his.

"Die slowly, Pig! And be thankful you aren't your cowardly Emperor. I am going to take great delight in inflicting pain on him and anyone else that stands in my way". She staggered slightly, the effect of two transformations in such a short time taking its toll on both their bodies. She turned and walked slowly to face Garlen, and as Ishtara gave way to Bex, the red skinned woman sagged into Bryn's arms. The tall warrior lowered her to the ground and held her as she gathered her breath.

She felt herself recover enough to sit unaided and took a fearful glance to one side to see the tattooed Cassalian kick wildly at the air as he struggled.

'*You are an evil one.*' She whispered in her head at Ishtara, echoing the Qoi's words as she had condemned the evil Yab M'Vil to a slow and painful death.

'*He deserved it,*' came the response and they shared a wry smile with each other.

21

Radnak swam in a thick, black sea, oblivious to all apart from the voice of the Damas, the angelic female demons who hunted with Crom Teder and carried away souls to the underworld. He moved effortlessly through the murky water, the viscous substance filling his lungs yet causing him no pain or hindrance. To hear the Damas was one thing, many warriors had heard their songs upon the battlefields, but to see one was to know that Crom Teder, the God of the Dead had finally called you to his dark world.

He turned towards the sound and became aware of a faint light in the distance. Kicking off, he swam towards it with powerful strokes. As he neared it, he noticed it was above the surface and was also the source of the haunting voice that called him. He felt himself become stronger as his strokes brought him closer to his goal. The voices became louder and clearer.

And then he broke the surface, the light causing him to wince and screw his eyes tight against the glare. He coughed, spewing forward the thick mucus that had invaded his body and he drew a breath of fresh air. Gradually, he was able to open his eyes, wanting desperately to set his eyes upon the Damas, eager to end his life of killing and violence.

It was not one of the guides to the underworld that met his gaze though, or if it was, then Crom Teder had moved into the business of recruiting them young. The dark-haired girl, a human girl at that, looked like an urchin. Her hair was unkempt, and her eyes were red from crying, her tears washing the dirt and grime from her face in little streams. Her dress, torn and stained, had once been fine and ornate. She couldn't have been much older than Igant. Seeing Radnak stir caused the girl to smile and she leapt to her feet.

"Lady Iga, he is awake!"

"One second, Ingren. I just need to finish your sister's dressing. I am sure though, our brave, strong warrior can wait a little longer." Radnak's heart pounded at the sound of Iga's voice. What had he been thinking? Eager to take the dark journey to Crom Teder? Tortured as he was with his forbidden love for the noblewoman, he knew he could never leave her. He lived, breathed and fought to keep her safe. He turned to look at her.

The tall, graceful goblin was kneeling in front of a young girl, younger than the one that sat near his side. She spoke softly as she wound a clean strip of cloth over the young girl's eyes.

"This poultice is a mixture of herbs and roots that the Old Ones passed down through the shaman of the Orc tribes. It contains elf glade and marsh thistle to guard against infection along with yellow rose to aid healing, amongst many others. There is also hypnost and mandrake root to calm the pain, my dear." The young girl spoke, her voice wavering as the words struggled to escape.

"Will they make me see again, Lady Iga?" The green skinned woman forced back tears as the young girl carried on. "It's so dark." Lady Iga reached down and took the young girl's hands in her own. She stifled a sob before answering.

"My skills and powers are not sufficient enough for that, my dear. Maybe there are some who can and maybe the Gods may take it into their hands to heal you and return your sight. That, though, I cannot say." The young girl clenched her fists at her side as the goblin noblewoman spoke.

"Sit, my child. Janis, please find something for Moren to eat. An apple perhaps, if we have some left." The young boy leapt to his feet from where he had sat, cross-legged, watching his mother like a hawk as she had dressed the young girl's wounds. Within seconds he had found not one but two apples and eagerly pressed them into Moren's hands.

Ingren stood as Iga rose and walked to Radnak's side. She smiled demurely at them both and nodded her thanks to Lady Iga. The young Princess walked slowly to her sister and sat down next to her, wrapping her arm around her shoulder.

Radnak looked up at Iga with a questioning look on his face. The tall goblin slowly swept a hand through her hair and sighed. When she finally spoke, it was in the guttural orc tongue.

"Janis found them. They were in a cell, all alone. They were the only prisoners he saw. The younger one, she can't be older than Janis. That young, and they have taken her eyes.... She will never see again, Radnak."

"Barbarians. I thought I had seen it all in the Southern Wars. How low Man and Orc would stoop." He levered himself to the side of the improvised cot that Iga had made for him when he was sick. Gritting his teeth, he started to stand. At first, he was a little unsteady but after a second or so he regained his composure and stretched. His muscles rippled over his stocky, grey body and he reached for his armour.

"Who are they?"

"They have said little. Igant seems to have more of a connection to them than the rest of us. They have said their names – Moren, that's the blinded one and the other is Ingren."

Radnak was the first orc that Ingren had seen and she stared now as the *sverd's* torso and arms were on display. Although shorter than the average human, half-orcs tended to share physical traits with their larger and more brutish looking cousins. From the size of the body covered by the blanket that Iga had conjured up from somewhere, the young princess had thought that the warrior was encased in armour. Instead he now stooped to pick his heavy mail hauberk up and managed to shrug it over his barrel chest. Igant ran to his side and helped him into his lamellar cuirbolli, a vest of armour made of hardened leather squares that were laced together by leather cord.

"I told you so, Moren. And you, Ingren. *Sverd* Radnak is fit again and ready. He will find this Karchek and then we will kill him for you."

It was the younger princess who answered, in between greedily biting chunks of succulent apple. She turned her head in the general direction of Igant's voice and almost getting it right, her shrouded face staring just to one side of where the young lord stood. She held the apple with two hands close to her mouth and spoke over it.

"Our brother is coming for us. He will find us and at his back will be the biggest army that you have ever seen. He will kill Karchek for what he has done." She searched hurriedly for terms that Master Tarnal would have used. She nibbled quickly at the apple before blurting out, "And I hope he feeds the dogs and crows with them all."

"And, pray tell, this brother of yours. Does he have a name?" Radnak enquired as he stretched and shrugged to make sure his armour was fitted true. He looked up as Ingren, the older one of the two, put her hand on her sister's arm as if to quieten her. She bent forward and whispered in her sister's ear.

"Come, girls." Radnak probed. "Who should Crom Teder thank for this impending rush of souls into his underworld?" Addressing them as girls suddenly hit a nerve. Ingen stood, thrusting herself upright in a pose that was undeniably regal, aside from the tears and grime.

"Girls? Girls!" The indignant tone almost reached crescendo level before Moren reached out to calm her sister. "I am Ingren Barstt, of the House Barstt, daughter to King Anjoan. My brother is Prince Garlen and he is riding here now with the Host of Tannaheim."

Radnak rolled his eyes. This was all he needed now, saddled with another two noble brats and with the Lord of the Inns on his way. He now recognized the names, though it was possible that any family may name their daughters after royalty, even the royalty of a neighbouring country. He had spent a long year in the south fighting the men of the Crossed Swords, as the Host of Tannaheim became known amongst the Orc army. He had traipsed the length of the West in his time and even set foot inside the fabled walls of the capital, albeit surreptitiously.

The Barstts, he knew. King Anjoan leading the men of the Crossed Swords would have made him more comfortable but maybe Garlen, Lord of the Inns, would leave the thinking and strategy to his generals.

"Sorry, your Royal Highnesses, for pissing in your wine...." He was cut short by Lady Iga who broke in with her authoritative voice.

"Radnak!" She rose and walked to Ingren, taking her hands in hers. "What *Sverd* Radnak was about to say, after he apologised of course, was that looks can be deceptive. In your current predicament, it was difficult to ascertain your position, especially with yourselves so far from home. We will do what we can to keep you safe until your brother approaches." She turned, glaring at Radnak.

The half-orc turned and reached for his sword and dagger that lay by his cot. As he did so he muttered under his breath, a little louder than he should have done.

"Let us hope he remembers his Orc War has finished."

"Radnak!" He raised his hand almost apologetically as Iga rebuked him.

"I know. We cannot stay here now their hostages have gone missing. They will be tearing this castle inside out to find them. We move tonight." Then it hit him. He had no idea what time of day it was. He had been out cold for several days and there were no windows or apertures in the walled in room the Janis had found them.

"Is it day or night now? Does anyone know?"

"It's day. A few hours after dawn." Igant spoke aloud. Radnak had noticed that his confidence had grown since the invasion night and smiled to himself, appreciatingly. "We will be safe in the lower passages when we move tonight. They tend to stay away at night. They tend to disappear." He looked across to his brother who stopped staring at Moren and smiled wryly at Igant.

"Good! If we can get to ground level, then Janis can take us through the walls. Then it will be just a case of escaping the city."

"I am afraid not, Radnak." Iga shook her head. "What Janis does takes great energy. When he moved us into here, he nearly collapsed. He won't be able to take us all through two walls." The young lord smiled apologetically as if ashamed that his wondrous power was limited.

"We still go. We will just find another way out. Now, get some rest."

Janis turned back to Ingren and motioned with his flat hand to his face, moving it away and towards his mouth. Ingren looked questioningly at Igant and Iga.

"He wants you to sing again." The noble lady spoke softly and hugged the two young girls. Ingren took a deep breath and began the same haunting tune as before.

. . .

"THROUGH FOREST AND VALE, *over river and dale,*
They marched under the red and gold.
Through forest and vale, over river and dale,
Our fathers, brave, courageous and bold.

THE COLD SUN *of winter kissed their steel*
And hastened them to Kani's embrace.
To the Bloody King, they swore ne'er to kneel,
Our fathers, the brave men of Heor Grace.

THROUGH FOREST AND VALE, *over river and dale,*
They marched under the red and gold.
Through forest and vale, over river and dale,
Our fathers, brave, courageous and bold."

22

Queen Sarsi stifled another yawn. Since the murder of her husband she had found, understandably, little time for herself. Every day was a constant turnstile of meetings with generals, councillors and dignitaries from other city states as she coordinated the defence of Danaria. Of course, she had Magus Vent to assist and she was thankful for it. He seemed to survive on less sleep than she had and was almost two steps ahead on any issue as it arose.

When the general in charge of one of the construction projects arrived asking for more men to complete the task, Vent had already issued the order conscripting wretches from the city's gaol. Messengers had been sent to outlying farmsteads and villages with a view to bring food and equipment to the city in return for a safe spot behind the famed Tannaheim walls.

The Hawk watched her from her side as she despatched another dignitary from the throne room. As the man bowed low and turned away, Queen Sarsi gave a furtive glance to her left at her husband's empty throne. He bent close to her as she turned back to look ahead.

"He will be proud of you, my Queen. He knows the Red Throne is in good hands." Sarsi looked slightly flustered as she realised her little glance had been spotted.

"Thank you, Marshall. I wish he were here by my side. But I could not have got through this without your help, Magus. I hope you know that."

'Aye,' the gaunt, old soldier thought. 'though I do almost feel sorry for whoever ordered the attacks on your family. You will prove a lot stronger than most of us in these dark days ahead, that I am sure.' He didn't make his thoughts known but saw an opportunity to broach a subject that had been troubling him since Anjoan's murder.

"Your husband, he is by your side," he left a slight pause and the Queen knew the question that would follow. "Is it not yet time for his funeral? It is time to lay his body to rest to give his spirit the energy he needs in the afterlife. He must be ready to fight with Kani and his brothers at the End of Time." Magus Vent referred to the belief that a time would come when the denizens of the Underworld would rise up against the Gods in one final battle that would signify the destruction of Maingard. Kani would enlist the swords of all those who feasted with him to battle against the trolls and demons.

Queen Sarsi looked Magus Vent square in the eye as she answered. In that one look and her words she portrayed all the vulnerability of the lover who had lost her love and the venom of the witch who thirsted for vengeance.

"I need him here by my side, Marshall. He is not yet ready for *that* Last Battle."

The grizzled veteran visibly gulped, unable to continue, unable to pass on the comments of the maids who complained of the unnatural chill in the corridors around the Queen's Chambers and the slight odour of death noticeable despite the pungent aroma of the herbs and incense that the Queen burnt. Neither did he say about the gossip that he had heard. Talk between staff mentioning unnatural liaisons between those living and those dead. The Hawk hurriedly changed the subject.

"Your son, when do you expect to hear from him?"

Sarsi started at the mention of Garlen and instantly the eyes of a mother returned.

"I think it is much too soon. I doubt we will hear for at least a week." An unsteady silence hung after her last word as if neither wanted to add the phrase that they were both thinking – 'If we hear from him.'

Her eyes flittered to a dumpy, older woman who had entered the throne room. She wore a peasant's black dress and a shawl of white wool that matched the silvery grey of her hair. In her hand, she clutched a small wicker basket. The woman had passed the guard at the door, any question of her validity of being allowed access to her Majesty had disappeared upon the showing of Sarsi's token, a ring with a garnet the size of a quail's egg set upon the silver swords of House Barstt.

"Master Smit," she called over the old man who, just a few days ago, had broached the awful news of her daughters' kidnapping. "I wish to take a break. I shall reconvene in one hour. Could you see that food is delivered to my chambers?"

As she rose, the throne room as one, apart from the newcomer, bowed or curtsied. She glided down the steps of the dais, pausing only to announce sotto voce to The Hawk.

"It will be alright, Magus. It really will."

As she made her way to the door which led to her chambers, followed by the silver haired woman, Magus Vent was not sure whether he could share her optimism.

23

"Garlen! You got to see this!" Gordin shouted from the gunwales of the skyship that lay at rest in the field by the village. The veteran waved and shouted again to his commander.

Garlen and Bryn stood a little way away from where Bex sat on the ground. The prince acknowledged his sergeant and held out his hand to the tall thief.

"Please, Lady Bex. I want you to see this. I value yours and Earl Kar's thoughts on what my men have found." Bex took his hand and he gracefully pulled her to her feet. She smiled demurely and strode past him towards the ship.

"Apology accepted, Your Majesty!" she called.

Bryn covered his smirk with his mailed fist as Garlen shook his head slowly. As he turned to follow the dark haired Samakan, he muttered somewhat loudly.

"I'm just glad that she is on our side, Earl Kar."

The way on board was rudimentary to say the least. A long, knotted rope hung over the side of the ship. Wooden ribs were set into what would have been the freeboard of the ship allowing Bex to 'walk' up the side of the ship as she clambered hand over hand with the rope. Gordin's hand was there to help her over the bulwark at the top.

She stood, slightly hindered for a few seconds by the slope of the deck. By the time Garlen and Bryn had reached the deck she had got used to the way the ship had settled in the soft earth of the field. From the centre of the deck rose a single mast, topped with a cross brace, albeit a small one. Two low cabins took up part of the deck with the rest of the deck space being taken up with stores and equipment all tethered down.

'*Do you know how this ship flies?*' she asked Ishtara. Her inhabitant demoness shook her head ruefully.

'*When I hitched a ride on the one that brought me to your world, I hid on the deck. It was not an experience that I would choose to repeat, though.*'

'Oh?' Bex enquired.

Ishtara opened her mind to Bex and a flood of colour and sound blasted her brain as she looked through Ishtara's eyes within the Qoi's memory of the interplanar journey. Even though this was all in her mind, Bex still threw her hands over her ears and clenched her eyes tightly shut. The speed of the colours as they hurtled past her eyes hurt and the noise seemed to irritate her very skin. The ship seemed to stretch and contract upon itself.

'*STOP!*' she cried, and the vision died instantly.

'*Why didn't you go below the decks?*'

'*I tried, once.*'

'*But?*'

'*I ... couldn't. I was ... scared. I could sense death and terror as soon as I opened the hatch to the decks below.*' The Qoi seemed ashamed of the fact.

'*We can face it together, Ishtara.*' Bex smiled inwardly to her compatriot and was pleased to feel the demoness return the smile.

"You needn't see this, Lady Bex." Gordin stood before her,

his body blocking the access to the shut hatch behind him. The hatch was set at a forty-five degree angle against the stern facing wall of the low cabin that was sited just in front of the mast.

"I'll be fine, Gordin. I have seen a few sights that would shock you."

'Aye,' the black clad soldier thought. 'But you haven't seen anything like this.'

By now, Garlen and Bryn stood on deck with them and silently Gordin pulled the hatch open. Bex could feel her mind suddenly feel empty, and a darkness start to envelope her thoughts. It took a few seconds before she realised what it was. Ishtara. Somehow the Qoi seemed distant, almost as if she had left. Over the previous week, Bex had got used to sharing her body and mind with Ishtara. The inane chatter and the feeling of someone else being able to recall her own memories had started to feel normal. She realised her mind was black or empty, it was how it had been before that fateful night at Yab M'Vil's villa.

'*Ishtara?*' She probed her own mind and called out again. '*Ishtara!*'

'*Yes, Bex?*'

'*What's happened? You feel different.*'

'*I'm not sure. I don't feel ready to see this. We Qoi, we are not used to this.*'

'*You aren't just Qoi anymore, Ishtara. Being human is about facing your fear and dealing with it. Whether it is fear of being hungry or cold, or a fear for your life, or something like this.*'

Ishtara nodded and Bex felt a little more of her presence. Bex steeled herself and stepped forward to the hatch. Ducking her head through the doorway she followed the others. The stairway led to a narrow corridor that ran towards the bow of the ship with several doors leading off on each side. The occasional torch sputtered a few flames to light the way. This corridor led to another set of stairs that doubled back round so they were facing the stern. Ahead of them was a pair of heavy wooden double doors.

A feeling of fear and oppression seemed to leak from behind the doors and when Gordin pushed them open, his three companions immediately wished he hadn't. A deluge of despair washed over them as they gingerly took a step into the room beyond.

The room was long, seeming to stretch to the far end of the ship. It was dingey, lit by a few torches that were fitted in sconces on the wooden pillars that were spaced down the centre. On either side were cages, the bars reaching to the very ceiling. The occupants of the cages stared out at the newcomers with vacant eyes. Bex's eyes quickly scanned the prisoners, vaguely counting them and giving up after three score. The majority were malnourished, the gauntness of their limbs and faces sickening to see. Every now and again she saw a healthy-looking captive in their midst. The prisoners were mostly naked although a few wore loincloths. She noticed several lying amongst the filth and detritus that covered the floor of the cages and wondered whether they were dead.

The stench was horrendous, the smell of death and decay mixed with the odours of fear and terror. The very essence of the stench seemed to permeate into their pores and Bex fought to keep her stomach from heaving.

One of Garlen's men walked to meet them, his face partly obscured by a leather mask that covered his nostrils and mouth. A short cylinder protruded from the mouth area with plant fibres woven over the end. He carried several more and handed them out to the three of them.

"These mask the smell," he said, his voice muffled by the device. "Something to do with the fibres. It's some sort of herb as far as I can tell." Bex inspected hers before buckling hers on. The cylinder was open at both ends but was densely packed by the plant fibres which carried a strong scent. As she put it on, she was welcomed by an immediate relief from the stench.

Garlen stared about him at the unfortunate wretches and then turned to Bryn and Bex. He saw tears in the eyes of the big soldier from Jacarna and realised why. Bryn finally spoke.

"This . . ." he indicated the captives caged like animals. "This is the fate of my people." He fell silent and Bex placed her hand on his arm.

"Set them free!" Garlen shouted. "Set them free and help them outside. Now!"

"Yes, Garlen." The masked Ghost snapped to attention. "But there is something else you need to see. At the stern." He turned and pointed. They could make out another three Ghosts at the far end of the room guarding four Cassalian prisoners who knelt with their hands on their heads.

As they approached the group, they noticed something else in the shadows behind the Ghosts. Gordin grabbed a torch from one of the pillars and held it aloft as they walked nearer. All three stopped when the creature was illuminated by the flame.

"Don't worry, it's surrounded by a ward. It can't breach that circle." Gordin motioned downwards with the torch and Bex and the others saw a dark blue circle etched into the deck. It gently pulsed with a mystical energy. In the centre of the circle sat, or so Bex thought, a creature. It was insect-like in appearance, its chitinous armoured body a dark copper red in colour. The dark carapace was crisscrossed in scars and its four legs were long and angled outwards and upwards from the thorax so that the body sat as if suspended. The legs reached a joint which Bex guessed was a knee, before stretching down to hooked talons that impatiently scratched at the wooden deck.

Two more limbs sprung from the upper thorax each with two sword-like claws. At the wide base of one of these claws was a short, stumpy opposing claw that looked like it could crush anything in a strong vice-like grip.

The head of the creature turned to face them, round and slightly flattened with two huge bulbous eyes on the sides. The mouth twitched as the two sets of horizontal mandibles flickered back and forward.

Two mystic chains crackling with energy stretched from the ceiling and floor to a wide collar that sat around the creature's neck. Two pulsing purple gems sat encrusted into jagged wounds in the creatures back. Part of the deck underneath the beast was an iron grid with holes a handspan across.

"Gruesome, isn't it"

"What is it?" Garlen spoke first. He didn't expect an answer, and none came. He paced the circumference of the circle ward staring at the strange being. Bex watched as its claws clattered against the deck as it tried to turn to watch Garlen.

'Bex, it is afraid. It fears us.'

'It is?'

'Yes, it does not want to be here, that much is evident from the magic that holds it and the ward suggests the Cassalians are as scared of it as it is of us.'

'Yet?' Bex sensed a 'but'

'It is here for a reason. They need it here.'

Garlen had finished his inspection and ended up once more in front of the kneeling prisoners. He asked his question again.

"What is it?"

The Cassalian, a pale faced man with jet black hair that was slicked back tightly over his skull stared upwards at the blond haired Garlen. And then spat at his interrogator, the phlegm landing on the Prince's black armour. It was Gordin who reacted first, his fist lashing out and striking the Cassalian in the face, splintering his nose and flooring him.

Garlen asked the next captive the same question. The prisoner looked up at Garlen, his eyes betraying the fear he felt. Bryn Kar, however, had had enough. He seized the Cassalian from behind, grabbing one arm and the terrified man's neck.

"Enough! We have no time for this! The Prince asked you what it was!" he pushed the soldier forward and he finally understood what the tall, chainmail clad guardsman was about to do. Bryn was shoving the Cassalian towards the creature, and he tried desperately to halt his progress. His feet slid on the deck as he was propelled forwards. He screamed as he tried to wrench himself from Bryn's grasp.

"Rexen! Rexen! I'll tell you what it is!"

"Earl Kar! Stop now!" Garlen commanded. Grudgingly, Bryn relaxed and the Cassalian dropped to the floor.

"Its name is Rexen. It is .... It's a Flyer."

"And what, by Bolam's Balls, is a Flyer?"

There was a loud clacking noise that emanated from the creature. Its mandibles clattered together ferociously and the small antennae on its head wiggled back and forward. And then it spoke in a very broken form, its words interspersed with clicks of its jaws.

"A Flyer, flies. This ship, I cause it to fly."

Bex approached the creature and it turned its head to her.

"You have a power, and they have harnessed you, so they can use you and your power?"

The insect-like beast lowered its head as if to acknowledge Bex's question.

"My wings. They took them. And their mages torture me with their magics." With a flick of its head, it indicated the pulsing jewels set into its back. Bryn stood tall next to the shapely Samakan woman.

"So, this is how their ships fly. There are more of your kind?"

Rexen once again nodded.

"Enough. We free these unfortunate wretches and then we

fire the ship. Let's move." Garlen pulled his mailed gloves back on and started to turn.

"Wait! You can't do that. Don't you see?" Bryn reached out and grabbed the blond prince by the shoulder. Gordin's hand dropped to his sword hilt but Garlen waved him down.

"I don't see what, Earl Kar?"

"This ship, this . . .", he indicated the creature, "this thing. We can use them to get to your sisters!" Garlen stared at the tall, dark guardsman and then his face cracked into a grin.

"I said I valued your counsel. And you prove me right." He turned to Gordin. "Get the men aboard and get these wretches unloaded. We leave at once!"

"Wait" Rexen interjected. "I am too weak. To fly, I need energy. I need to feed. After I help, please free me."

"Well, feed first and then we leave." He started to leave.

"You must feed me." The giant insect waved one of his sword-like claws at the mystical ward surrounding him. "I cannot leave here."

'I have a bad feeling about this, Bex.' Ishtara quietly spoke to Bex. The thief nodded back.

"Where's your food?" Bryn Kar spoke slowly, the same thoughts coming to him as had come to the Qoi. The creature lowered its head once more, this time in shame rather than acknowledgement.

"I eat life. Life is my energy." As if to accentuate his point he waved his claws slowly at the cages to the side of the ship. Garlen followed his gaze and sighed.

"Garlen! You cannot! These may not be your subjects, but they are people, citizens of Maingard!"

"Bex, Lady Bex, you think too little of me. I wasn't thinking of those poor wretches. Dead as they are in mind and spirit. As much as my sisters mean so much to me, I would not.... Could not...condemn these people."

The prince nodded to Gordin and made a gesture that Bex could not see.

The black garbed soldier grabbed the Cassalian that Bryn had threatened and threw him at Rexen. The mystical ward was one way, allowing anything to enter but nothing to escape.

Bex and Bryn watched, sickened even though they knew the capacity for evil that the Cassalians had. The unfortunate soldier was caught in the claws of Rexen who deliberately snapped through his arms. The man wailed, his voice hitting a falsetto screech as the insect threw him in the air and then sliced him in two with his bladed claws. The upper half of the body still seemed conscious as Rexen lifted it to his mandibles and started to tear and chew.

As he fed, the purple gems on his back glowed brighter and brighter until they discharged their mystical energy in an arc to a similar gem on the ceiling of the ship. The ship seemed to purr.

"Satisfied?" Garlen inquired.

"Yes. For now," Rexen answered. "I will need more," he added in between bites. The blood and small pieces of carcass fell to the deck and disappeared through the grill below.

"Fine. We have these." Garlen reached down and patted the cheek of the Cassalian who had spat at him. "Just make sure this one is last."

J erone opened his eyes as the early morning frost chilled his face. By the light of the fire that was now just ash and embers, he could see the figure of Risas-tu's companion, the silent boatman. The quiet figure sat with his back to a tree, his head hanging low and covered by his dark cloak. Placing his hand upon his own chest, just below the cut that Janda had given him, he slowly counted twenty heartbeats whilst he studied the sleeping figure. Once satisfied that he saw no sign of movement, he turned to look for Risas-tu.

The big frame of Risas-tu lay next to the dying embers of the fire. His chest rose and fell with each breath and the silence of the pre-dawn was only broken as the bald merchant spluttered into his matted beard.

Late into the evening, they had made camp, pulling the boat towards the shore and tying it to one of the trees. They had shared a meal of salted lamb and ale around the fire and the barrel-chested man from Nordal had sung some ballads from his homeland, long, slow and mournful. Eventually he had persuaded the forestman to sing as well and Jerone had offered a somewhat less than tuneful rendition of 'The Hunter's Life'.

Despite the camaraderie around the makeshift camp, Jerone felt that something was amiss. The warning that Risas-tu had given him about not looking below deck on the boat had pricked his curiosity and there was something about the man that Jerone did not like.

As silently as possible he rose and padded slowly towards the boat. He had decided to leave his warhammer back next to the blanket that he had slept under instead taking the short-bladed knife that he had killed the warrior with in Janda's home. Looking back, he made sure the sleeping forms of Risas-tu and the boatman were still at the camp. Taking a deep breath, he nimbly jumped on board.

He skirted to the far side of the boat. Keeping the black and white canvas between him and the riverside camp, he knelt and started to lift the canvas. The hold below was dark and the smell that emanated from the gloom gave credence to Risas-tu's statement that he carried livestock. Jerone, though, wanted to make sure. He slipped beneath the canvas to stand in the hold. The space extended from one side of the boat to the other and nearly from bow to stern. If he moved from where he stood, beneath the canvas that covered the only opening into the darkness below, he would have to bow his head.

He immediately wished he hadn't. The stench was unbearable, made worse by the confine of the hold. He raised his hand to cover his mouth and nose as he fought the urge to vomit. He heard the occasional clink of something metallic, possibly chains and then some shuffling from every corner of the gloom. As his eyes became accustomed to the darkness, he noticed the forms that lay huddled on the floor of the hold.

They were livestock as Risas-tu had said but not as Jerone knew it. Chained together in the blackness of the hold were slaves; men, women and children. Jerone counted nearly a dozen in the line to his left and there was another line at his feet and one more on the other side of the hold. As the gloom lifted, he could see the fear in their eyes. Everyone was naked, yet many were either too weak to cover their nakedness with their hands or had had their dignity ripped from them like their very clothes.

They sat together in filth, their bodily waste collecting in gutters between the three lines of captives. A soft groan escaped from the lips of a few of the slaves as they noticed that this was not Risas-tu. They wondered if they had reached another cross-roads in their pitiful and painful journey and if Jerone was their new owner. Some reached out with their manacled hands, the pitiful look upon their faces imploring Jerone to be their saviour and release them.

He carefully picked his way through the bodies, noting their features through the grime. Most were not of the Forest, at least that much he could see. Not many were black haired, indi-cating that they were not his folk, or from any of the twelve tribes. The white hair of Anders was an anomaly, seen by many as an unnatural occurrence, but with the blessing of Herne as he was the son of the chief. Though not an expert on the geog-raphy of Maingard, he guessed that most would have come from the Wolf Mountains, to the north and west of the Forest. The snowy caps of these were visible from some parts of the Forest in certain conditions.

"Herne protect them." He whispered as he passed amongst them. A short prayer that they should fall under the protection of the Deity of the Forest People. Some of them babbled, and some grasped at his legs as he carefully placed his feet between their scarred and emaciated legs.

"Shhhh!" he brought his finger to his lips, afraid of the noise that they were making. He stood up, lifting his head away from the squalor of the hold and looked out from beneath the canvas tent. From where he was, he could just make out the campsite, the angle of the low gunwales of the boat and the riverbank making it difficult to see properly. He stood tall and his heart leapt as he could make out the blanket that the red-bearded boat man had slept under. It was thrown to one side, the bedding underneath empty.

"Herne protect me," he muttered. But the Forest God was not listening that day and he felt the blow to his head just before he blacked out completely.

A THOUSAND MILES AWAY, past the Great Forest and close to the ends of the earth, Janda swam through the cold air. Try as she might, she couldn't feel it. Her consciousness stretched out across the forest to the south, hearing the inane chatter as the world progressed on its way. Nowhere could she feel her next Channeler. Her mind washed over the fate of Jerone, her Witchguardian. Again, she had faith in him to come through his ordeal. Besides, she had problems of her own to worry about.

Could she have already missed it? Surely not, when it finally happened it would be completely unmissable. There can have been no chance of the unveiling already occurring and that she had missed it. The tremor would be like nothing else she had felt in her fifty lifetimes. It would be as if the ground cracked open and the mountains moved. The air too. Like a thousand thunderstorms unleashing their energy all at once. Then it would be quiet. Quiet except for the singsong sound of the Channeler's soul announcing that it was ready for her.

A beacon to guide her across the many miles to her new body. Momentarily she wondered who Herne and Maya had chosen for her this time. Would it be a warrior, one to help take the fight to the invaders? Or a guide, to lead the folk of the Forest to safety?

And then it happened. The world exploded into a cataclysm of sound and Janda shuddered in midair. She screamed in ecstasy then soared high into the sky, spiralling round and round as she did so, mixing with the many birds that were sent flapping into the clouds in shock. The same skies became charged with the power of a thousand suns and that power seemed to soak into her very spirit.

And then, silence. The trees stopped shaking, the birds eventually settled, and peace reigned once more. Janda felt herself sink towards the icy ground in a post orgasmic rapture. The silence reigned for several minutes before the calling of Maya broke it. The sing song call of Herne's long forgotten soulmate rang out, calling to Janda.

She looked up, noticing the direction that the call had come from and rose again to the skies.

25

"Your Majesty, I have what you requested – though the price I had to pay to obtain them was higher than either of us imagined." The woman known as Murag held out the wicker basket to her Queen who motioned for her to place it upon a side table. Murag looked about her as she stood in the Queen's antechamber. The room was sparse, just a sofa which the Queen was currently perched upon and a table with four chairs. The door through to her bed chamber stood open and the older woman could see the form of Anjoan laying as if asleep on the great bed. A brazier stood at the foot of the bed and herbs sat smoking upon it, lending a heavy perfume to the sweet smell of death.

"Thank you, Murag. Though I did tell you that money was no obstacle to your mission. These mystical components are essential to my plans – but gold or other worldly trappings of greed are not. I shall have a clerk reimburse you for your expenses immediately." The older lady bowed her head in reverence to the Queen.

"That is kind, my Queen. However, I was not referring to the cost of items in gold, considerable the cost of some of them.

Some of the items have cost me dear in other ways. My mind, soul and body will pay the price." Murag bowed her head once more and added, "My Queen."

Queen Sarsi rolled her eyes. She started to peel the soft, thin gloves from her hands.

"I may seem to be in disarray with the chaos that surrounds me, Murag, but I am very aware what is going on in my kingdom. Do not treat me as one of your apprentices." She threw the gloves at Murag's feet and the startled woman looked up at her. Sarsi rolled the long sleeves of her plain dress up over her arms to reveal blackened veins standing proud of her pale skin. They crossed her skin like rivers on a map, and her once clear complexion was mottled in places by bruises and sores.

"Do not talk to me of the cost to your body and mind!" her voice raised in pitch and volume as she held out her arms in front of the older woman.

"I know that most of these components and ingredients have been in the possession of your little coven for many years, so little cost for you there. And as for your soul?! Don't play games, Murag!" Sarsi seemed to gain height as she ranted, and a chill air seemed to invade the proximity of the two women. Sarsi smiled as she saw the older woman tremble slightly. Murag had been a witch for longer than Sarsi had been alive, yet the Queen had gained more power and ability than Murag's entire coven put together.

"I don't think that your soul felt pain when you tortured that unfortunate wretch to obtain Virgin's Tears. More like pleasure, you perverted crone. I have eyes and ears everywhere and I know what you did to her."

Murag regained part of her composure and stood tall. She pointed at the red-haired queen and scowled.

"Don't forget who schooled you and kept your secret for so many years, Sarsi! I taught you everything you know!" She felt her breathing slow as Sarsi whispered arcane words. Her muscles ached and became unmoving, leaving her standing, pointing accusingly to her one-time student.

"And that is where you are wrong, Murag. You have stood still, as I have run on before you. Your teachings were not the only schooling I have received. Whilst you and your pathetic little coven dabbled with your precious little charms and incantations, I sat at Nyx's feet." The old woman's eyes flickered as Sarsi mentioned the dark King of Hel, the Witch King Nyx.

"I learnt more those few nights I sat with him than all the years I spent with you. I learnt how to bring death and cheat death. If you were half of the witch that you proclaim to be, you would know what I need these ingredients for," she paused as she picked a thin bladed knife from the table and approached Murag. "And you would know what ingredient I omitted."

Sarsi smiled as she saw the terror in Murag's eyes. The frozen witch, held immobile by a power greater than her own, struggled to speak, trying to cast forth some spell that would break the Queen's hold on her. Sarsi stroked the side of her face, her hands cold to the touch and rough where the distended veins had erupted from the surface.

"Did your grand-daughter's eyes look like that when you extracted those Virgin's Tears from her? I just wish I could string this out a little, but I hope you understand, Murag. I am in a hurry."

Slowly, Queen Sarsi pushed the blade into Murag's stomach as watched as the old witch's eyes opened wide.

26

L ady Theres raked the embers of the fire and added more coal from the scuttle that sat next to the tall plain fireplace. She had managed to 'volunteer' for the duty of attending the fire in Count Dutte's bedchamber. The Count was at court, but he preferred his chambers warm and toasty, especially during the chill winter months. Hence she found herself alone in his room several hours before his return. She carefully placed several more logs on to the coals and watched as they caught. Satisfied that the fire was under way, she turned her attention to the room. It was dark, with heavy drapes drawn across the two windows. A heavy four poster bed occupied the far end of the room. Apart from the large wardrobes that sat to each side of the bed, the only other piece of furniture was an ornate, heavy-set desk covered in scrolls and vellums.

She hurriedly scanned the top documents, loathe to move anything and leave proof of her espionage. Nothing seemed out of the ordinary, mainly reports from Tar Dutte, the Count's lands in Marneheim. Details of monthly payments, in and out along with rosters of duties and patrol reports. Clearly the

Count liked to keep his finger on the pulse of running his ancestral home when he was in the capital. Theres resorted to leafing through the pile on the left-hand side of the desk and found her eye drawn to a small vellum scroll. The broken seal indicated it had come from Marneheim, but the appearance was different than most on the desk.

Lady Theres unrolled it and discovered it was a personal letter, devoid of the numbers of the other reports it was written in a small, but neat script. It was signed by the Seneschal at Marneheim and asked the Count that he might say a prayer as he had a recent death in the family. A brother, Frar Stenos, known personally to Count Dutte, had passed away a few days before. There was something about the letter that caused Lady Theres to read it again before she rerolled it up and placed it within her dress.

She next slid open the top drawer of the desk and gasped as she looked down. A large copper coin sat on some papers, a king's face from centuries past looked up at her. His features had been cruelly obliterated by a crude skull scratched into the surface, a skull that had been crossed through itself. Her orders from Tikar had been to look for anything out of the ordinary and this certainly fitted the bill. She palmed the coin, passing it into a hidden purse under her gown.

Theres took a step back, making sure the desk looked as it did before she entered the room. Even though she had only placed the coin beneath her gown a few seconds before, she patted it to reassure herself, then turned and left the room.

27

L ord Remoh's ship approached Tannaheim shortly before dusk and made a slow circle of the walled city before hovering several hundred yards from the Eastern Gate. The tall figure of Remoh stared impassively out over the city as the rooftops passed underneath. He knew it would fall to Karchek and the Emperor's Host, just like the countless cities and lands before.

The knartevilder followed a familiar course, first a lightening attack to strike fear into the very hearts of all who stood in their way. Then, seemingly peaceful negotiations to neighbouring states and cities to bring them under sway without further bloodshed. That is, until the subjugation begun. The weak and the infirm were stripped from the land to be sent to the slave pens, fodder for the Flyers and a living cargo doomed to return to Homeland to feed the Emperor's infernal machines and demons. Anyone worthwhile would be sent to the quartermasters and enrolled into the Host, replacements for the inevitable corpses left at many a city wall. The rest would be conscripted to strip the land of every resource possible – wood, steel, iron, gold and silver – not to mention food and livestock would be crammed into the large cargo and work ships. There, the goods would either be sent back to Homeland or manufactured into weapons of war for the next city, land or planet. Once done, the luckless workers would be condemned to the living hell of the slave pens.

Remoh stroked his black beard, wondering how this one would go. He never tired of the fighting, the struggle from street to street once the skyships had landed and then the inevitable realisation of defeat from the defenders. What he enjoyed most, however, was the spoils. Tearing the women away from their men and throwing them to his blood gorged troops. Choosing the fate of the wailing and tormented. Watching as the defeated trudged to their fate or screamed and clawed as they were dragged away.

He tried to imagine this Sarsi, this queen that his commander had bade him to meet. He had heard that she was beautiful but dangerous, a magician or witch. He felt sure that he could meet and give his demands in some security though. For a start, her daughters were in the hands of Karchek. Secondly, his father always had told him to fight fire with fire. He had his own magician, one of the Emperor's Adepts. He turned to the grey cloaked man who stood behind him. The Adept had his cowl down, his bald head gleaming in the evening sun.

"Your first negotiation, Turkbour?" he asked.

"Yes, Lord Remoh."

He hadn't struck Remoh as the most talkative soul, every conversation during the flight had been one way with the young Adept adding only a few additions to his mainly 'yes/no' answers. Remoh wished Brant was to stay with him, but Karchek had requested that the senior Adept was to make his way back to Jacarna as soon as he could. He wasn't all too sure about the younger Adept, but he had seemed to handle himself well in the initial invasion.

"Just stick close to me. You know your task when we land, yes?"

"Of course. I am to stand vigil on the psychic plane. To protect you from any attack, physical or magical."

"Are you nervous, Turkbour?" Remoh asked

Turkbour shook his head.

"The Emperor forbids it. An Adept is always to be fearless and dedicated to the Emperor's Way."

Remoh shrugged.

"We will approach tomorrow and enter the city in the morning."

28

L ady Theres slipped out of the kitchen area of the large town house that belonged to Count Dutte and made her way across the small back courtyard to the stables. The cobbled yard had a covered area to store carts and wagons in and was surrounded by other outbuildings that formed the perimeter. With a furtive glance to make sure that she wasn't seem, she pushed the large door open and darted inside. The stable had a central area that was surrounded by several stalls on each side.

The occupants of each stall looked over their doors at the newcomer. One or two snorted and nickered, expecting food, whilst others pawed the ground, striking the wooden doors to their stalls with their hooves. She was wary at exciting them more, in case they should bring attention to her. There was a noise from the hayloft above, and within seconds Churt slid down the ladder, his face beaming at the sight of his adoptive mother. He rushed over to her and threw his arms around her, his face buried within the folds of her servant's dress.

"It's good to see you as well, Churt." She stroked his mousy brown hair as she spoke.

Churt had been sent to the kitchen as an assistant, his duties included fetching wood for the fires and washing up. His quarters, though, were now the hayloft of the stables. It wasn't exactly what he had hoped for after his last mission for Tikar Welk, as a lowly servant boy in the employ of the slaver Yab M'vil. At least, he thought, there wasn't any flaming demons here in Tannaheim.

"Did you find anything?" He asked, his grip still tight about his mother.

"I did. No-one seems to want to talk about Dutte though. Most of the staff hate him, some are indifferent."

"What did you find?" Finally, he let go and stepped back, allowing her to breathe again.

"This." She took the scroll from her dress and passed it to the boy. He didn't bother to look at it further. If Theres said it was important, he would believe her. And besides, he hadn't had the fortune to learn to read.

"Tikar said that he was looking for any news from Marneheim. That letter fits the bill."

"I should take it straight away to the Brandyman." He went to hug her again, but she stopped him. She took the coin from within her purse and handed it to him. He stared at the obliterated face of the centuries-long dead king and said nothing.

"I found this as well. I think this is more important."

"What is it?"

"I am not sure; I haven't seen anything like it. But it was in the Count's bedchamber."

"I'll take it as well. The Brandyman will know what it is." He closed his grubby fingers about it and shivered at the touch. It was only copper, but the evil it seemed to emanate made him shudder.

"Be careful, Churt." There gave him a big hug and smiled at him. Being one of Tikar's agents was certainly dangerous, and whilst the young lad had grown up on the rough streets of Tannaheim, she always worried about him.

"I always am, Theres. I always am."

He spirited the coin into his belt purse and turned to the ladder to the hayloft. She watched him start to climb it and sighed. Relieved to be free from the evidence that she had collected, if it was evidence at all, she left the stable the way she had entered.

As she crossed the yard, a voice broke the night-time silence.

"What have you been doing in there? Asking more questions?"

Under Steward Harte stepped out from the shadows of the covered cart area and into the courtyard. With him were three men, not dressed in the livery of House Dutte, but all in black. Two of them carried short clubs.

"Nowhere, Under Steward." She looked at the unsavoury types that stood behind the Under Steward.

"You've been very nosey since you arrived. Asking questions that you shouldn't have been asking. Now, I need to make sure that you don't have a big mouth as well."

She made a quick glance back at the stable door, praying to all the Gods that Churt was on his way. Harte noticed and followed her gaze.

"Of course, her son. Get him." He turned to one of the men behind him, who started to walk to the stables.

"No!" She screamed out as loud as she could, and darted forward, striking the middle-aged man right in the centre of his face. He coughed and spluttered as blood flooded from his nose.

"Churt, run! Run and don't look back!" She called out, even louder than before. There was a clatter of tiles as Churt clambered through a dormer vent onto the roof of the stable. Like a mountain goat, he skipped and ran over the slightly angled slope until he disappeared from view over the roof of a storeroom.

"Get him!" Blood poured from Harte's nose as he held his hand to his face in an effort to deaden the pain. Two of the thugs turned and ran for one of the side gates that led to the street alongside the property. Theres turned and tried to run to the back door of the house, all other avenues of escape being blocked. The thug who had been making for the stable had turned at the sound of her screams and now made after her, egged on by Under Steward Harte. The man was much fitter and athletic than Theres, who only made it to the door before being grabbed by Harte's man. She struggled viciously, trying to kick him or headbutt him as he held her in a bear hug from behind.

"Get off me!" She screamed again, twisting and turning as much as she could. The thug held her fast, then turned her towards Harte. Before she could lash out with her feet at him, the bald steward struck her across the face. Another scream earnt her another slap across the face and she tasted blood. Whether the blow had cut her lip or whether it was from Harte's hand, she did not know.

The corpulent form of Under Steward Harte waddled to a cart set by the courtyard wall. He retrieved a short stick, the width of a wrist and the length of a man's forearm, from a pile. Viciously, he drove one end into her stomach causing her breath to erupt from her lungs. The thug who held her, threw her to the floor, then accepted the stick from Harte.

"Let her know that we don't tolerate thieves, scum and liars in this house." He spat at Theres before stepping backwards. The brute raised his stick, before raining blow after blow down on Theres. Mercifully, she blacked out after the second or third hit.

29

The wretched contents of the slave pens had been unloaded and were now in the care of the villagers that Bex and Garlen's troops had saved. The Prince had given them instructions to head for Tannaheim and seek shelter within its walls.

The skyship had risen from its resting place, Rexen's power lifting it into the gloom of the Maingard dusk. To say that Col had mastered the strange craft was an overstatement. The fisherman turned soldier had spent a few minutes experimenting with the controls before announcing that he had the basics. The skyship turned its dragon-headed bow towards Jacarna and started to accelerate.

All around her, the Ghosts prepared for war. Armour was repaired and tightened, and the steel of their weapons was rubbed clean and polished. Some sat in quiet meditation whilst others sung the tales of heroes from old, loudly, proudly and repeatedly.

Bex had already donned her mail shirt again after removing it earlier to check for damage. The weirdsword *Caladmorr* was sheathed and strapped to her belt. Her two ever present grecks were thrust into her boots. She crudely daubed a black band of soot over her eyes before strapping her spider over her mail. She stretched to make sure the leather straps and buckles didn't constrict her movement and then made her way from the cabin down to the long room that was the prison of the demon-like creature known as Rexen.

She paused outside the double doors to steel herself and also to pull the herbal mask over her face. Pushing the doors open, she strode inside. Even though the long cells stood empty, she could still see the faces of the incarcerated wretches who, until only an hour or so before had wished for a quicker and easier death than the end that awaited them.

The insectoid creature was resting as she approached, its limbs seemed jumbled up beneath the armoured body. The gems on its back pulsed rapidly, the purplish glow eerily reflecting from the glossy carapace. The blackhaired warrior looked about. Only two of the prisoners were left. Despite the horror that they had visited upon her world, she couldn't imagine the thoughts that crossed their minds as they waited their grisly demise.

An image of Ishtara's world flashed into her mind, lines of shackled *Qoi* being forced onto skyships. It was quickly replaced by the murdered girl from the hamlet, her long, red hair blowing in the wind as she reached out to Bex, before hands grasped her from behind, ripping the clothes from her body. She started to cry, but the tears that flowed from the corner of her eyes were blood. Her once beautiful features decayed rapidly into dust that dispersed in the ever-increasing wind.

'Don't waste your grief on them, Bex', Ishtara spoke to her. Before she could reply, Rexen raised his head.

"Ahh, the one with one inside. Welcome to you, Lady Bex."

Rexen pronounced the words stiltedly, its mandibles adding clicks between words and syllables.

"You know about Ishtara?", Bex queried, trying to think whether her symbiotic 'twin' had been mentioned when they had first encountered Rexen.

"Yes, I can sense. We are alike, you and I."

"I don't think so. I don't kill innocents." Bex spat back, annoyed about the comparison.

"That I didn't mean." The insect-like monster lowered its head, its bulbous eyes closing. "I do not wish to do these things, but the pain...." The sabres of his claws tapped out a little staccato on the metal grating below, the sharp tips picking out the steel bars.

"...You do not know the pain. It is not you that I am alike, Lady Bex. I meant the one within. She knows my torment."

Ishtara stayed quiet. Rexen continued.

"In your eyes we are horrors. However, quietly we lived, unaware of other planes, of other worlds. And then true horror arrived. Once we lived, but now we are dead. Our kind are dead or form part of the evil that brought death to our worlds." Bex felt Ishtara start at Rexen's words.

'Our kind form part of the evil.... Does he mean that he knows of some Qoi that are still alive?'

"Rexen, Ishtara asks whether you know of any *Qoi* that survived her world's destruction?"

"Free me and I will say what I know."

"You know that your freedom is not in our power, Rexen."

'Bex! Please.' Ishtara implored.

'We cannot trust this creature just yet, Ishtara.'

'But Bex....'

'You know what I say is true, Ishtara. We can always speak with Garlen when we have found his sisters.'

Ishtara harrumphed, knowing that Bex was right.

"Do what you can to help us rescue Garlen's sisters and we will set you free then. Until that point, we can do nothing."

The Flyer seemed to contemplate Bex's words but before he could respond Rica appeared behind Bex and announced that Jacarna was in sight.

———

30

T he figures oozed out of the stone wall of the dark corridor. For Radnak, it was the first time that he had done this conscious. Even before he had fully emerged from the rock, he had made his mind up that it would be the last time as well. Janis had urged him to keep his eyes shut and he had been glad that he had. He didn't know whether his body slipped through the rock or vice versa, or whether it was a mix of the two. He likened the whole experience to having sand rubbed over his skin, eyes, and mouth. And that was before he got to the sensation of feeling the fine particles pass through his pores and into his body.

He shook violently, the aftereffects of the cat man's poison still lingering. He reached out with his hand, resting against the wall to catch his breath and sanity. From the corner of his eye, he caught Janis start to pass through the wall again on the second of his nine journeys to bring the whole party out of their self-made prison. As soon as Janis had disappeared, the half-orc retched.

By the time the young Lord had reappeared, this time with

his elder brother, Radnak had regained his composure and the warrior in him had taken over. In comparison to Radnak's consternation with the passage through the rock, Igant was in awe, despite having made many more journeys than his *Sverd*. Radnak grunted, 'definitely a youth thing'. Igant nodded to the experienced grey skin and Radnak indicated that he should take up station further down the corridor, guarding the rear.

Next to appear were the two princesses. He noticed that both girls seemed unperturbed by the short journey. The older girl, Ingren, kept her eyes shut but her face was set hard as she appeared from the rock, her arms around Janis. The orc tried to smile at her but it came out as an embarrassed grunt.

When Moren appeared, her terrible wounds covered with a fresh piece of cloth torn from the hem of Iga's dress, she alighted from Janis' grasp. Radnak noticed the tenderness that the young goblin lord dealt with the injured princess. It seemed reciprocated as she slid from his grasp, but the spell was quickly broken when her sister silently reached out to her and touched her. The young girl jumped but after a glare from the silent Janis, Ingren quickly reassured her little sister.

"It's okay, Moren, it's only me." Radnak had sensed a little awkwardness over the last few hours between the sisters and it may have been the light, but he swore he could see the younger girl stiffen slightly at her elder sister's words. She didn't pull from Ingren's touch though.

"My Ladies. Please wait whilst Janis brings out Iga. Then we will need to move silently but quickly. Stay together – I will lead and Igant will bring up the rear," he went to pass by but turned back and reached to his belt. He unclasped a curved blade in a leather sheath and passed it to Ingren.

"You may need this, if any comes close," he paused and then added a little louder so Igant could hear as well, "or if I and Igant should fall." He knew he wouldn't have had to add anything if the lords and princesses were the battle veterans he had once stood shoulder to shoulder with in past wars and skirmishes, but the youngsters had not seen the evil of war. He could only just bring himself to think about the further brutalities that any soldier, fresh from the adrenaline rush of battle, could visit upon the young girls and his beloved Iga.

31

C hurt ran. He had heard the cry of warning from Theres whilst he was in the hayloft and had immediately taken flight. He had always planned on leaving via the roof, having scouted out possible exit routes just like Tikar had taught him. He hadn't looked back at all, not even when he slipped over the edge of the storeroom's roof and slid down to the adjacent street. As he landed on the muddy ground, he heard the gates further down the wall open. He hurtled off in the opposite direction, hoping that he would stay ahead of them.

He stole a glance back over his shoulder to see the two men who followed him. They were big. He knew he wouldn't stand a chance if they caught him, so he had to make for the inn on Cheap Street, and thence to the secret rooms below. His feet splashed through the puddles that pooled in the cartwheel ruts.

He dashed to his right down an alleyway that led to one of the many marketplaces in Tannaheim. As he did so, he noticed that they had gained a little in the hundred yards or so that he had run so far. At this rate, even he could work out that he wasn't going to make it.

His heart pounded, like a drum in his ear. By Tomnar! What would they do if they caught him, when they caught him, he corrected himself? He knew he couldn't let Tikar down. If he was caught, then it wouldn't just be the Phantom that he would be failing, but Theres as well. The Gods only knew what they were doing to her right now. If they did catch up with him, then whatever fate was befalling her now would be in vain.

He turned the corner into the near deserted marketplace, only to be sent sprawling as he collided with a passer-by. He rolled over the ground, coming to rest on his backside, his hand bloody from the fall. As he staggered to his feet, the man he had hit lashed out with his cane.

"Watch where you are going, you brat!"

Churt threw his arm up to block the blow and yelped as the cane bit down on his arm. He fell again, only to be hit once more. He could hear Tikar Welk speaking in his mind, recalling the lessons that the Phantom had imprinted on his agents.

'Use anything you can to make sure your mission succeeds. Anything within reach or anything out of reach.' At the time, it sounded like mumbo jumbo. A lot of the things the hooded mystery man had said wasn't always clear until you needed it, that much he knew was right. This was one of those times. He knew he only had seconds before the men came around the corner into the marketplace and he those seconds already mapped out in his young mind on what he had to do to avoid capture.

As the old man raised his cane again, Churt grabbed a handful of mud from the ground and turned and threw in one action, hitting the old man in the face. In the time it took for the old man to throw another curse word at him, he had scrambled to his feet and was making for the opposite corner of the marketplace. Not a moment too soon, the thugs came bounding out of the alleyway, and nearly collided with the old man. As they passed him, still wiping the mud from his face, one gave him a hard shove for good measure, sending him sprawling. Any other time, Churt would have guffawed with laughter. But right now, he had other things on his mind.

He dived down, rolling under one of the market tables and into the next lane of stalls. The men behind split up, one sprinting to the end of the line, parallel with his own path, and the other clumsily climbed over the stall to follow him. He dived again, heading for the street that left the marketplace from one of its corners. This was Cheap Street; he was nearly there.

He felt the ground jar his arm as he rolled and came straight up to carry on running. He pushed the pain from his arms out of his mind and forced every bit of energy into his legs and lungs. As he ran onto Cheap Street, he could hear the footsteps behind him, and he knew that they were close. He could see the Inn ahead, and hoped he had enough distance between him and his pursuers to enable him to get to the door and open it. His legs ached and he felt that, if he stopped, his body wouldn't start again.

Then, a hard swipe of a cudgel hit his legs sending him crashing to the ground. His face smashed into some of the rough cobbles, dislodging a tooth and tearing his lip. He looked up, the door to the Inn of the Luckless Wench was only a few yards away. He was next to the opening of an alleyway that snaked down the side of the old building. He groaned at being caught so near and tried to summon the energy to move again or to shout for help. His attacker stood over him, cudgel raised in one hand and the other on his knee as he panted hard, trying to catch his breath.

"Fucking brat. I hate running." The other man, a little slower than the other, ran up and came to a halt next to them, on the opposite side of the Inn.

"What did you take, brat?" He launched a hard kick into Churt's side, causing bile to rise in his throat. He coughed and spluttered, blood and vomit splattering into the puddles on the road ahead.

"I think you need to leave him alone and to face someone your own size." The voice cut into the silent air around them. Churt's addled mind tried to place the sound. The pain rocked through his body and he gasped as his lungs tried to return to a peaceful rhythm. He was sure he had heard that voice before. He turned his head to the right and saw a pair of boots walk out of the alley by the inn. A sword trailed alongside, the tip causing a slight ripple in the puddle as it moved towards him.

"It's not your business, stranger. Now, fuck off!"

Churt looked up, his eyes failing to focus on the blurred image. Above the boots, he could make out white legs and a white body.

"It is my business when a young lad is set upon by two cowards. If you think that you have the balls, then you should stand before me."

The brute standing over Churt stood tall, pointed his cudgel at the newcomer.

"I don't think you understand. This little shit is *our* business." He empathised the word by pointing at his chest. "Besides, you don't know who we work for. Our employer will want this little thief."

The newcomer laughed and Churt finally started to focus on the figure.

"I know exactly who you work for. A coward and a traitor to the Red Throne. One who will pay dearly for his crimes." The two brigands took a step backwards as the white clad figure moved closer to them.

"Now, my employer is a different matter. Scum who get themselves under the scrutiny of the one I work for, tend to end up dead."

Churt saw the bladed flash up, and a spray of blood landed on his cheek. There was a cry of protestation from behind him and a curse, before the blade flashed again and something thudded to the ground beside him.

"Churt! Are you okay? It's me! Gavan!" He felt someone start to lift him. He tried to help his rescuer by supporting some of his own weight, but he fell limp.

He came to a few minutes later. Someone was wetting his brow with cold water. It was Yanna. The old, withered figure of the Brandyman stood behind here.

"Churt, you're awake. You had me worried there for a minute. Where's Theres? Is she alright?"

He closed his eyes and slowly shook his head. His lip felt numb and he could still taste the saltiness of his own blood. The door behind them closed and Gavan appeared. He was wiping his sword clean with a cloth.

"That's the bodies disposed of. I doubt anyone will miss scum like that." He looked over at Churt.

"Oh, you're awake! What news do you bring?"

The injured boy tried to answer, but his words were clumsy and didn't come. His cut and grazed fingers pointed to his belt pouch. Gavan reached for it, taking the few contents that it contained and handed them over to the Brandyman. His old hands wavered as he opened the scroll to read it. He nodded and let the scroll roll up in one hand. He held the coin up, turning it so they could all see the skull etched crudely over the King's face, a deep scratch crossed through both images.

"Tobe's tits!"

"What is it?"

"It's trouble, and the answer. Tikar was right." The old man sighed. "What assets, if any, do we have in the Brotherhood of Karnast?"

"The assassins? None, it has been impossible to get anyone

planted in the guild. We have definitely tried many times." Gavan answered.

"I do have one, not in it, but very close. Not an asset, but a friend." The little mousey Yanna spoke up. The Brandyman and Gavan looked at her, an incredulous look upon each of their faces

"Fferyll at the Red Tart, she helps pass information to the Brotherhood. Sets up meets." Yanna shrugged

"How in Tomnar's name do you know that?"

"Oh, I pick up loads of information. I'm small and just a messy brat. No-one pays me any attention."

The Brandyman smiled, his mouth a horror of crooked and rotting teeth.

"Yanna, can you take some men and collect this friend of yours. Then meet me at the gates to the Palace. You need to pass this information to the Hawk. Gavan, take your squad to Dutte's townhouse and find Theres. Eliminate anyone who causes you problems."

"Even Dutte himself?"

"He won't be there. Sarsi has all the Lords at the Palace. They are making final preparations for the invasion."

32

Bex and Ishtara led the way, guided by Bryn Kar, down the seemingly endless stone staircase. Garlen and half of his Ghosts followed at a short distance in a loose formation. Rexen had lent his experience to Col to help guide the large skyship to a safe landing on top of the roof of the vast palace complex. There were already four ships berthed there, but Garlen had directed Col to land apart from them. Leaving a dozen Ghosts to guard the ship, Bex and the rest had made their way to the unguarded doors leading to one of the several spiral staircases winding their way down into the palace.

On every floor, the staircase opened out onto a wide landing. Several times Bex and Bryn had to pause, bringing the retinue to a halt as they heard Cassalians moving on the landing below. They had waited until they moved on before proceeding.

Ishtara had stayed mainly quiet, leaving Bex in an eerily silent world. She had been used to the almost incessant chatter since that night at Yab M'vil's villa, when they had joined together.

'*You're quiet.*' She pointed out to her companion.

'*Yes.*' Ishtara replied bluntly. Neither spoke for a few seconds until Ishtara carried on, filling the uneasy silence.

'*This is your area of expertise. I do not want to distract you.*' There seemed to be something more, so Bex inquisitively raised her mental eyebrows.

'*And I feel the despair. Bad things happened here. I can feel it and it brings back memories.*' Bex nodded, you didn't have to be an empath to sense the anguish and sorrow that seeped out of the cold stone. They had passed, stepped over in many cases, evidence of battle from the invasion several days ago. Dark stains of dried blood marked the places where defenders had been cut down in their futile attempts to stop the invasion.

She looked back at Bryn, seeing that he sensed it too. His face was set in steely determination, his eyes flickered between anger and sorrow, and his grip upon the hilt of his sword and axe seemed to tighten with every floor they passed.

'*There are soldiers below, Bex*'. Ishtara dropped her internal voice to a whisper, showing she was still getting to grips with the fact she had no body of her own. '*I think they are on the stairs.*'

Bex paused, holding her hand up to bring the procession to a halt. She whispered Ishtara's concerns to Bryn.

"I'll deal with them." He took a step forward before Bex stopped him, her hand upon his arm.

"What level are we on?"

Bryn looked quizzically at her.

"About halfway."

"Then we leave them. You remember what Garlen said – avoid any confrontation until we have no choice." She noticed the despair in his face as his mind registered that she was right.

"There will be plenty of chance to get your revenge, Bryn Kar," she unwittingly echoed his advice to Namot from days earlier. "Now, is there a way round them?"

Bryn nodded and indicated that they leave the stairwell and

moved into a wide corridor. This corridor ran along one side of
the palace and they were able to see fire still burning
throughout the city through the narrow window slits. They
moved quickly through a large ante chamber only to come to a
quick halt as the door at the far end opened and a thick set,
grey skinned warrior walked through.

He wore a hardened leather cuirass over chainmail and, as
he saw Bryn and the others, he snarled displaying a pair of
short tusks that protruded from his lower jaw. He hefted his
vicious looking broadsword but seemed to motion behind him
with his free hand for his companions to withdraw. Rica and a
couple of the archers pulled out to one side and readied their
bows, one of the soldiers shouting out as he did so.

"Orc!"

Just then, a blur burst forward, knocking a slimmer, green
figure through the doorway. It screamed out as it did so.

"Garlen! You came!" She ran straight for Garlen and threw
herself at him. It was all the blond prince could do to drop his
sword and to sweep the young girl up in his arms.

"Ingren! I had to; I couldn't leave you here. Is Mori with
you?" His heart sank as Ingren sobbed in response.

"Oh, Garlen!"

The grey skinned orc helped the young goblin lad back to
his feet, making way for a tall and elegant female goblin to
enter the chamber. Her dark hair and green skin contrasted
with the light grey dress that clung to her figure, covering all
but accentuating every aspect. One arm was cuddled round the
shoulder of a young child, grimy but with her face wrapped in
bandages.

"The one you ask about is here, Prince." Lady Iga addressed
Garlen, making her way to where the prince held his sister.

"Mori!" he darted forward and crouched down as he
reached out to his youngest sister. "What have they done to
you?"

"Beware, Prince. It is bad; they hurt her terribly." Iga spoke softly.

"Garlen, she's blind! They blinded her!" Ingren sobbed loudly.

Garlen raised his hands to the bandages as if to remove them. The young girl placed her hands on top of his, stopping him, then moved her hands slowly to his face, her fingers slowly moving over his features.

"It hurts." The young girl cried and then shook.

"I did what I could with what limited resources I had, but she is still in shock." Iga still stood with her arm around Mori's shoulder.

"And who are you?" he snapped at Iga. "Goblin!" he spat out the addition as he stood.

"Watch what you say, Inn Lord!" Radnak came forward, standing level with Iga with Mori. "If it wasn't for Lady Iga, your sister would have died days ago. And Igant and Janis here, rescued them, else they would both be back down in that cell." The short half-orc stood face to face with Garlen, the blond Danarian slightly taller by a hand's width.

"It's true, Garlen! Radnak is on our side." Ingren came back and grabbed the young goblin's hand and brought him forward to stand with the woman.

"Janis here dragged us both through the stone!"

"Is this true?"

Janis and Mori nodded, Janis more vigorously than the injured girl.

"Then I owe you all an apology and much, much more. Forgive me. You are more than welcome to come with us." He shifted his sword into his left hand and held his right out to Radnak. The half-orc grunted and grasped Garlen's forearm, which the prince reciprocated; an age-old sign of acknowledgement and friendship.

"Whilst this is all nice, Garlen, we are standing in the

middle of an enemy stronghold. I think we should be moving before the Cassalians find us." Bex interjected. The prince and the mercenary released their grip.

"Of course! Col, get the men ready to move. Mathor, take point." He turned to address Bryn Kar. "There is no need for you to guide us back, the way should be simple – straight up!" He smiled.

A young voice interrupted, a young goblin sprinting into the chamber from behind Radnak. He was a tall adolescent, carrying a short sword that dripped with blood. His left hand clasped his bicep, and all could see the blood coating his hand.

"*Radnak! Radnak! Ap arg durant tag!*" he exclaimed in a language that was completely foreign to Bryn and Bex. He came to a skidding halt as he realised that strange soldiers seemed to have his family and friends covered.

"*Igant! Du huk gnart.*" Iga swept to his side, slowly and carefully pushing his sword down from the defensive stance he had taken upon noticing the others. She took his hand away from his arm and muttered under her breath. Bex noticed the other Ghosts were readying arms.

"What did they say?" she asked, gripping her curved greck tighter.

"Iga pointed out that he was hurt" Radnak said, turning to acknowledge Bex for perhaps the first time.

"And the young lad was warning that they had found us." Garlen added.

The gristled half-orc nodded and looked at the young prince with a little more respect.

"You speak goblin tongue?"

Garlen nodded and directed his next question to the young injured goblin.

"*Tyen qwe?*"

"*Yang-tui.*" Igant garbled back.

"At least twenty."

Ishtara purred inside, obviously glad that the skulking around was about to end.

"Garlen, get your men and sisters back to the ship. I'll deal with these, but please wait for me."

'I think Bryn Kar could well do with staying with us. He needs to, how do you say, deal with some anger?'

'I think that would be a good idea, Ishtara.'

"Earl Kar, would you do me and Ishtara the honour of fighting by our side?"

The chainmail clad giant smiled and hefted his handaxe to his shoulder.

"There are twenty of them. Maybe we should all stay?" Radnak enquired, as the Ghosts started to retreat.

"I don't think we will be needed." Garlen called over his shoulder as he ushered his sisters from the room. He noted how Ingren and Iga fussed over the older goblin boy and how the younger goblin had clung to Mori. He scooped Mori up and held her close. "Don't be late, Lady Bex!"

"You better wait, Garlen! Or I am going to send Ishtara after you!"

Bryn was to Bex's left, sword and axe ready. Radnak took up guard to her right, both of his massive gloved hands on the hilt of his sword, lifting it to his shoulder. He glanced at her, as she slowly coiled into her standard stance, left foot forward and left hand raised, with her sword hand level with her chest, the curved blade pointing towards the doorway.

"You do know how to use that, do you?" he grunted.

Bryn Kar laughed.

"Your only worry, Radnak, is whether they leave any for you and me."

With that, the enemy poured through the doorway, and Bex darted forward with a quick brace of thrusts leaving a man dead on the floor before Bryn and Radnak had moved. She jumped back nimbly between the two men.

"They?" Radnak asked

'*I think it is time for me to take over, Bex.*' Ishtara purred once more, a definite lilt to her voice. Igant had been right, there was at least twenty opponents who faced them. A dozen or so swordsmen had entered the chamber and Bex could see more bunched the other side of the doorway.

'*You are starting to like this a little too much, Ishtara. You once told me that the Qoi weren't warriors.*'

'*We aren't. But you saw that young girl, what they did to her. There isn't much you can do with monsters like that.*'

"They call these the Chosen. Soldiers taken from vanquished worlds." Bryn announced, staring at the motley assortment of races that faced them. Warily the Chosen stared them down, shuffling over and around their fallen comrade. Bryn feinted an attack, skipping a couple of steps forward, then back to his place in line, hoping to draw them forward.

The ruse worked, with a cry and a shriek that called out for Death, three charged forward whilst the rest clattered their swords upon shields, raising a clamour that filled the chamber. Bryn dropped his shoulder, smashing into the shield of his attacker. The man, a pasty individual whose thin black eyes glared at Bryn through a mess of black, facial hair found himself unbalanced and unable to deliver his overhead blow. The guardsman shoved him brutally to one side then brought his longsword down onto the hip of the warrior that was closing in on Bex.

Radnak waited until the last second and dodged nimbly inside his attacker's space, closing his massive, mailed fist around the blue skinned hand that held the man's sword. The blow was stopped in its tracks and the impetus of Radnak's immense strength almost lifted the man of his feet. The half orc's other fist, wrapped round the hilt of his own broadsword, crunched into the Chosen's face. The man's face disappeared into a bloody pulp, accompanied by a sickening crack. He sagged in Radnak's grip and the bodyguard made sure of his kill by bringing the huge blade down quickly onto his exposed shoulder blade. What little armour the attacker had was ineffective and the blade cleaved through bone and flesh. More of the Chosen now surged forward, whipped into a frenzy by their leaders behind.

Bex felt the now familiar warming of her skin, the heat rising to an almost unbearable level as the smoke started to seep from the openings of her armour. As the final metamorphosis neared, she had a strange thought.

'I wonder what happens to my clothes when we change?'

'An obscure pondering, Bex. Really? At this time?'

'As long as they keep coming back!' she chuckled within as Ishtara burst forth. The change nearly cost Radnak his life. Shocked by the abrupt appearance of the fiery Ishtara, he stumbled backwards and fell, two of the enemy moving in on him. He threw up a hurried parry as one attacked, catching the sword blow and turning it with a grunt to one side.

Ishtara swept both her swords up in a cross to block an attack from a swordsman whose grey skin was darker than Radnak's and whose nose was large and scaled. Hate blazed in his eyes and even the strength of Ishtara was starting to wane as he forced his sword down with both hands. The blade grated against the two curved grecks. She pressed forward, directing her knee hard into his groin. He grimaced but nothing more, spitting curses and phlegm at her. From all around came the clash of steel upon steel as Bryn and Radnak engaged more of the enemy.

She pushed upwards and danced to her left, leaving her left sword raised to continue the block, the right swept back and down then she thrust it viciously into the gut of her opponent. His momentum not only carried his blow harmlessly over where she had stood, but also propelled him onto the point of her greck. She gritted her teeth and shoved harder, watching the blade sink into the soft flesh up to the hilt.

"Pig!" she snarled at the Chosen, who sank to his knees, wrenching the greck from her grasp. She dropped the remaining greck from her left hand into her right.

'Perfect, Ishtara.' Bex called from inside her mind. There was little time for respite. Two more attackers closed down on her, one of them jabbed his spear at her whilst peering out from behind a round shield adorned with a blazing star.

She grabbed at the haft of the spear and caught it in a vice like grip, dancing to her left to pull the spearman between her and the second attacker. She felt someone collide with her back, knocking the wind out of her. She kept her grip on the spear and gave a nervous look over her left shoulder.

"Bex!" It was Bryn who called out, raising his axe to smash it down on her, catching his strike just before delivering it. They stared at each other for a split second, suddenly aware that there was no room for error in the tight confines. She saw movement behind the big guardsman and called out a warning.

"Bryn! Watch out!" she twisted her torso. Still gripping the spear in her left hand, she thrust the curved sword deep into the throat of another grey skinned soldier, as the man raised his sword to strike Earl Kar. As she drew the blade back, a hiss of air escaped from the wound, bubbling blood as it did so.

Bryn Kar returned the favour, launching an attack on the spearman, reaching over her lithe body with his long arms. The axe crunched down through the pitiful leather cap the soldier wore. He dropped instantly, the blow sending him to his long-forgotten gods even before his body and brain registered. Bryn managed to keep hold of the axe, tugging it free from the gaping wound, then turned to find a new target. Ishtara did likewise, turning to meet the swordsman's strike with a raised parry. Steel upon steel rang out as she forced the attacking blow upwards, before slashing downwards twice across each thigh.

As the man stumbled to his knees, she drew the blade across his throat.

Within a few minutes, the enemy lay dead or dying with a few taking the view that discretion was the better part of valour, retreating from the swirling swords and the fiery visage of Ishtara. Now the half-orc turned and regarded Ishtara as he cast the corpse of a Chosen to one side, pulling his dagger from its armpit.

Flames licked across the surface of her skin, a skin that slowly swirled in patterns of red, orange and black lava. Two twisted horns rose from her head. She looked back at him, his face was reflected in her black eyes. He gave a simple nod as an acknowledgement.

"Crom Teder! Can you give some warning next time!"

"Where would the fun be in that, Radnak?"

Ishtara's form slowly changed to Bex's and the redskinned woman sagged against Bryn. Her body steamed as she regained her composure, almost gasping for breath.

"We should get moving." Bryn said, turning towards the corridor that led to the stairwell. "Take the lead, Radnak."

They made good time on the stairs, only meeting two guards who Radnak dispatched quickly. At one point, they heard pursuers behind and Bex urged them to halt for a second. Her fingers fluttered over the spider's web, pulling a handful of small metal objects from one pouch. She sprinkled these on the stairs behind them.

"Calthrops," she explained. "It won't stop them, but just make them a little slower once someone steps on one." They picked the pace up and broke through the door onto the roof. Bex was relieved to see the ship still on the rooftop.

Three Ghosts were running towards them, and Bex recognized Rica among them. The young soldier had his bow readied as he ran. Bryn was nearly carrying Bex as they ran, with Radnak panting hard behind. One of the soldiers with

Rica called out a warning and Rica stopped and raised his bow. The arrow whistled as it flew past them, its path so close and true that Bex could see the fletching as the arrow flexed and spiralled past them. She heard a grunt from behind as the arrow hit its target.

A volley of arrows flew overhead, fired from the top deck of the ship. The three Ghosts protected their retreat and Bryn lifted Bex up so she could grip the boarding ladder further up. Willing hands hung down from the gunwales to haul her up, so she only had to climb a few feet to be safe. Bryn followed, quickly hauling himself up hand over hand.

As Bryn clambered over the side, Bex pulled herself up to see what was happening. Her calthrops had not slowed the pursuers much and there were now twenty or so Cassalians on the rooftop charging towards the ship. Radnak was nearing the top of the boarding rope, whilst one of the Ghosts has started to climb as well. Rica stood at the foot of the rope, unleashing death on the approaching Cassalians.

"Rica, time to move!" Garlen called over the side and then shouted to the archers on the deck. "Keep him covered, take out those troops!" Finally, he turned to Mathor near the wheel-house. "Tell Col to get this shitbucket moving!"

Radnak turned and gripped the soldier below by the scruff of the neck, pulling him over the side. Bex watched Rica sling his bow and turn in one movement, grasping the knotted boarding rope. The ship lurched as Col and Rexen finally got it moving, its huge bulk lifting ungainly into the dawn air. Radnak reached down again to offer his hand to the climbing Ghost just as an arrow hit the hull near him. He flinched and reached again, gloved hand just tantalisingly out of reach for the Ghost. Two more arrows hit, this time true, and the soldier was swept from the rope.

"Get rid of those archers!" Garlen called, directing the fire of his men. Rica scurried up the rope, and then screamed as an arrow hit his left shoulder and it was all he could do to keep his grip. He desperately tried to grab higher with his other hand, imploring Radnak to reach further down for his hand. The half-orc grunted an expletive in orcish and then beckoned the archer to reach higher.

"Your hand, lad! Quickly!"

Garlen's archers unloaded another volley of arrows, a volley that cut down several of the approaching archers on the rooftop. Unfortunately, a second too late, as several had already unleashed their own arrows at the stricken Ghost as he clung precariously to the side. One hit, punching through his leather armour, missing the steel discs that added extra protection, and knocking the breath from his body and the strength from his fingers. The young face looked up, the gaze of the old eyes flitting from Radnak to Bryn, then finally settled on Bex.

As Garlen bellowed out orders and directed fire from behind her, Bex clung exhausted to the gunwale of the ship, her face framed by the wooden railings. She reached out pathetically to offer hope and help to the young warrior. She screamed his name as their eyes locked and she saw the desperation in his face fade to mirror the horror on hers as he realised his fate.

His grip loosened as the ship lurched again, clanging him against the hull. Another volley of arrows splintered against the side of the ship, sending shards in all directions. Finally, his strength left him and as he fell, he seemed to open his mouth to scream but hit the rooftop before a sound escaped.

And with that, the skyship leapt forward into the dawn air, and Bex watched as the Cassalians swarmed over the unmoving body. And Bex and Ishtara wept.

33

G avan made sure his men were ready before turning his attention to the doorway of Dutte's townhouse. A dozen of Garlen's Ghosts backed him up whilst several more covered the back alleys that could offer escape for anyone within. Their black armour was in direct contrast to the off-white of his own, yet they all had the same determined look as their sergeant though. One of their own was within the building and in peril. The Ghosts were aware that the work that the Phantom's agents carried out, unmasking traitors and scum who feasted on the misery of others, was as dangerous as their own. At least, as soldiers, they had their arms and armour for protection.

Gavan's face twisted in anger as he pounded the door with his mailed fist. Due to the late hour and the noise of the visitors, a guard opened the door rather than a servant. Pushing his way in, Gavan shouted out for Theres.

"Lady Theres! Are you here?" The guard protested but thought better of reaching for his sword as the black garbed agents of Tikar Welk swarmed into the entrance hall. A wide stairway opened out before them, whilst several doorways gave access to further rooms on the ground floor.

"What is the meaning of this intrusion? Do you know whose house this is?" The stout figure of Under Steward Harte appeared at the top of the stairway, hurriedly wrapping a gown around himself to cover his night clothes. A wad of cotton was protruding slightly from one of his nostrils. A guard stood behind him, whose own bravery was limited to resting his hand on the hilt of his sheathed sword.

"By order of the Red Throne, I have power to search this premises for a servant; a woman by name of Lady Theres." Gavan answered, his voice overpowering the outraged Harte's. The Under Steward swept down the stairs to confront the intruders, confidant of the protection offered by his employer.

"She no longer works here. She was sacked yesterday. She was nothing but a common thief. Tomnar only knows how she had such a perfect reference."

Gavan seethed. Every second counted and the corpulent figure of Under Steward Harte irritated him. He snapped, stepping forward and slapping the bald man across the face. Harte recoiled; his eyes wide. He seemed more shocked due to the unexpected insolence of the intruders than the pain itself, though his cheek reddened. 'Where were the rest of his guards?' he thought.

"Enough!" Gavan screamed. He turned to his men, barking further orders. "Rouse everyone and assemble them here in the hallway. Question every servant for the whereabouts of Lady Theres."

Two of his men stripped the guards of their weapons and bound their hands behind them. The rest rushed through the house, banging on chamber doors and shoving the startled occupants towards the ground floor.

Gavan glared at the smug figure of Harte, who had, at least, stopped protesting. The veteran soldier was becoming frustrated as the hallway filled with servants and guards, brought in by his men. Much of the talk from the servants gave the impression that most had last seen her the hour before he had rescued Churt outside the safehouse. His only hope was that she was locked away in the depths of the house or had escaped and was on her way to the Phantom's network.

Havert, one of his men, pushed his way towards Gavan. He was one of the young ones, recruited to Garlen's men in the last few days of the Orc Wars. His blond hair set him aside from most of the others and drawn comparisons with Prince Garlen. Though the agents that carried out the dangerous task of working undercover with the scum that they hunted knew nothing of the real identity of the Phantom, the Ghosts were all well aware of the identity of Tikar Welk. Havert looked distressed, and Gavan's heart sank. The younger man whispered in his ear.

"We've found her. Out in the yard." With the sad, almost ashamed way he carried the news to his sergeant, it was obvious to Gavan that it was the worst news. He nodded for the young soldier to lead the way. As he passed Under Stewart Harte, he grabbed him by the scruff of his neck, dragging him with him.

"Bring them all out." He called to his men as he made his way through the servant areas towards the back yard of the town house. A smattering of rain had given the dawn a melancholic feel and the yard, enclosed by the walls and stables at the end seemed to close in on Gavan as he dragged Harte to where Havert and another Ghost stood by a small cart. A tarpaulin covered the back, and the old soldier threw Harte to the wet cobbles as Havert lifted the corner of the oilskin.

The battered body of Lady Theres lay underneath, her striking features obliterated by the force of the blows. Havert pulled away the tarpaulin completely and placed it on the cobbles. As the body was revealed to all, a whimper arose from the watching servants. Gavan lifted his friend from the cart and laid her on the oilskin, as delicately as one taking his true love to bed. He gently folded her hands over her chest and stood, wiping a tear from his eye.

"Check their hands," he snarled at his men. Hurriedly, they carried out his order. They had seen this look on the veteran's face before, all too often when confronted with one who had overstepped the mark with innocents unable to defend themselves. Many of the Ghosts carried out their duties for pay as well as their loyalty to the Prince and the fact that they were ridding Danaria of scum. Gavan, however, seemed to take it personally. They all had their stories, of who they were before they become soldiers and Ghosts. Gavan had kept his past to himself, but the demons of whatever it was, still haunted him.

One of the guards was found to have blood on his hands and he was pushed to his knees in the rain. He started to protest his innocence until Gavan spoke and addressed the waiting crowd.

"Tonight, your companions murdered a young lady whilst another two tried to murder her son. Normally, the culprits would be hauled off to the dungeons, then hung. However, we are at war. And so, this city is under Martial law, until the Queen decries so. Because of this, you are all found guilty by association. By rights, I could have you all hanged now." There had been murmurings of protest from the assembled guards, whilst Harte had been shoved to the floor next to bloodstained guard.

"He ordered me to! He said Count Dutte needed protection! Please..." The guard that had been pulled forward with Harte started to beg for his life, as his hands were tied before him.

"Shut up!" Harte spoke again, only to receive a kicking from one of Gavan's men.

"I take it, that that is a confession!" Gavan had said, then divided the assembled guards into two groups. "Instead of hanging, you will dispense the justice instead."

He made his way to the cart and picked up several of the cudgel-like sticks. The first was still slick with Lady Theres's blood. He tossed them to floor in front of the assembled guards. Nervously they picked them up and surrounded the two men, who knelt on the ground, their hands tied in front of them. Tears had flowed from the guard accused with Harte, whilst the Under Steward just spat at Gavan's feet.

"Anyone who refuses will join them."

The men of the two groups looked at each other in nervousness and worry. Then one swung a stave at Harte, catching him across the top of the arm. That seemed to spur the others on and soon the two men were submerged within the group, the staves rising and falling with deadly accuracy. Gavan gave them five minutes before calling them to a halt. The battered figures lay, almost dismembered by the force of the blows.

"Take the rest of the guards into custody. I'll get the Palace to conscript them into one of the regiments for defence of the city. Stay here and question the staff about Dutte. The Hawk will be grateful for any information about him."

"Where are you going?" Gavan looked up at the question, his mind distant.

"I have to tell Churt we found Theres." He swallowed, having carried the grim news of so many deaths to so many wives and mothers, he now had to tell a child the worst news imaginable.

YANNA SAT at a small table with the Hawk opposite. She had brazenly walked to the gatehouse of the Palace and demanded to see the Hawk. When the gate guards had laughed at her, she had handed a note to be passed to him, stating it was the utmost urgency. The guards had choked on their laughter as the Hawk made an appearance within minutes, ushering the young girl through to his offices.

He now stared at her dirty face and appearance, noticing that she had fresh blood on the cuffs of her tunic. Marshall Vent finished pouring himself a goblet of wine and carried it to the table, along with a glass of milk for Yanna. She bobbed her head in an exquisite gesture of servitude and mumbled her thanks.

"Thank you, Ser Vent."

He peered gravely at the little girl, down the edge of his nose that gave him his nickname. She squirmed slightly, as here, in the opulence of the palace, away from the poverty of the under city, she was out of her depth. Not only in class, but this was a whole new world; and she wasn't in control. On the streets, she knew every hidey-hole, every rat run, every friend and every foe. Here, she was a rat in a trap. No, not a rat, she thought to herself. There was only one rat in the palace, and it was time to set the Hawk on him.

"Now, young Yanna. What is the meaning of this?" He held out the small note, written by the Brandyman, that she had passed to the gate guards to get access to the Marshall.

"I know the identity of the arda archer. Yanna." He read aloud. "I take it you are referring cryptically to our arda game, comparing it to the assassination of King Anjoan."

"Whatever cryptically means, yes. I am."

The Hawk sighed and reached for his goblet.

"Who is the murderer?"

"It's Count Dutte! He arranged for the murder of the King. He met with the Brotherhood of Karnast. You must stop him, before he hurts the Queen as well." Yanna gabbled her message, her hands talking excitedly as her mouth ran away.

"Accusing a man of noble birth, or indeed any man, of such a heinous crime is a serious matter. Do you and your employer have any proof."

"Tikar told me that he had met with the Prince, and he had told him, that he – that's the Prince, had met Dutte's son on the road outside Tannaheim with a man claiming to be Frar Stennos's brother. But it can't be, he's dead."

The Hawk shook his head and took another sip of wine.

"You've lost me, young Yanna. Who is Frar Stennos, and what does he have to do with Count Dutte?"

"Frar Stennos is the seneschal of Tar Dutte, in Marneheim. Dutte's son, Earl Monteith, told the Prince that the old man he was riding with, was Frar Stennos's brother. But this letter," she reached into her pocket for the scroll that Theres had found in Dutte's chamber, "says that he was dead."

"Granted, that is odd," said the Hawk, his eyes running up and down the scroll. "But could he mean another brother?"

"The Prince seemed to think his other brothers were dead as well. But he also said that Monteith had ridden out to meet him from Marneheim, but this was outside the East Gate. Near where the Prince found the wagon his sisters were taken in."

The Hawk still looked doubtful.

"And the old man was riding a warhorse, not a riding horse. Tikar thinks that the old man had smuggled the princesses out of the city, took them to one of the Cassalian flying ships, and then met with Monteith on the way back." She added triumphantly. The look of victory soon subsided as Magus Vent cast a doubtful look at her. He could sense her disappointment.

"Look, it's not that I don't believe you in what you are saying. But if we are to accuse Count Dutte, his life would be forfeit." He drew his finger across his neck in an obvious gesture to the young girl. "We need to be certain."

Yanna's hand dived into her pocket again, withdrawing the coin that Theres had found.

"Lady Theres, Tikar's agent that was murdered tonight at Dutte's house, also found this." She handed it over and Vent took it without looking, as he stared straight at Yanna.

"Murdered, how?"

"She was beaten. Gavan, he is Tikar's lieutenant, he killed the men responsible. Though if I was you, I would execute Dutte straight away, because when Tikar's back, and he finds out, he'll do it for you."

"By Tomnar!" Exclaimed Magus Vent, as he stared at the coin of Karnast. He knew exactly what he was looking at. The coin that sealed the contract between the Brotherhood of Karnast and the Client. It symbolised that a job had been accepted, with a similar coin being shown or left with the victim that would show the job had been completed. It could only have meant that Dutte had had some dealing with the Assassin's guild.

"Now, do you believe me? Are you going to arrest him and torture him?" Yanna was on her feet, her arms waving excitedly again. The Hawk pondered.

"Not yet, we have enough to take him, but I will watch him," he paused, "well, like a hawk." He laughed. "To see if we can draw out any more accomplices. The Throne has tried to infiltrate that damned guild for years. If only we had someone there!"

"I do, and she is on her way here now."

The Hawk peered at the snotty, dirty faced child. She seemed to surprise him at every turn. What an excellent recruit she would make to his own network. If he could tempt her away from her mysterious employer, that was. And he very much doubted it.

"My young girl, you do know some very extraordinary people!"

Yanna looked up at him, her hands grasping the glass of milk.

"Do I?" she enquired innocently.

34

Turkbour gripped the gunwales of *The Sword of the Host* as it lazily circled the city below. The young Adept reached out with his mind and explored the air surrounding the ship, ready to ward off any attack from below. Turkbour was certain though, that such a backward society couldn't pose a threat to the Host.

He stared downwards as Tannaheim grew under his gaze, and *The Sword of the Host* slowly descended. Black specks came into view as the city hurried along in its day, unsuspecting of the menace that hung above them.

"They have no idea." Lord Remoh spoke, making the young Adept jump. Turkbour had been so focused on guarding from attacks from the city that he had been unaware that the warrior had left the sanctity of the cabin. Turkbour didn't answer.

"I like to watch them at this point. The moment their lives change. The beginning of the end." He clapped his hands, then spat over the side. He nodded towards the younger man.

"Although we fly a white flag at the bow and stern, we should return inside. There is a possibility that these barbarians might start throwing something at us."

"The Almighty Emperor does not allow…"

"You are no use to me dead, Turkbour." The old warrior interrupted. The young Adept nodded in agreement, though the fire in his eyes showed otherwise. Silently, the pair withdrew to the main cabin, where Lord Remoh ordered his helmsman to continue the landing.

A thousand pairs of eyes watched *The Sword of the Host* finish its descent and settle gracefully upon the central courtyard of the Palace. The green tableau was empty except for the dragon ship and a small phalanx of spearmen drawn up 'at guard' by the gateway that led from the courtyard to the interior courtyards of the palace.

Slowly, a hatch opened on one side, lowering to the ground to form a ramp from the newly formed opening. A low murmur hummed around the troops that waited nervously, the shields and spears glistening. This ceased immediately the first pair of boots marched out. Thirty-nine more pairs followed, and the forty troops made an inverted 'V' either side of the ramp. Lord Remoh waited some way back in the confines of the ship, anticipating his theatrical appearance. He turned to his grey-cloaked Adept standing behind him.

"Can you sense Brant from here?"

"Yes, Lord Remoh," Turkbour nodded.

"Tell him General Karchek requests his immediate presence back in Jacarna."

"The Emperor's Will." Turkbour acknowledged Remoh's order. Momentarily his eyes glazed over and then the pupils returned to their natural dark colour.

"He will leave immediately."

"Very good. Let us find out what this Witch Queen is about and deliver the terms of her surrender. If she values her offspring, then this should be a quick affair. And then I want to find a noble woman who wants to convince me not to send her to the slave ships." With that, he strode forward into the sunlight. Turkbour pulled his cowl up over his head, hiding the disgust on his face before following the commander out. He squinted in the low sun and looked about him.

The dragon ship had landed in the middle of a walled courtyard, an immense area covered by a well manicured lawn. An archer would have struggled to hit the ships from the walls that surrounded the courtyard, such was the size. As it was, a contingent of bowmen lined the walls, facing Remoh and his men, their longbows poised with arrows loosely nocked. The troops facing Remoh displayed the crossed swords of Tanna-heim on their oval shields. They stood close to the wall, either side of the central gates. Ahead of the right-hand side, was a rider on a white horse whose impatient hooves scratched at the earth.

Turkbour looked down, the grass soft and luxurious under his feet. As he watched, minute creatures made their way from blade to blade, and he was reminded of how the citizens of Tannaheim had looked as the ship had descended. Insects, he believed they were called. Many worlds had similar, though not many had them this small. He was mesmerized as the small, six-legged creatures strayed onto the leather webbing of his boots and crossed from one side to the other. Several disap-peared from view as they did so, the young Adept assumed that they were hidden by the strapping and material of his boots.

A veteran of many knartevilder, Remoh had grown accus-tomed to the reaction of every tribe or nation he had faced. He had seen many: shock, anger, awe, and despair – but the main one was fear. He hoped to see that in the eyes of the watchers opposite. Fear always made the knartevilder run smoothly. Whilst the Empire spread by violence and bloodshed, Remoh was more content if the acquisition of slaves, ship-fodder and new recruits for the dragonships could be completed with as little loss of life to his own men.

He scanned the troops opposing him, eager to note some

form of fear, an omen that the knartevilder will proceed efficiently. There was nothing. Not a soldier wavered, fidgeted or
shook. From beyond the courtyard walls floated the sound of
maidens singing and laughing. The only movement came from
the solitary horse as it pawed at the ground. Slightly perturbed,
Remoh turned his head to the cowled Adept who stood silently
to one side.

"Can you sense anything?" Remoh asked. Turkbour looked
up as he heard Remoh's voice. The ants were forgotten for a
moment.

"The spearmen facing you are an illusion. A very clumsy
illusion at that. The witch Queen has been probing since we
disembarked. Should I deal with her?"

"Not at the moment, keep your guard up and be ready to
shield us if she attacks."

"I can cope with her, Lord Remoh. She is clumsy and
amateurish. The Emperor's Way will prevail. Make your negotiations."

Lord Remoh nodded and strode forward. As he did so,
another twenty soldiers marched from the ship escorting four
wretched souls shackled to one another by chains about their
necks. They wore robes of office, the pale blue of Jacarna, albeit
soiled and torn. Their eyes stared blankly ahead as they shuffled forward, each one holding a wooden casket. The magic of
the Emperor's Adept Sinister amplified Remoh's voice.

"I am Lord Remoh, envoy of The Almighty Emperor's Lord
Commander of the Host, His Excellency, General Karchek. I
have come to negotiate your surrender – and wish to do so with
your queen face to face." He paused as his voice reverberated
around the courtyard.

"Failure to do so will result in your city falling to the same
fate as Jacarna and Tarim. If you doubt my words, I bring
messengers and gifts from Jacarna to convince you." He
gestured towards the four prisoners.

"I must advise that I am protected by the Emperor's hand and a swift retribution will be dealt should any harm be visited upon me or my troops."

He waited patiently as his words echoed around the courtyard. When they fell silent, he turned to Turkbour and nodded. The Adept raised his hands and pointed them at the gates ahead. Bright arcs of lightning flashed from his hands, lancing their way towards the wooden gates. Not one of the soldiers moved as the spears of light flashed past them, nor when the gates exploded in a cataclysmic blast. Splinters of wood showered the courtyard, some passing right through the immobile guards. As the echo of the explosion died away, the spearmen and rider flickered and disappeared, leaving the courtyard to Lord Remoh and the Cassalians.

On the battlements surrounding the courtyard, the archers stepped back, dropping the readiness of their longbows. An older man with greying hair and the features of a hawk appeared on the tower above the shattered gate. He called out to Lord Remoh.

"There is no need for more theatrics. Queen Sarsi, Ruler of Danaria will accept your request for negotiations."

35

'I can't believe he's dead, Ishtara.' Bex thought. The thief sat with her back to the gunwales of the ship as it flew over the Great Asken Forest.

'The same, Bex. I'm really sorry.'

'But it's like Garlen doesn't care. Did you see him as we left?' The prince had quickly made his way around his men who were still on deck, before making his way to the wheelhouse to see his sisters.

Bryn Kar had stood at the stern of the ship since their escape to watch the inevitable pursuit. He turned and walked back to the wheelhouse, pausing to stand over Bex. He noticed the way she glared at the squat cabin, as if she could bore a way through the wood to the occupants beyond.

"He suffers as well, Bex."

"Why doesn't he show it? Rica was one of his men, they fought with each other for years."

"Because we have to stay focused on the 'now', so we have a future. No doubt Rica was valued by Garlen, but this is war, Bex. If Garlen breaks down over the death of a friend, a warrior, one of his own – then he is not concentrating on the safety of the rest of us. And that could get all of us killed." The Earl lifted his gaze from Bex and looked out to the cloudy skies. Bex was certain that there was a glint of moisture in the corner of his eye as he did so.

"Believe me, Bex. It isn't easy being responsible for others. But Garlen will find a time to raise a flagon for Rica, and maybe shed a tear. And for every other one of us that dies in this cursed affair!"

'*Maybe he is right, Bex.*' Ishtara sighed.

'*Maybe, but it still doesn't feel right.*'

'*But Bryn Kar is upset, and I don't think it is just Rica.*'

'*No, I think it is his men that he weeps for. His men and his city.*'

She raised herself to her feet and stood by his side. The tall thief ran a hand through her hair and then placed it gently on the warrior's arm.

"Is this your time, Bryn Kar?"

"Yes," the chainmail clad warrior straightened his back and seemed to stare further out to the horizon far way. "Right now, your Rica is being led to Kani's Hall, where my men already are, feasting and drinking. I hope from where they are, that they can see me as I avenge their deaths."

'*I'm sure they will, Bex. It will be my vengeance as well. Right now, Bryn and I are exactly the same.*' Ishtara swirled about in Bex's mind.

"Ishtara feels your pain, Bryn. We all do, but especially her."

A voice cut into their reverie. It was a beautifully, soft voice that seemed to float on the crisp morning air.

"I hope I am not intruding, but this is the first chance I have had to thank you. For our rescue, I mean. I know you came specifically for Moren and Ingren, but you ended up our saviours as well." It was Lady Iga, elegant as she always appeared to be, her slim figure covered with a fur mantle.

"It was our pleasure, Lady Iga." Bryn stammered slightly and bowed his head to the noblewoman.

"Well, we have you to thank for rescuing the princesses and starting the escape. I am not sure I could have managed anymore of those stairs!" Bex smiled back as the waiflike face of Iga broke into a smile of her own.

"*Sverd* Radnak says that you two fought hard and well. Or should that be you three?"

"Ah, I see he has told you of Ishtara." Said Bex.

"Oh yes, he said she was a sight to behold, an absolute wonder. And reminded him of Yuth-gur, the shield maiden of Crom Crade."

"Crom Crade?"

'*Shield Maiden? Let me go to speak to that half-orc now!*' Ishtara snarled.

"Yes, Crom Crade is one of the trinity of the Gods of Goblinkind. From what I know of the human pantheon, I would say he would be similar to Tomnar. And Yuth-gur is his wife and shield maiden."

'*Wife?*' Ishtara was nearly boiling over.

"She is the leader of his army and bodyguard, the wielder of the sword Hurng, which means 'Heart stealer', and the most ferocious warrior known to any goblin."

'*Oh, that sounds a little better.*'

Bex smiled inside.

"I think that Ishtara is warming to the idea of Yuth-gur."

Just then, the ship banked to the right, a little less gently than any manoeuvre that Col had managed so far. Iga was flung against Bryn who stumbled backwards but wrapped his muscular arms around the delicate woman. Bex steadied herself.

"Why do that?" she cursed.

Bryn looked astern, the two ships that had launched from Jacarna after they had made their escape still trailed them, neither catching up.

"It can't be because of our pursuers. They aren't gaining at all." The tall guardsman answered, helping Lady Iga to regain her composure before adding, "We should get below decks, getting thrown overboard is not going to make the day any better."

Bex fired an inquisitive look at him.

"Is that wise? When Bryn seemed puzzled, Bex continued, "Not with Rexen?"

"Of course not, there are plenty of cabins below deck, but first the wheelhouse to find out what Col and Garlen is about!"

It was Lady Iga's turn to look puzzled.

"Rexen?"

Bex paused, not sure what to say and then decided the truth is best.

"Rexen is part of the magic that allows this ship to fly and to also cross the planes. He is a creature, imprisoned and tortured by the Cassalian, that is somehow connected to the ship. But I think we should keep the younger ones away from him."

"Why is that?"

"Well, to get his power, he needs to eat, as we all do, I suppose."

'Not all of us, Bex.' Ishtara interrupted.

'You're not helping make this part easy!'

"It's what he eats and how he eats, that makes it awkward for the younger ones."

"I'll have to see for myself." Said the goblin lady, pulling the fur cloak tighter around her to fight the cold air.

Bex just raised her eyebrows as the goblin and Bryn made their way to the cabin door. She sighed and followed.

As they entered the squat room, Garlen was in discussion with Col as the black armoured warrior stood at the control wheel of the ship. Mathor stood looking thoughtfully out of the cabin window at the bow of the ship. The bald sergeant greeted them all.

"Lady Bex, Lady Iga, welcome and come in. Earl Kar, Garlen was just about to call for you."

"What has happened? Why the sudden manoeuvre?" Bryn Kar strode to Mathor's side and followed his initial gaze out to the clear sky ahead. The Great Asken Forest passed them by underneath, the canopies of the trees a distance below them. The sky as they had left Jacarna was clear and blue, only the fires and smoke from the burning pyres and workshops marred the beauty. However, the way ahead was grey with great clouds rising up like walls to obstruct their way.

"The bow lookout saw a ship ahead, looking to catch us between our pursuers. Now, we aren't sure if they have a way of communicating between these ships, but we thought a course change would be prudent. Garlen wants to head north and then cut west again over the hinterlands."

The prince looked up, acknowledging their appearance for the first time.

"Ah, Bryn and Lady Bex. Good to see you. Yes, a ship was ahead of us, so I wanted to avoid being stuck between the hammer and the anvil, so to speak. Also, Mathor seems to be wanting to avoid ship to ship combat." He grinned at his sergeant, who just shook his head.

"We've all fought ship to ship, Mathor. Remember the pirates of the coast at Worte?"

"True, Garlen, but when you lose a ship at sea, some of it sinks, some of it floats – and generally, the sailors float in the sea waiting for someone to come along and save them. I can't see that happening with this ship."

"You're an old woman, Mathor!" he laughed and slapped the smaller, thicker set man on the back.

"My initial plan was to fly along the King's Road, all the way to Tannaheim, but this way, up the hinterlands and then across to the Wolf Mountains, then back home approaching Tannaheim from the north, will be slightly longer. I have already let my mother know that the rescue is successful." He noted their questioning looks and touched a locket that hung from his necklace.

"With this, it's one of her special lockets, imbued no doubt with the tears of an executed man and a magical incantation read under the new moon, or some obscure magic like that," he sarcastically spoke. "When I got back on board with Moren and Ingren, I used it to relay a message back to my mother. She knows we have my sisters, and that we are on our way home."

"Garlen." One of the Ghosts climbed the stairs from the lower decks, resting his hand on the railing and addressed Garlen from there. It was the small wiry figure of Kardanth, the knife thrower, his blades strapped across his chest.

"Message from Rexen. He needs to eat – but we are out of prisoners!"

"Bolam's balls!" The prince exclaimed.

"He, It," Kardanth shrugged, "reckons another couple of hours and then . . ." The small man made a gesture by drawing his finger across his throat, then turned and disappeared down the stairs.

"Prisoners? What did he mean by that?" Lady Iga enquired.

36

Jerone Witchguardian awoke with a groan. He was in darkness and his head hurt. The smell of Herne only knew what hit his nose and he retched, coughing bile into his mouth. The only blessing to that was the smell and taste of vomit confined the stench of human excrement and decay only to his nose.

Slowly his memory came back to him as his eyes accustomed to the darkness and the forms of his new travelling companions came into sight.

How could he have been so stupid? He shook his head. Chances are, even if he hadn't stumbled onto Risas-tu's cargo himself, the red-haired slaver would have added him to it at some point.

Jerone tried to raise his hand to his head to touch the lump that Risas-tu's blow had left, but his hands were manacled to a long chain that ran along the ship to his neighbour and beyond. He focused on the man chained in similar fashion lying next to him. He wasn't a forest man, probably an unfortunate from the hinterlands or the mountains, who had crossed paths with the slaver.

There were over thirty other occupants of the small hold, chained in three lines, the outside lines lying with their heads against the curved sides of the hull. Apart from the man next to him, none of them looked at him.

"Jerone," he said, trying to indicate himself which wasn't the easiest task taking into account the lack of slack in the manacles and chain.

The man's eyes lit up in terror and he shook his head from side to side. Undeterred, Jerone carried on.

"It's ok." The cover above was ripped up, causing sunlight to flood in and blind them. Jerone squinted, unable to cover his eyes from the sun's glare.

"Quiet!" The face of Risas-tu loomed over the edge, looking Jerone in the eye. "Oh, it's our new guest." His face cracked with a great booming laugh. The face and beard disappeared for a moment and then the giant boatman dropped down into the hold. He landed with a wet thud in the human detritus that pooled in the bottom of the barge. Without warning, he raised one foot and stamped hard on Jerone's stomach, causing the young man to curl up in pain.

"I'll kick ye only the once this time lad, since nobody told you the rules. No talking. Next time, it will be a real beating for ye." He spun around and glared at some of the others, who all cowered in fear. He roared with laughter, throwing his head back, then spat at Jerone before climbing back onto the deck. The canvas cover was pulled back, enveloping the hold back into darkness.

Jerone coughed, still doubled up in pain. Slowly, he extended his legs until he was laying straight and tried to turn onto his side. As he did so, he realised he was turning his back on his neighbouring prisoner, so he flipped round to face him. The slack in the chain gave his hand a little more freedom and they brushed against something that lay under the muddy, brown liquid in the small space between the captives. It was his small hunting knife he had been holding when Risas-tu had hit him. He must have dropped it, and the slaver hadn't noticed. It had come to rest against one of the ribs of the barge, helping to hide it from view.

Waiting until nightfall, when he felt the rest of the hold had fallen asleep, he managed to bend his leg towards his hand and then slowly slip the blade down into his boot. He then fell into an uneasy sleep.

THE CALLING of Maya had stopped again, causing her to pause in her flight. This high up, soaring on the ethereal wind and dipping in and out of clouds, Maingard seemed peaceful. Focusing on the air and leaving the noise of the ground to one side, she heard only the chatter-like song of birds as they called to each other. That and the wind pushing against the air. Of the Calling, nothing.

When it had happened, it was the strongest that she had ever heard, that seemed to tell her of the strength of her next Channeler. That could mean only good news in the struggle ahead, either to defeat the invaders or to lead her people to safety. The disruption to the Calling though, bothered her. It was as if her Channeler wasn't quite ready. And with the peril that faced Maingard that worried her.

She waited, circling in the sky, an invisible vulture high in the air. It had stopped once already, causing her to panic searching frantically for any sign of the Calling. Just as she had given up hope, it had started again and had stayed constant until now. This time, she was anxious rather than panicky, her only consternation was not if it would start again, she knew in her very soul it would, and not when – as long as it was soon.

No, her anxiety was purely on whether the Channeler was ready. In her fifty reincarnations that had never happened. She hoped it wouldn't matter. Her anxiety grew when she realised that she would find that out sooner, rather than later.

Just then, the Calling started again, a long drawn-out song of joy and sadness. She quickly orientated upon the origin and sailed on, allowing the wind to blow her along.

37

The thirty Cassalian soldiers marched in perfect time through the destroyed gates, Remoh and Turkbour at their head. The four emissaries from Jacarna shuffled along in-between, still chained together. Remoh had chosen to split his force, leaving half stationed outside the skyship. After all, he thought, the Danarians were not in a position to negotiate. The tale of the destruction of Jacarna and Tarim had now reached the city, and of course, Karchek held the Witch Queen's daughters as hostages. And there were still the eyewitness reports from the four Jacarnans to come, along with their 'gifts'. Remoh smiled at that thought.

However, it was initially the Cassalians that were taken aback. Sarsi had chosen not to meet them inside, but outside in the chill air. The inner courtyard had been set up to reflect the throne room above. A long table had been placed upon the damp grass and a raised dais sited at the head. Sarsi sat upon her throne, overlooking the entrance of Remoh and his men. She wore a simple dress of white fabric with long elbow length gloves, and a gold and silver crown. On one side of her was a hooded figure who sat upon a stool, the other side was the older man who had answered Remoh from the battlements. He wore chain and an exquisite breastplate with bas relief of the crossed swords of Tannaheim. Several other lords sat at either side of the table, with a rank of spearmen and archers lined up at each side.

Lord Remoh, at that moment, had a morsel of respect for his adversary's attempt to throw him off guard. He whispered to Turkbour.

"Keep your guard up. I do not trust her."

"She is still clumsily probing, and the guards are more illusions. The Emperor's Will shall be done." Turkbour folded his arms across his chest. Remoh nodded and stepped forward.

"Sarsi," if he noticed any reaction to his simple address and lack of manners, he didn't show it. "I will not waste time here. You will have no doubt, heard of the destruction that has befell other cities of your world. I am hoping that you will see sense, that your forces will be no match for our own if you do not surrender and swear fealty. If you do this, General Karchek will allow you to continue to rule in his stead. All he asks is that your forces are placed at his disposal. I do not need to remind you that your daughters are held hostage and General Karchek hopes that you will not need any additional persuasion. However, I have brought some persuasion of my own, in the hope that these negotiations pass as quickly and peacefully as possible." Lord Remoh addressed the Queen and the court.

He clapped his hands, and the four shackled men approached the table, placing the small wooden chests on it before retreating as one. They did so silently and without an upward glance, not daring to look any of the Danarians in the eye. As they ungainly moved back in line, a Cassalian pushed each one to his knees. The old men collapsed, broken in mind as well as body.

"Talk." Lord Remoh commanded.

One by one, they announced who they were and what rank

they had held in office. Tarak Marshad, Master of Coin; Bannon Kar, Lord of Swords; Clar Nylo, High Maester; and Jat Cinner, High Merchant. At the name of Bannom Kar, Sarsi's eyebrows raised.

In turn, each gave an account of the destruction, in very graphic detail. They told of the devastation wrought by the Cassalian weapons along with the futility of resistance. Each one gave their own eyewitness account of the attack, for example, Clar Nylo disclosed the gruesome details of King Renta's death. Sarsi sat impassive throughout but Remoh could see that the detail was distressing some of the Lords around the table. He nodded to one of the guards who slid the small caskets across the table towards the Queen.

It was General Klebb who reached forward to the first casket and flipped the lid open. He immediately retched, lifting his hand to cover his mouth. He seemed transfixed by the contents.

"What is it?" The old man next to the Queen stepped down towards Klebb. "Come on man, spit it out!"

"It's. . . . It's King Renta!"

The Hawk looked down and nodded. He slowly closed the lid, before opening the other three, one at a time.

"It is indeed King Renta, Your Majesty. Or, at least, his head."

"And the others?" inquired the Queen, her voice completely neutral.

"I believe them to contain his wife and two of his daughters." The Hawk closed his eyes as he spoke, unable to look upon his Queen.

Lord Remoh smiled and raised his hand. At the signal, the four Cassalians standing behind the kneeling men, drew their daggers and slit each throat, pushing the bodies forward.

"Your answer, please." Lord Remoh pulled his gauntlet of one hand, proceeding then to do the same with the other.

Queen Sarsi stood. She slowly made her way down the steps to stand at the head of the table.

"Well, Gentlemen. Your advices please." She placed her gloved hands on the table and stared at each one of the Lords. Several looked down, unable to meet her gaze. It was Eglebon Dutte who spoke first. He defiantly stood, returning Sarsi's stare.

"It is obvious we should surrender. We stand no chance otherwise – any resistance is pointless." There were a few nods from around the table.

"Well, you would think that, Dutte." The glare from the red-haired queen seemed to bury itself deep in the heart of Dutte, who faltered to reply. She pulled at each finger of her glove, stretching the fabric out in order to slip the glove off.

"Anyone else?"

A young Lord stood up from his seat opposite Dutte.

"Better to die a freeman rather than live a lifetime in servitude!" He slammed one fist into the palm of the other hand

"Thank you, Lord Kyl Dantice. Tell me, Lord Remoh. My daughters are unharmed and are well?"

"Of course," lied Remoh. "It is senseless to harm hostages before negotiations require that course of action." By now Sarsi had removed both gloves, displaying black veins worming their way from her fingertips to her forearms.

"You lie!" she threw her right arm up and pointed her open hand at Remoh. Her fingers slowly closed, and even though she was at the opposite end of the table and nowhere near him, Remoh could feel her fingers slowly crush his windpipe in a grip like a vice. His hands flew to his throat, to try to wrench the invisible hand open. His face reddened and he spluttered.

Sarsi's left hand now pointed at Dutte and he felt the same invisible force push him backwards.

"Sit down! I'll deal with you in a minute." She turned her attention back to Remoh. "One of my daughters has been blinded, her eyes taken by the man you serve." The Cassalians seemed to awake from the reverie, drawing their swords as the realised their leader had come under attack.

Turkbour started to lift his hands to counter Sarsi's attack but, to his dismay, found that he was unable to move them. It was like he was attempting to lift blocks of stone with just the muscles in his wrists. He tried to speak instead but without success; his jaw stiff and his tongue dry and swollen. Beads of sweat broke out upon his brow, and he struggled to control what he saw. Sarsi was walking slowly down the table length, one hand dragging over the backs of the chairs. Even though he could see her there, ahead of him, she was whispering in his ear; her breath warm against his skin.

"You poor complacent fool!" Her tone was more pitying rather than hateful. "You dared think you could come here and walk over us, walk over me?"

He looked down at his hands, almost willing them to work. His fingertips had gone black, a strange sensation burning within them as the blackness crept further up his fingers. He watched in horror as the blackness seemed to be the same small insects he had seen earlier on his boots, but this time crawling under his skin. The burning sensation continued and spread along his hands and arms, chasing the insects along in front of it. He answered her in his mind, his voice slowing and drawn out.

"But you were so clumsy in your attack." His mind avatar turned to face her, only to find her gone. Her voice in his other ear caused him to jump.

"You were the clumsy and amateurish one. My attack started the second you alighted from your ship. My mystical energy layered the air and ground by the hatch in your ship and you walked on through it. Since then, I have burrowed cell by cell into your body to layer those particles deep within you – all without you knowing.

"You have failed, Turkbour. Just like your Emperor will."
With that, he watched helplessly as the troops that he had
moments ago confirmed to Remoh as phantasms, were instead
proven to be real as they let loose a volley of arrows from either
side. Cassalians fell to the ground, two or three arrows
protruding from each. The handful that were left threw down
their weapons and sank to the ground. Then she was back with
Remoh, the grip on his neck loosened slightly.

"You came to my world! My land! My city! My court!
Murdered my husband, abducted and mutilated my daughters!
Yes, I know exactly what your Karchek has done to my
daughters."

She came close to Remoh, the blackness in her hands
starting to seep into the veins of her arms.

"How do I know this? Because a few minutes ago, I had
word from my son that his rescue mission has been successful,
and he is on his way here with his sisters. You have nothing left
to bargain with. Your kind will rue the day they came to this
world. You, however, I have other plans for you." She raised her
hand and pointed it at Turkbour, and he sagged in her grip as
his heart burst inside him. She then clapped her hands.

Remoh looked up as the doors to the Palace proper opened
and a procession of six men wearing leather aprons and black
hoods walked down to the table passing the seated Lords. They
surrounded the captive Cassalian and started to cut his armour
and harness away using thin knives.

"Butchers? Your Majesty?" questioned one of the seated
Lords. "You are going to execute him with commoners?"

"You mistake my intentions, Lord Ghan. These men aren't
here to kill him. Though I would recommend that my Lords
stand and move away, especially if you are squeamish."

By now the butchers had stripped Remoh bare, his
muscular body showing scars from numerous battles. They
knotted ropes around his wrist and two of them pulled him

face down onto the table, Sarsi's hold on him relaxing. Those still seated jumped backwards, their chairs overturning. Remoh gritted his teeth, Sarsi's grip on his throat relaxing. One of the butchers looked at the queen from under his hood, only his eyes visible through the small slits. She nodded, acknowledging his silent question.

Remoh gritted his teeth as the men got to work. The thin blades cut into the skin at his shoulders. The cuts were deep enough to send an eruption of blood to the surface. His nostrils flared as he fought the instinct to cry out, his breath escaping as a snarl instead. Two of his torturers pulled his arm tight whilst a third pulled the tip of the knife down the inside of his arm, opening a wound from armpit to wrist. His brain clutched at some distant part of his memory as the pattern of the cuts seemed familiar.

And then his mind uncovered the horror, the long-forgotten memory remembered. Images of a race long vanquished in an earlier knartevilder. Soldiers, now long dead, executing a deserter; slicing and peeling the skin from his flesh. Bile collected in his mouth as he remembered the deserter had screamed for nigh on an hour before falling silent.

Remoh clenched his eyes tightly shut, trying fervently to block the sight of the razor-sharp tips being inserted into his wounds in an attempt to cut the layers of skin from his muscle beneath. His mind and nervous system awakened the agony, images of the deserter being flayed alive now burnt into his consciousness.

His eyes jolted wide open, and the scream stuck in his throat as he felt pincers grab the upturned skin. Steel flashed in the sunlight as the master butchers attended to their art, one slicing away under the layers of skin as another pulled his very essence from his being. The scream finally escaped, gushing forth as the dam broke and the torment flooded from every cell of his body. The butchers remained impassive beneath their masks, their eyes focussed fully on their grisly task. Their arms were soaked in gore to the elbow and blood splashed upon the table.

As Remoh's tongue lolled from his mouth, his eyes met Sarsi's. The red-haired bitch stared straight into the depths of his soul as the skin was pulled from his arms like sleeves. He saw hate in her eyes, the twin dark pits that showed her revelation in his exquisite pain.

A sloppy mess was thrown down in front of his eyes. Blood splattered his face as the mess slid away from him. His tortured eyes broke from the gaze of the witchqueen and he realised that the bloodied mess was the skin from his arms. As the cold air bit into the unprotected flesh he shivered, both from the cold and from shock.

Sarsi and the Lords seemed to disappear into a mist of fog like spectres as his vision clouded. His heart hammered wildly as he was pushed harder against the cold wood. He felt the knives dig into the back of his neck and shoulders. And he screamed again, his mind hurling incoherent curses at his torturers. Then, as his confused and afflicted mind finally realised he had bitten through his tongue, he passed out into blackness.

He jolted awake a second later to find himself standing at the end of the table, his throat squeezed by Sarsi's power. He was aware that he wore his armour and that, apart from his throat, he wasn't in pain. He tried to clear his head; what trick of Sarsi's magic was this? The pain had all been too real. The Danarians still sat at the long table and it was as if nothing had happened. Turkbour still stood immobile to his side.

Sarsi raised her hand to the Adept and squeezed, killing him instantly. Again. She clapped her hands. Again. And the doors to the palace opened again, with a procession of six butchers starting to approach him. The only difference this time, was that Remoh screamed whilst he awaited his fate, Sarsi's power stifling most of the noise.

Sarsi turned away from the collapsed and gibbering form of Remoh. The once proud and confident Cassalian was reduced to a wreck, occasionally screaming, his eyes bulging and his face red.

"What have you done to him?" Asked the Hawk, as Sarsi returned to her throne.

"I've had him flayed alive, time and time again," she saw his quizzical look, "only in his mind though. He experiences every single second of pain, and now he will relive it for as long as he lives." She raised herself up in her throne and addressed the seated Lords.

"We now have another matter to address." She nodded to the Hawk, who in turn beckoned a sergeant of the guard over and whispered in his ear. The sergeant moved away and spoke to two guardsmen. "I have received new information, and evidence, regarding the murder of my husband. Yes, he was murdered on the orders of Karchek, but with the help of a traitor." She let her words sink in before adding, "who is at this table now!"

The Lords around the table erupted into chaos, clamouring for an answer. Surreptitiously, the guard sergeant and his men had made their way to stand behind Eglebon Dutte.

"Dutte, you had a vested interest in the Cassalian proposal for capitulation, no doubt. I wonder why?"

"Preposterous!" he exclaimed, rising to his feet and banging the table. "I suggested it would be sensible to accept their offer as resistance seems completely futile. You may well have condemned this city, and all of us, to death." He seemed to calm down a little and started to sit. After all, he had made sure his tracks were covered.

"Stand, while I address you! You are on trial here, Ser

Dutte!" Sarsi's voice cut through the murmuring and background noise. Dutte reddened but managed to respond.

"On trial? What is the charge?"

"Murder. Treason."

"What? That is madness, I am innocent! Where is your proof?"

Sarsi reached to her side and touched the hooded figure to her side. It spoke clearly, the feminine voice coming from within the voluminous folds of the hood.

"The one that said the following words; 'It is obvious we should surrender. We stand no chance otherwise – any resistance is pointless,' is the voice that I heard before."

"I am the Master of the Privy Council, your Majesty. It is all possible that she could have heard me at court." He had heard the woman's voice before but couldn't place it. When she replied, the woman's voice changed. There was an added inflection and an accent more akin to the rougher side of the city.

"But I'm not the sort of girl to be seen in the court, Ser Dutte!" And then he had it, he remembered where he had heard that voice before. It was the blind girl from the Red Tart. Fferyll, but she couldn't recognise him, surely?

"The word of a whore over the word of a noble? You are surely jesting, Your Majesty?"

"Who said anything about her profession?" The Hawk interjected. Dutte thought fast.

"She said her sort isn't to be seen in court, Marshall. I'm just assuming that is what she is."

Sarsi stood, her figure tall and graceful as she descended the steps. She took Fferyll's arm and bade her to stand.

"I would rather welcome a thousand whores to the palace than one traitor, Dutte." The Queen retorted before raising her hands to Fferyll's hood, pushing it back. The girl's blond hair tumbled out, framing her beautifully perfect face, perfect that is apart from her glazed eyes.

"Tobe's Tits, she's blind. How can she be your evidence against me?"

There was a murmur from many of the Lords about the table, evident that something was amiss. Could Dutte really be the traitor that Sarsi indicated?

"She was born with that affliction, yes. But I have been led to believe that she has a memory for voices and words. Is that true, girl?" Sarsi addressed the trembling Fferyll.

"Yes, Your Majesty. A curse and a blessing." She stepped forward and raised her hands to the side of her head. She then took to recollecting the entire conservation from when Remoh entered, word for word and indicating the general direction of the speaker at the time with her hands. She had just finished Dutte's advices to Sarsi regarding the Cassalian proposal when he slammed his fists on the table.

"Enough! This is a witch hunt and you all know it. Enough of these tricks with your paid whore, Sarsi. You have doomed us all with your mistakes."

"But that is not all I can do," Fferyll stood tall, stepping forward away from Sarsi. "My employer is not the Queen. I am an agent of Tikar Welk."

"Even better," interrupted Dutte. "The mysterious Phantom, a figment of someone's deluded imagination." Fferyll glared at him.

"Tikar Welk planted me into the Brotherhood of Karnast, the guild of assassins. One of whom you met that night on that roof on Fish Lane."

"Well, do you deny that, Dutte?" questioned the Marshall.

"Of course! I have never been to Fish Lane, never set foot in that despicable part of the city, never met the guild of assassins and certainly have no dealings with common whores!"

"Your man Sato says different. We picked him up last night. He told us he was there with you." Vent stood at the side of the blind girl.

"A confession under torture? By Danarian law, you need more evidence than that!"

"Remember when I fell against you, before you climbed out onto the roof?" Fferyll held out her hand, her fist clenched.

"Preposterous, girl. I told you, I was not there!"

"I fell against you and cut your cloak. This is the piece I took." She opened her hand to reveal the piece of dark material. Marshall Vent took the piece and handed it to the guard sergeant. The two guardsmen grabbed Dutte by the arms and unclasped his cloak, throwing it to the table. Matching the piece to the cut edge of the cloak, the sergeant nodded to the Hawk.

The Hawk threw a coin on to the table. Dutte watched it as it spun on its edge in front of him. The large copper penny fell flat, the face of a long dead king overwritten by a skull, which in turn had been crossed out.

"This is the final piece of evidence. A coin from the assassin's guild. For those who are unlearned in the way of the Brotherhood of Karnast, it denotes that a job has been accepted and marks the contract between the Client and the Brotherhood. It was found at Count Dutte's house last night." He reached into his tunic and threw down a second coin. It was a twin of the first.

"It matches this coin, that was found early this morning in the cabin of *The Dagger*, a ship owned by Count Dutte, and tasked with taking orders to Lord Visney and Shales in the Isle of Winds, ordering them to return at once to aid in the defence of this city. I put it to you, you vile piece of scum, that it is you who has endangered this city and potentially, condemned every last man, woman and child in Tannaheim to death!" The Hawk returned to Queen Sarsi's side.

Dutte stood tall, thrusting his chest out. He spat towards Sarsi, his phlegm landing short.

"Curse you, witch queen. You have brought this kingdom to its knees."

"You are mistaken, traitor! You have hurt this kingdom more than anyone, murdering my husband. But know this, all of you Lords here now. I will give my life for Danaria. Danaria will never kneel before these or any other dogs. I will not yield to Karchek or any other. Who is with me?" Queen Sarsi stood as she addressed her court. A great cheer erupted from the watching soldiers and Lords, many thrusting swords in the air.

"For Danaria!"

Sarsi quietened the crowd, taking her seat on the throne again. She waved her hand at Remoh, still writhing on the floor in his mental anguish.

"Send this lapdog back to Jacarna as a warning. Let us make Karchek worry for a while." She turned to the young Lord who had made the comment about freedom. "Kyl Dantice. I am delivering the prisoner into your hands. Not only was he responsible for the murder of my husband, your King, but also your nephews, the Lords Klush and Dirian Dantice. I have had my fill of revenge today. Make an example of him."

The blond Dantice rose, grinning.

38

G arlen had followed Kardanth down the cabin steps into the hulk of the ship. He had practically flown down the steps, placing his hands on the rails and taking the narrow steps four at a time. Bryn and Radnak followed him, whilst Bex stayed in the cabin with Lady Iga. She thought it would be best if she answered Iga's questions before she saw Rexen.

The wiry figure of Kardanth stood to one side as Garlen burst through the door into Rexen's chamber. Even with the cages empty to each side, Garlen could still feel the presence of so many wretches who had lingered their last few hours away in the chamber. He gagged slightly as the foul stench hit him, and he wished he had put one of the masks on. Bryn, who stepped up beside him with Radnak, had grabbed one of the leather masks, holding it over his face with one hand. Radnak just stared at Rexen, his contorted visage showing disgust at both the smell and sight.

"Crom Teder! What the fuck is that?"

Rexen turned to face them, his sword like claws clicking and waving in front of his insectoid features. The gems on his back, where once the glowed brightly, now were a dim purple. The mystic chains still crackled with energy as the held the Flyer tight by his collar. His bulbous compound eyes fixated upon the half-orc.

"What the fuck is that?" he mimicked, his mandibles clicking as he spoke.

The half-orc roared with laughter.

"Prince Garlen, I need to eat."

"There is no food, Rexen. Everyone else on the ship is with me."

"Then we must stop."

"We must have some food somewhere, Garlen." Radnak interjected before continuing, "Surely?"

"Are you volunteering, Radnak?" laughed Bryn.

"Volunteering, what do you mean by that?"

Bryn waved his hand around the chamber, indicating the cages.

"These cages held the prisoners of the Cassalians. Those too weak to fight or work. They fuel the Flyers so these ships can fly."

"Bryn Kar, please do not explain more. I am embarrassed." The Flyer bowed his head as he spoke.

"Crom! It eats people? Those bastards feed slaves to it?"

"We all have to eat something, Radnak!" Bryn thumped the orc on the back. Garlen gave both a stern look and they fell silent. He turned back to the Flyer.

"Rexen, how long do we have?"

"Not long, Prince Garlen."

"Bolam's balls!" Garlen cursed and turned to walk away.

"Wait, what are we above?"

The prince paused and thought.

"Are we over the Hinterlands yet, or still over the Forest, Bryn?"

"Still over the Asken Forest."

"Then trees, big trees."

"Trees aren't good. I need clearings."

"Then we'll head for the Hinterlands and pray to Tobes we'll be in time! Send a message nearer the time we have to land." He paused before adding, "If you can."

There was an uneasy silence as the trio walked back to the wheelhouse cabin. There, the prince gave the instructions to head straight to the Hinterlands. Bryn left the cabin to aid the lookouts keeping watch for pursuers.

Garlen stood next to Bex and sighed.

"I had hoped I had left these days of terrible decisions behind me, when the war ended, and I brought the Ghosts back to the city. As Tikar Welk, I was still fighting a war as such, but for most of the time I had the upper hand."

"You are doing a great job, Garlen." She placed her hand on his arm. "Believe me."

"It doesn't feel like it."

"One day, you will make a great king."

"That never interested me, I always planned on letting that curse pass by."

They were interrupted by the door crashing open and Igant bundling in. They all turned to face him and noticed he was shaking, his face red. His hand rubbed over the bloodstained bandage wrapped around his right arm as he blurted out his message.

"*Garlen, vienta nat. Tyonag!*"

The tone of his voice was enough to deliver the urgency and meaning of the message, even if the words weren't clear to Bex. The words were clear to Garlen though, '*Garlen, come now. Quickly!*'. The blond prince flew past the stricken goblin Lord and out onto the deck. As he did so, he called to Col at the wheel.

"Keep her steady, we've got to make the Hinterlands!"

'*What now?*' inquired Ishtara.

Bex followed. The false promise of a bright, sunny day had faded, and the clouds were closing in. But that wasn't why the goblin had called the prince to the deck for.

Bex was met with the prince being restrained by Radnak, the bulky frame of the half-orc struggling to push Garlen away. Mori was laying on the deck, her body convulsing and shaking. Iga and Ingren were kneeling by her head, the goblin lady bent over the young girl's face, gently consoling her. Ingren cried as she slowly stroked her sister's hair. Moren's head was resting on Iga's cloak, the heavy fur bundled up to form a pillow for the young girl. Her scarred face shook and turned as spittle drooled from her lips.

Bryn hurried to Bex's side.

"Let me hold her! What is happening to her!" Garlen shouted as he tried to shrug Radnak off.

"Leave her be, Garlen. Iga knows what she is doing." Hissed the half-orc, his dark grey face blushing darker as he pushed the slighter man away.

'*What is happening to her, Bex?*' Ishtara's voice was distraught. '*I don't know, but it doesn't look good.*'

The young girl's convulsions started to appear less violent and the soft voice of Lady Iga took on an authoritative tone.

"Radnak, you can let the prince go now, if he agrees to follow my words. He can come to his sister's side but must not hold her at the moment."

Radnak stared into the prince's eyes. The anger had flowed away, there was now only a sense of distraught as Garlen slowly nodded. The half-orc's grip softened and released and the young man, who had led his men into war and terror, sank to his knees next to Iga. The slim fingers of the goblin guided Garlen's hands to his sister's face.

"Stroke her face, Garlen. Let her know that you are here. Let her know that everything will be alright."

The tortured face of the young prince turned to face her.

"Will it?" The words struggled to leave his lips. Iga nodded and rested her hand upon his arm.

"Yes. Yes, it will." She said softly as she stood.

39

R emoh's ship had not wasted time in flying back to Jacarna. The crew, along with the remainder of the soldiers who had been left to guard it whilst Remoh had conducted his ill-fated negotiations, were relieved to do so. Many times, when his screams had punctured the near silence of his constant babbling, had they contemplated in putting him out of his misery. The overhanging threat of Karchek's response to his favoured lieutenant's death stayed their hands. Instead they resorted to a gag and bindings, and only removed them when the small ship was about to land on the palace rooftop.

Word was sent to Karchek that Lord Remoh had returned. The giant general had been awoken that morning after his feverish coma had subsided. Narki the hag had taken control of his healing and convalescence, and had banned all entry to his chamber except for slaves bringing water and bandages.

He managed to make his way to the throne room unaided, a huge improvement from several days ago when he had to be virtually carried to his bed. The cut above his eye still throbbed and the scar had turned black, but at least it had started healing. His other wound was more serious, and it still ached when he walked. But he hadn't commanded the Emperor's Host during the destruction and pillage of three dozen worlds by showing weakness, so he paused before entering and steadied himself. His guards pushed open the great doors and he strode to Renta's throne. His first command of the day had been just after he had been told of the princesses' rescue, and he was glad to see it had been carried out. The surviving guards who had been on duty when Janis had plucked the princesses out from under their noses, had been arrested and dragged to await their fate. They now stood in chains, bare chested with their heads bowed. Twenty-three were arranged in a semicircle facing the throne with the two officers standing ahead of the others.

Karcheck slowly took his seat and then addressed his court. His voice carried to all corners and the prisoners trembled at his words.

"I detest failure. It is an affront to me and more importantly, it is an affront to the Emperor. In allowing my hostages to be taken from their cell and then to allow their rescue mere days later, you have all failed me. You have failed me, and you have failed the Emperor. I pronounce you all guilty and the Adept Sinister will now carry out the sentence."

Standing to one side of the throne was Brant and another of the Adept Sinister, their grey cloaks making them nearly as one with the stone columns that held the great balcony up. Brant made his way to stand at the bottom of the dais, whilst his somewhat younger looking companion went to one end of the line and stood behind the first prisoner. The older man nodded to his companion, and then started to speak.

"Jakash min drorn tut." The pain flashed through him, almost dropping him to the floor. He started to glow, a fierce white glow that momentarily blinded all in the hall. And then the wolf-like creature that had ripped apart the muggers on the streets of Tannaheim appeared, much slower this time. It crept out and approached the two officers on its hind legs, sniffing the air as it did so.

Meanwhile, Brant's companion withdrew his hand from his robe to reveal a short mace, headed with three flanges. He raised it, smashing it down on the unprotected head of the first man, who crumpled to a heap. He then walked silently past the second, third and fourth man before striking again. He did so at random, dispatching eight of the prisoners without a sound from any of them. He noticed that several lost control of their bladders as he padded behind them. When he reached the other end of the line, he could almost hear the exhale of relief from the lucky ones.

Brant's wolf circled the two officers, drool dripping from its menacing jaws as the yellow eyes glared at the two men. Finally, it stopped behind them, its breath lapping at the back of their necks. The man on the right could bear it no longer and collapsed to his knees, raising his chained hands and beseeching his general.

"I have failed you, my Lord. It is true. But a chance to prove myself in the next phase of the *knartevilder*, please I beg of you. I will not fail you again!"

"You think you can be of use to the Emperor when we assault Tannaheim?" Karchek leant forward, his hand rubbing his chin as he spoke. The kneeling prisoner nodded, his face almost showing relief through the terror. Karchek flashed his eyes at Brant and nodded, almost imperceptibly to his right. The Adept snarled one word, again in the old language and the wolf snapped at the still standing prisoner, tearing him to shreds.

"You would lead the assault on the walls? You would face certain death by the side of my captains?" The man nodded again, his eyes staring straight ahead trying to avoid the temptation to turn and view his comrade's demise. The sound of tearing flesh and screams echoed about the hall.

"So, you would face certain death for me. Exactly like you have done just now? By throwing yourself to the floor and begging for your life? You are of no use to me as a sword, but there is a way you can assist the Emperor." He held his hand up to Brant, who started to call back the lupine creature.

"Guards! Take him to Soshin. Make sure he is on the slave quota for the *Emperor's Scythe* tonight. His men can lead the assault without him. At least they stood their ground." The red cloaked guards stepped forward and grabbed the one-time officer under his armpits and dragged him off. He screamed as he went, his diatribe ranging from begging to threats.

Karchek beckoned to one of the slaves who stood to one side of the throne for some wine. He drained the goblet in one gulp and demanded more. Whilst his goblet was refilled, Remoh was led in.

As the once proud and strong warrior was led in, Karchek stood and slowly descended the dais to meet him. His face was in shock, one of the few times that Brant had seen it like that. He raised the goblet and drained it again, flinging it away as he emptied it.

His lieutenant sank to his knees, still babbling. He then raised his hands out in front of him as if to inspect them and screamed. It was a horrid sound, like a stuck pig. He then writhed on the floor, still screaming for several minutes. Karchek circled him and then crouched down beside him, lifting his head to look him in the eye. Remoh shrunk back, cringing away. He scooted away on all fours, and Karchek thanked the almighty Emperor that the screaming had stopped.

"Sarwent, what have they done to him?"

Karchek addressed the Adept Sinister who had executed the eight guards earlier. The younger Adept stepped forward and approached Remoh, muttering softly. The litany he recited seemed to calm the tortured mind, and Remoh fell strangely silent. He knelt, his grey cloak spreading out on the floor as he did so, and gently touched Remoh's forehead. Sarwent's eyes bulged as his mind linked with Remoh's. He blinked a couple of times and then flung himself backwards with an exclamation.

Brant hurried to his side. He reached down and helped the younger man shakily to his feet. Sarwent's stomach heaved and he retched bile, the acrid taste fouling his mouth. Brant called for water for his colleague.

Karchek asked again.

"Well, what have they done to him?"

"I don't think he is reachable."

Karchek screamed at Sarwent.

"I asked what they had done to him, not whether he was reachable. What has that fucking witch done to him?" He jabbed his finger first at Sarwent, then at Remoh.

"She flayed him. In his mind. She flayed him alive in his mind. Then brings him back to the beginning of that memory so he experiences it again and again." Sarwent was shocked at the outburst from the Lord Commander of the Host and stammered his reply.

Karchek turned back to Remoh and raised his left hand to the cheek of the smaller man. For a brief second, there seemed to be a flicker of recognition in Remoh's eyes. And then he screamed again. Karchek slid his hand over Remoh's mouth to cover it, stifling the scream. Then, with a quick twist, the giant snapped his lieutenant's neck bringing relief to his tortured mind.

"Sound the horns and arrange for the ships to load up. We will leave four ship's companies here. The rest will leave for Tannaheim." He addressed the new adjutant who waited by the throne but didn't take his eyes from the dead figure of the man who had accompanied him on so many *knartevilder*.

"How many slave hulks, Your Excellency?"

"I won't be needing any. I am going to annihilate the whole city!"

"General Karchek," Brant turned to address him. "The Emperor will be most displeased. Homeworld needs slaves, the Host needs slaves. The Emperor demands it."

"Fuck the Emperor, Brant. Don't stand in my way." With that he stormed from the throne room.

40

"They will be coming tonight, Marshall." Sarsi sat back in her throne, her hands lightly gripping the arms.

"Then we need to make sure that you are safe, Your Majesty. Have you contemplated the proposals to move you away from the Palace?" Marshall Vent stood facing the two thrones, King Anjoan's throne on the right of Sarsi's had not yet been moved. The Hawk was the only other person present in the throne room.

"I have, Magus. And I will be staying here at the palace." When the Marshall made to comment, she raised her hand, silencing him immediately. "I will hear no more of it, Magus. This is my throne, and I will not be leaving it for some invader to take."

"But, it isn't. . ."

"I said, enough!" Queen Sarsi snapped; her face flushed as she admonished the older man. She immediately felt guilty as Magus Vent had given so much in the defence of the realm. He had served her family, and especially her husband, extremely well over the years and she was aware that he was only trying to do his duty and keep her safe.

"How are the defences progressing? Is everything in place as we have discussed?"

"Yes, Your Majesty. Every ship in the harbour have had their ballistae removed and they have been installed on certain buildings throughout the city. Lord Smit and his engineers have finished six siege catapults and they are working on two more."

"Very good. Are they in place?"

"They will be by dusk."

"Excellent."

"All the other preparations are in hand as well. I would still like to bolster the Palace defences for tonight. Your Majesty."

The Queen slowly sat forward and removed her cloak to reveal her bare arms and shoulders. The veins in her arms were now black to her shoulders, and the whole of her forearms were a mottled grey. Magus Vent took a sharp intake of breath as he saw the state of her arms.

"Your Majesty, the disease is taking hold and spreading. You must listen to reason. You are in no state. . . ." Again, she cut him off with a raise of her hand.

"I have listened to reason for the whole of my life and where has it got me? My husband has been murdered. My eldest daughter was taken so many years ago. My youngest has been tortured and mutilated. My city has been threatened. Do I need to go on?" Vent shook his head, a sorrowful look upon his face. Sarsi, however, continued.

"This," she lifted her hands. "is not a disease. It is a curse, and a gift. The rumours that have hung around the court for years are true. I am no minor magician or common witch. I practise the Dark Arts, Magus. It is a trade I have made with Nyx, the Witch King. A payment for the power he has lent me. It is consuming me. I just pray that I have time." She uttered the name of one of the Dark Lords of Hel. A Dark Lord who traded powers for souls; Nyx, the King of Witches.

"Nyx," Magus Vent spat on the floor between them as he

mentioned his name, "does not exist. It is a word delivered to unruly children in order to bring them into line."

"Really, Magus. Do all you hardened warriors always spit for good luck then, when you mention a fairy tale?"

He chose to ignore the question. Whether Nyx existed or not wasn't important. The thought of Nyx scared him, and the blackness was spreading on his queen. At first, it had been the odd vein on her hand or arm, and he had taken it to be a sign of ageing. But then it was more pronounced, and she had taken to covering her hands with gloves, longer and longer ones as the blackness crept up her arms.

"If you are going to stay in the Palace, then I will need to post another regiment of guards here."

"You need do no such thing, Magus. In fact, you will divert the guards to other parts of the city. All of them. Including you."

"I will do no such thing, Your Majesty. I swore an oath to your husband to defend him, his family and the city. My place is here!" The Marshall thumped his chest as he spoke. His voice was in total dismay.

"Your place is at the side of your family, Magus. You should be there in case the invaders get a hold in the city. You have served my family well and you have fulfilled your oath." Sarsi's tone indicated that the audience was over.

"But who will protect you?"

"I don't think I need much protection, Magus. Do you? Besides, I am looking forward to confronting this Karchek. However, I do have someone else here who will stand with me." She smiled sweetly, her eyes gleaming with a venomous tinge. She clapped her hands and the Hawk could hear movement behind the throne.

"Who's there?" he cried out, his hand dropping to his sword. A sweet, stale smell pervaded his nostrils and his mind struggled to place it. A figure loomed from behind Sarsi's throne, a tall, immense figure in shining steel plate armour, a scarlet cloak thrown over one shoulder. In his mailed hands he carried a great two-handed sword.

Magus Vent stared at the figure, transfixed by the face framed by the dark hair and the bushy beard. The skin was discoloured, with the appearance of dark black and purplish bruises and the Hawk was now aware what the smell was. It was the sweet smell of death, masked by once pungent herbs. Marshall Vent took a step backwards, automatically bowing as the figure of King Anjoan took his throne.

41

"It was a seizure, a misfiring in her brain. Poor girl, as if she hasn't suffered enough." Lady Iga mopped Moren's brow as she slept, a large wolf fur pulled up over the young princess to keep her warm.

"What would have caused it?" Bex asked, standing at the door to the small cabin. The only furniture in the room beside the rude cot, were two stools occupied now by Iga and Garlen. The prince was in deep thought, his chin in his hands and his face pensive.

"It could be anything, possibly a delayed reaction to her injuries. I can't tell for sure. I can only give her an elixir to help with the pain now."

"Lady Iga," the prince started, "you have done so much for my sisters and I cannot start to thank you enough. If you could stay by her side whilst I see to my men. I need them to be ready when Rexen has to land."

"I can see to that, Garlen." said Bex. "You should be here with Moren."

The soldier stood, gently leaning forward to plant a soft kiss on Moren's forehead.

"As callous as it may sound, Bex, I can't stay here. I have seen so much war, death and destruction that I don't think I can show emotion or sit still. Moren is in the hands of the Gods and only Iga can help her regain the balance to this side of the scale. There are another forty souls on this ship that need me right now."

"You are right, Garlen. It does sound callous." Bex gave him a scathing look and stood her ground for a tense few seconds before standing aside and letting him pass.

'I can see his point.' Ishtara added.

'Can you?'

'Yes, he is right. He can't do anything for his sister right now. He should be doing something that he can affect with his actions.'

'Bolam's balls, girl. You are as callous as him!'

'Pfft!'

The whole ship jolted, as if it had struck a wall and then the bow started to dip. Bex grabbed the doorframe to keep herself upright.

"Crom! What was that?" exclaimed Iga as she leant forward, wrapping her arms around the young Moren.

"I'll find out, but it doesn't feel good." Bex stepped out into the corridor. She could hear shouts of confusion coming from the deck above and staggered to the stairs up to the wheelhouse.

"Col! What's going on?" she called up the stairs.

"Something has hit us! I can't keep us in the air!" With difficulty she made it up the steep steps to the cabin above. A Ghost was lying face down at the top of the stairs, a wound on his head. She didn't need a second look to see that it had been fatal.

Col was standing feet splayed at the wheel, pulling it back, desperately trying to keep the ship from plummeting bow downwards into the earth below. Mathor was next to him, his right arm lending strength to Col's attempt to save the ship. His left arm was hanging by his side and he had a grimace upon his normally cheery face.

"Keep her steady, boy, or we have had it!"

"Tell me something I didn't know, Mathor."

Bryn came crashing through the door, followed by two of Garlen's troops. They saw the situation straight away and leapt to the aid of Col and Mathor. Slowly the combined effort pulled the bow of the ship up to near horizontal flight.

"What happened, Bryn?"

"A ship came out of the clouds above. We'd lost track of it earlier, but it suddenly appeared again. It hit us with that cursed weapon of theirs before they turned back towards Jacarna. The stern has gone completely. We lost a couple of men over the side."

"Aye," one of the Ghosts added, "Mayak and Stim. Both gone."

"Brace yourselves!"

Bex looked ahead out of the cabin window. The ground was coming up fast, but at least they had left the Great Asken Forest behind and the land ahead was wide, rolling grass land. She watched as the ground came rushing up. The big figure of Bryn dived on her, pushing her to the floor as the ship hit.

The sound ripped through the ship as the hull split and cracked. Splinters rent the air causing horrific injuries to anyone in their way. As the occupants of the cabin managed to get to their feet, they could hear others from the deck below calling to abandon the wreckage. Bryn pulled Bex to her feet and they looked about the cabin. Mathor was on all fours, the big, old soldier coughing hard. Col was down, the heavy control wheel of the ship lying across his legs. He didn't seem to be breathing. The other two Ghosts were staggering about, faces blooded from being flung about in the crash.

The ship appeared to be in three main parts. Snapped in half across the beam, the stern of the ship – or what was left of it – was upright. The bow half of the ship had broken into two, but there only appeared to be survivors from the larger half. The survivors started to clamber from the wreckage and Bex was relieved to see that Garlen emerged holding Moren, clutched to his chest. Iga, Radnak and the two young goblin lords appeared with Igant holding the hand of Ingren.

The prince immediately took charge, shouting for a head count and a list of injuries as well as supplies. As he rattled out his commands, his Ghosts leapt into action, Kardanth taking a tally of the able bodied as they returned to the wreckage to grab weapons and food. The blond prince jogged over to Bex and Bryn, expressing delight that they had come through relatively unscathed. He then turned to Mathor, grinning as he saw the older warrior holding his left arm at an angle.

"See, my old friend! At least falling out of the sky, you manage to walk away. If this had been a normal ship at sea, you would never had swum with a broken arm!"

"Col didn't make it. Jappa, Mayak and Stim have gone as well."

"Aye," the prince's face darkened, "and there will be a few more as well. It is a heavy toll I have asked you all to pay."

"We knew it was only a matter of time when we took the King's gold, Garlen. We have been a long way, you and I, as we all have. We may all end up in Kani's Hall before this is all over. But I am going to feed as many of these whore-sons to the crows as I can before I go." He turned to attend to the wounded with Iga.

"Killing and dying. Killing and dying." Bryn muttered softly to himself.

"What was that, Earl Kar?" asked Garlen.

"Nothing, Garlen." He walked a few yards away to stand on his own. He faced the Great Asken Forest, a wall of green on the horizon, in the general direction of his home.

'*What about Rexen? We need to find him?*' Ishtara chirped up inside Bex's mind.

'*Is that wise?*'

'*He said he knew about the Qoi.*'

'*But.*'

'*I need to know, Bex. I need to know if I really am the last of my people.*' Ishtara pleaded. It was something that Bex hadn't heard before from the Qoi. Sadness, yes but this tone that begged the Samakan sounded torn.

'*We'll have to hurry.*'

Bex dashed over to the stern part of the ship. Due to the ship being torn apart, the door to Rexen's chamber now formed the outside wall. She tentatively pushed it open, stepping inside. It was a mess. The cages to either side had buckled and split with wooden frames scattered across the deck, along with planks from the deck above. The stern of the ship had been destroyed by the Cassalian weapon, leaving the end open to the elements. This now left the air a little fresher as she approached the insect. The ward about him was still unbroken but a beam from above laid across one of his legs and a green ooze seeped out from the damaged chitin. The chains that had once seethed with energy, shackling Rexen to the ceiling via the iron collar about his neck were broken, now just dull and ordinary. As Bex approached, he raised his head.

"Ah, the one with one inside. You have come to help me." He paused as he saw she was carrying her greck. "Or kill me?"

"No, not kill." Bex had drawn her sword subconsciously upon entering the room. His comment surprised her and also embarrassed her. Had she intended to kill him?

"Then the sword, why? Are they here?" Bex guessed that he meant the Cassalians.

"No, but they will be soon. We need to move."

"Ah, so you still trust me not. Because of what I look and do?"

Bex blushed and sheathed her greck.

"You said you would help Ishtara. You said you would tell her all you knew about the Qoi, whether there are others."

"I did. And Prince Garlen's sisters I helped rescue."

'*Let him loose, Bex. Please*'

"I said that I would free you if you helped, you have my word. So, tell me now!"

'*Bex!*'

Rexen's mandibles clicked away as his sword-like front limbs tried to move the beam. As he grew more frustrated, he snapped back to Bex.

"Yes, I know of more. They live."

'*Bex, now get him out of there.*'

Bex took hold and strained against the beam to shift it. It seemed to be too heavy. She heard a voice behind her. It was Bryn.

"Bex, we have to go. There's another two ships coming." He saw what she was doing and moved to help her.

"Is this wise?"

"Wise or not, Bryn Kar, you seem to be helping me. I suppose all logic has died today." She grinned and they strained together. They managed to lift the beam, so it was no longer crushing the Flyer's leg, and then twisted it to one side to roll it away.

"Break the ward." The Flyer instructed.

Bex placed her foot on the etched runes that circled the Flyer. They were no longer glowing, but whatever magic was left in them still held Rexen captive.

'*Ishtara, can you burn these away?*'

'*Of course.*' replied the demonic voice of Ishtara.

Bex held her hand close to the runes and the skin started to blister and smoke. Flames crackled over her fingers and she lowered her hand, so the flames touched the wood. Bryn turned away, unable to watch. Rexen looked on, transfixed as the wood started to smoke before catching light. As the runes burnt, the circle became broken and the Flyer tentatively stepped out.

"Thank you." He said simply.

They exited the ship from the gutted stern and walked round to where the rest of the Ghosts were preparing to move out. Rexen clattered about in delight.

"Fresh, fresh air. Sunlight. Do you know how long I have craved this?"

"Bolam's Balls, Bex!" Garlen shouted and drew his sword. Several other Ghosts also turned to face the trio and readied their weapons. For Iga and the children, it was the first time they had seen Rexen and they stood in shock and awe.

"Wait! He does not mean any harm! He helped get your sisters back!" Bex stood in front of the large insect and waved her arms in the air.

"It's a monster, a fucking monster!"

Rexen seemed to take umbrage at that remark and stopped, turning to face the prince.

"No, Prince Garlen. There are the monsters." He twisted his upper thorax and waved a sword in the direction of the Asken Forest, specifically at the two dots in the sky that seemed to be getting bigger and bigger.

"It eats humans!" Garlen pointed his sword at Bex as he swore some more.

"On my world, there are no humans. Yet we live. To you, I am an animal, yes? You eat animals, yes? Perhaps I should be afraid of you, yes?"

Garlen sheathed his sword in a snarl. Looking up at the approaching ships he continued.

"We need to move out. If it threatens one of my men, Bex, I will kill it. Then you." He turned and waved his hand over his head in a circular motion to get his men moving. Bryn walked past Bex, patting her on the shoulder.

"Charming!" he grinned.

Rexen brushed one of his swords along Bex's arm in a crude imitation of Bryn's gesture.

"Thank you, Bex and the one inside. I pledge to you my swords. Also, I won't harm you or the others. Except Garlen, maybe him." He mandibles clicked together animatedly as he seemed to exhale through the chitinous jaws and Bex swore that she had just heard an insect laugh.

42

They marched on, keeping a loose file. Two Ghosts took point and guided them on. They all kept an eye out behind to keep watch on the chasing ships.

Garlen's Ghosts were down to twenty-eight soldiers. Three of them, including Mathor, were badly injured. What was worse, the terrain they were moving through left them badly exposed. The rolling hills of the Hinterlands were hard to move fast on. The ground was uneven, and the weather had closed in, bringing a light rain making the grass slippery. And the ships behind were closing in.

"They are transports. That is good." Rexen said, after pausing to study them. They were still too far away for Bex to make out any details on them, but they were visible now as ships and not black dots.

"Why is that good?" Bex was keeping close to Rexen as the troops made their way over the hills. She felt honour bound to keep an eye on the Flyer, as she still wasn't sure about trusting him.

"Transports only have troops onboard. No energy weapon."

Bex nodded and decided to run forward to give Garlen the news.

"I was starting to worry about that. If we are caught out in the open like this, we wouldn't stand a chance. Not even Tobes would be able to save us."

Several of the Ghosts were taking turns to carry Moren and Ingren. Radnak was carrying the youngest goblin Lord, Janis, whilst Igant ran with his mother. Both were as fleetfooted as hares, with the constitution to keep up with the stronger soldiers.

Bryn jogged forward, to pass on another message from Rexen.

"One of the ships is landing, about a mile or so back."

"And the other?" asked Garlen.

"Keeping coming for the moment." The prince nodded in acknowledgement then called for Mathor.

"Get the men on point to find a defensive position, high ground if possible. We are going to have company very soon."

"What's happening?" Bex asked.

"Cavalry. There's no point landing so far behind unless what you are unloading can move fast enough to catch us up. That means cavalry. Being out in the open against cavalry would be about as bad as being caught out in the open with those damn magical weapons."

The Ghosts on point swung to the left, aiming for a small hill, that as they got closer looked more like a large rocky outcrop.

"Tobes tits, maybe she is looking out for us today," exclaimed Garlen as they reached it. A rocky slope led up to the outcrop which had vertical drops on the other three sides. There were a few sorry looking trees on the top with several large rocks offering some protection.

Kardanth gave a quick scout whilst the other Ghosts fanned out to cover each side. He came back to advise that only the opposite side offered anything like a way up or down. He also reported that a fog was starting to lay down north of the hillock.

"You could hold this with only a few men." Garlen discussed with Mathor.

"Aye, if you had enough food and water."

"We just need to draw the Cassalians in and then we should be able to slaughter them. How many troops could that ship of ours carry?"

"Fully armed, about sixty. Cavalry probably twenty or so."

"If we assume that those two ships are similar size, then its three to one. Not too bad odds. We have had worse. Do you remember Chater's Bridge? Or that fort outside Dumnotia? We got through those. We can get through this."

Garlen went to see his sisters who were sitting with the goblin lords and Iga. Mathor beckoned Bryn and Bex over.

"I'm just going to check every position. Could you just take guard here for a moment?"

They squatted down, peering out over the hinterlands and noticed a small cloud of raised dust a way out. The other ship was starting to descend, over to the west. Bex turned to tell Mathor about the ship, only to see the bald head of Mathor speaking to the Ghosts collected about him in the middle of the outcrop. Several were nodding, before they all started rolling dice.

"What in Tomnar's name are you all doing?" Garlen strode up to Mathor.

"It's your idea, Garlen. So, quieten down and let me do this."

Garlen looked like he was about to explode, but one of the Ghosts rolled his dice, then held his sword up.

"A three. Look like I'm in with you, Mathor." A few others clapped him on the back.

"This is not my idea, Mathor. Now stop pissing about!"

"You said remember the fort outside Dumnotia. You also said that we can hold this with only a few men. I reckon about eight. That's me, Gant and Tarktay," he indicated the other two injured Ghosts, "and now Than and Harkoan to start with."

"And what are the rest of us going to do whilst you fight off a small army?"

"You are going to go. Head north into that fog and get back to Tannaheim. Beat these Cassalian pricks so hard they rue the day they came to this shithole of a world, then drink a round in memory of us heroes." He gestured towards the men he had named.

"We are all in this, Garlen. Mathor asked for volunteers. We all volunteered. That's why the dice to decide." The Ghost who had just rolled three on the dice, Harkoan, calmly spoke to his prince. Mathor faced Garlen, his imposing bulk squaring up to his commander.

"Now, as I see it. You and your sisters are more important to Danaria than eight of us." He looked at Iga who had joined the throng. "And this is going to be no place for a Lady and her children. And you are going to need her over there. I can feel it. She is essential for Danaria. You said yourself, she could be the most dangerous of us all." He pointed over to Bex to accentuate the last point.

"Now, Garlen. I don't care what you say. This is happening. There is a slight way out to the north that Kardanth found and that's where you are going. I wasn't afraid to give your father a slap if he needed it, and I'll beat your arse as well if I need to, broken arm or not."

Garlen didn't know what to say as he knew what the old soldier was saying was true. He retreated a short way and sat down, a solitary figure with what felt like the whole of Maingard on his shoulders.

It took only another minute to decide on the other three men to stay and the farewells were quick. Garlen hugged each of them and Bex could swear that she saw a small tear as he gave the bulky figure of Mathor hug. Before she went, Bex threw the rest of her calthrops down the slope. She looked at Mathor and half smiled.

"It's not much, but I hope it helps."

"Don't you worry, Lady Bex. I meant what I say. You and that fire demon, you are important here, you are needed. I can't say why or how I know; I just do. You try to take good care of the prince, though."

'*We will, Mathor.*' Ishtara purred away and Bex relayed the message to the old warrior.

Bryn beckoned for Bex to follow him, and she half turned to go, then gave Mathor a quick kiss on the cheek. He reddened slightly, then laughed.

"As soon as we've beaten this lot, we will be hot on your tails." The other seven Ghosts cackled between them.

Bex left, finding it hard to do so without turning to look back. If she had done so though, she felt she wouldn't have been able to leave.

The route down was steep and covered in shale but they managed to navigate it without a hitch. They managed to make the fogbank before they head the cries of battle behind them. She gave a prayer to Kani for the eight and hurried along.

'*He was right. you know.*' Ishtara spoke, breaking the silence.

'*Was he now.*'

'*If we had stayed there and repulsed the Cassalians, what would you do as the Cassalian commander?*'

'*I don't know,*' Bex's head swam with many thoughts and emotions. She was sure that the eight were doomed, and that halved Garlen's forces. So many men dead to rescue two girls. She hoped that they would be worth it.

'*Well?*' questioned Ishtara.

'*Maybe try again?*'

'*I hope Garlen doesn't hand over command to you, Bex. By the all-giving fire!*'

Bex harrumphed.

'*There's only one way down. Sit there and wait for us to starve or for us to come out. Then their cavalry can cut us to bits. Or they could wait until another ship comes along with one of those energy weapons.*'

'*Amazing, the Qoi aren't warriors, yet you know that?*'

'*I am just trying to take notice of what is going on around us.*'

The fog closed in about them and it was all they could do to keep in contact with those in front.

43

The gaunt face of Koopler looked out over the wall. The light from the setting sun cast an eerie glow over his angular features, accentuating his hollow cheeks. He nudged his companion with his foot. Morga was sitting with his back against the parapet, his eyes almost closed.

"What is it now?" the older guard muttered.

"Do you think they will come tonight?" For once, the brashness that Koopler had always displayed seemed gone. Morga detected fear in the young lad's voice.

"Maybe, maybe not. But they will come. If not tonight, it will be soon. The old Queen might have pushed them over the edge."

"What did she do?"

"Sildur the Red knows someone whose brother works as a page in the palace. This Karchek, sends one of his top men to push her to surrender. It appears that the Queen's daughters are missing. I think they've been taken. Little beans to barter with. Anyway, this Cassalian turns up with a small army to ask Sarsi for her surrender. She looks at him. Clicks her fingers and they all drop down dead. Straight down, Sildur said."

"Really?"

"That's what he said. The page saw it with his own eyes."

"So, she is a witch! I told you so."

"So Sildur's friend said. Do you believe in all that? Have you ever seen a witch, you ever seen magic?"

The young guard thought about it for a while and then shook his head.

"No, no I haven't."

There was an uneasy silence, as Morga closed his eyes again. Koopler nudged him with his foot again.

"Have you?"

"Have I what?"

"Seen a witch."

Morga chuckled and shook his head.

"No, son. Not unless you mean one of those girls down near the dock. Some of the things they can do can be mistaken for magic!" He chuckled again.

"Do you think she'll do that when they do come?"

"Who?"

"Sarsi, you idiot. I didn't mean your girl down the fucking docks, did I!"

"No, I suppose not."

"But," he paused as if putting great thought into his forthcoming utterances, "she could do it again, click her fingers and kill 'em all?"

"No, Koopler. You think she's a witch, Sildur the red thinks she's a witch, but she is not a fucking witch."

"But."

Morga interrupted the youngster.

"But nothing. Do you see her up here with us, keeping guard, on vigil for the Cassalians?"

Koopler shook his head.

"No, you don't. She's over there, sitting pretty in the palace, surrounded by her guardsmen. Whilst we sit here." Morga continued.

"That's where you're wrong, Morga. She ain't surrounded by her guard. My girl, she's a maid at the palace, remember? She says Sarsi sent everyone away. Even the Hawk. She is in that palace all alone, waiting for them to come."

"Now that is strange." said Morga, closing his eyes for the third time.

"Morga!" Koopler nudged him again.

"Will you shut up!"

"No Morga, you need to look at this!" Morga looked up at the young lad, his blond shoulder length hair blowing gently in the breeze. He realised he was pointing, out over the wall. Slowly, and grumbling, Morga stood up, following the line of Koopler's arm and finger.

"Bolam's balls!"

The horizon above the rolling hills that led down to Tannaheim from the east was filled with black shapes, far enough away to hide any detail, but close enough for Morga to see that they couldn't be anything else other than the Cassalian ships. He counted quickly but gave up when he got to fifty, even though there were many more.

"Bolam's balls!" he repeated.

"Morga." The young guard's voice was wavering as he spoke.

"Morga. I don't want to die."

44

The skyships closed in on Tannaheim. The city surrounded by its high walls that had deterred many an attacker in its long history, now awaited its fate. The Cassalians were eager for battle, desperate for the pillage that would start as soon as they landed. Karchek had promised them something that hadn't been offered before. The chance to put the whole city to the sword. No slaves, no prisoners – just wanton destruction. This was unprecedented, never before in any *knartevilder*, had the commander of the Emperor's Host given a similar command.

Small ships darted forward, as fast and as agile as the dragons they resembled. Bolts of energy cascaded down from them destroying the city gates where the King's Road entered the city. Others crossed the city walls and rained destruction down upon the city beneath. Buildings within the once impregnable walls started collapsing. Fire spread fast and the Danarian's ran in chaos.

The slow, ponderous skyships that carried the assault troops finally arrived at the city walls. Whist several came to rest on the plain outside the East Gate, the rest started to descend within the boundaries of the walls. Karchek's own skyship, The Emperors Scythe, headed straight for the Palace. It was a ship so big that it had four Flyers held captive within. Their pain powered its flight and propelled it towards Karchek's destiny with Sarsi. Three other ships accompanied it.

The ships that had landed outside the city opened their hatches and disgorged their cavalry. Horsemen swarmed like ants as they chaotically formed into a loose formation before starting to trot towards the city gates that had been destroyed by the barrage in the opening few minutes of the engagement.

But Queen Sarsi and her generals had not been idle since Bryn Kar had briefed the court about the attack on Jacarna. The responsibility for the defence of the city had been passed to General Divoc, a very capable leader with years of experience in defensive warfare. Sarsi had promised him whatever he needed, and Marshall Vent had delivered. Now Divoc's plan was put into action.

Soldiers on top of some of the larger buildings threw off canvas sheets that had covered ballistae, taken from the galleys moored in the harbour, and moved to defend the city. Great steel tipped bolts from these engines slammed into the sides of the transport ships, tearing onto the hull and sending shards and splinters of wood flying through the interiors.

Oil had been seized throughout the city by order from General Divoc himself, and barrels of the flammable substance were now hurled at the descending ships by the siege catapults that were sited by the palace. The barrels smashed over the decks and hulls of the ships, spreading the sticky oil. Archers located on the walls and towers of the city, then used fire arrows to set them alight. Soon, a dozen of more ships were falling from the sky, many set ablaze.

The cavalry that charged through the main gates were forced into ever narrowing streets by barricades until they came to a dead-end. They circled, whooping as their horses reared, the latter ranks causing more confusion and obstruction as they arrived. From the upper floors of the buildings on either side, the people of Tannaheim attacked, some unloosed arrows from their bows, others threw rocks. On the ground floors, the doors and windows of which were boarded up, small flaps opened, and the soldiers stationed there thrust outwards with spears, butchering man and horse alike.

However, these little successes were outnumbered by the sheer weight of numbers against the defenders. For every ship downed, several more landed. The heavy siege weapons that the Danarians used were targeted by the faster, smaller ships and they were soon destroyed.

Above the palace, The Emperor's Scythe started to descend, finally settling on the same courtyard that Remoh had landed on when he had tried to negotiate with Sarsi.

45

M on Baxt lifted the flat chest out from under her simple bed and placed it on top of the mattress. She reached under her dark hair and lifted the thin leather cord from around her neck. Hanging from it was a small brass key that she now used to unlock the strongbox. Inside was a leather jack that she removed and held out to inspect.

Memories of her distant past flashed before her eyes and she smiled. She donned it, strapping it over her undershirt. The laces needed a little loosening, but it still fitted. In the past, this had offered her protection in so many ways. It wasn't just the physical protection the leather gave her, but also emotional and psychological. When wearing it, she was no longer the plain daughter of the village smith, but a heroine, capable of any feat. Ogres, orcs, wolves and worse, she had faced and beaten, outfought and outwitted. Often alone but sometimes with others, but never subservient; always as equal to her companions.

She reached back into the box, removing a bundle of

oilskin rags, laced together. Placing it on the mattress, she unlaced it, revealing a sword. She picked it up and felt its balance and weight. She gave it a few swishes through the air, more memories flooding back. She thrust it through a loop on her belt and went downstairs to the bar area.

Above the bar was the only item from her past life that she displayed. A long bow hewn from yew. She reached up and took it down from the wall, restringing it and flexing it. Satisfied, she poured herself a flagon of strong ale and downed it. Wiping her mouth with the back of her hand, she stood and then picked a quiver of arrows from underneath the bar counter. Strapping it over her shoulder, she made her way through the kitchen area and out into the alley that ran behind her bar.

She remembered her words to Bex, that she wouldn't leave 'Ol' One Eye' but knew that this was right. The Inn wasn't the most important thing here, it was the city. Without Tannaheim or her denizens who made up the clientele of The Black Dragon Inn, then the inn was nothing. And if the inn was nothing, Mon Baxt was nothing. All her past meant little if she didn't act now.

She looked up as a ship flew overhead, flames alight down the hull on the port side. She shrunk into the shadows automatically, even though she knew that they wouldn't see her. Stretching above her, she grabbed the balcony terrace of the building next door to her beloved inn. Pulling herself up, she made another leap to grab the edge of the roof, praying that the tiling wouldn't give way. Within seconds, she was on the roof, her heart pounding.

Fear had given way to anticipation, anticipation of battle ahead, but also the chance to pit her body and her wits against the most fearsome enemy she had ever encountered. This was the true Mon Baxt, not the innkeeper, but warrior, archer and hero.

She stood up on the parapet and surveyed the Tannaheim from the rooftops. The city had welcomed her and now she was determined to fight back to protect it. She was one, but one of many.

46

K archek heard Sarsi's voice purr inside his head. It, she, was starting to annoy him. The Emperor's Scythe had descended in the palace courtyard some fifteen minutes ago and so far, they had encountered no defenders inside the palace building. The three hundred soldiers that the general's immense ship carried, along with more from the other three transports pushed through the palace.

'*Not that way, Karchek. Straight on.*'

He growled as the soft purr reverberated inside his skull. His head still throbbed as it was, his eye so swollen that he had removed his helmet as it constantly rubbed and irritated the wound.

"*Come to me, Karchek.*"

"I am, bitch! Wherever you are hiding!" As he spoke aloud, his troops moving with him wondered about his state of mind, even through the fog of war that had descended over them. Normally, they would be berserk by now, looting and killing indiscriminately, but the absence of defenders had started to unnerve them.

They came to a wide, ornate staircase with white marble steps disappearing upwards, whilst the corridor split either side and looped behind them.

'*Up the stairs, Karchek.*'

He grabbed one of his soldiers, who loitered too long in front of him, shoving him headfirst onto the marble stairs. He swore and urged his men to unloose their 'hounds', the rabid, unliving beasts that were held in check with mystical chains. They loped in front of the invaders who clicked their leash handles, making the enchanted blue chains to disappear. They tested the air with their noses, slavering at the mouth. The beastmasters lashed out with their whips, sending them off in a frenzy, howling as they chased up the stairs, some on all fours. Karchek and his men followed.

'*That's right, Karchek. We have unfinished business to attend to.*'

"Too right, I'm going to snap every bone in your body, then I'll fuck.."

'*Now, Karchek, that is no way to speak to a Queen, is it.*'

He raised his clenched fists and threw his head back, howling madly.

"Bitch, come out and fight me!"

'*Ah, your pets have found me. How sweet.*'

He lifted his sword, pointing the long double-edged blade up the stair way. He howled once more, then screamed to his men, who cheered and charged ahead.

"The bitch-queen is up there. Kill her defenders, but she is mine and mine alone!"

47

The Hawk looked out from his bedchamber window at the fire and destruction over the city. Effectively banished from the court by his Queen, he had returned home as she directed. He couldn't believe that she had given up, not whilst the forces of Tannaheim carried on their desperate rear-guard action. Sarsi had known what her action would drive Karchek to do.

Every man, from high general down to lowly soldier had been told what to expect. They knew the consequences; they knew that their futures lay at the point of a sword or in a slave pen. They also knew that their Queen was undefended in the palace, willing to allow the soldiers normally stationed there to defend their own homes, their own families by being moved to the city itself. She had signed the order herself, passing on that all Danaria should believe in themselves and also in their queen.

He clenched his fists tightly by his side as he watched, ships still circled the city, more transports as well as the smaller, faster ships. He was torn. Magus Vent had dedicated his life to the crown, serving first King Dirian, then Anjoan, and briefly

Sarsi. At this dire time, he should be there with his Queen, protecting and assisting where needed. But also, he was glad to be at home. His family were in the cellar, not wanting to see the devastation visited upon their city. And he was here to protect them, and if necessary, die with them.

There was a rustle from the garden below. He gripped his sword and looked out again, trying to pinpoint the location of the noise. There it was again. The sound had come from the bushes along the garden wall. He scanned the area outside the garden but couldn't see any sign of the battle getting that close. He made his way downstairs, calling down through the cellar door that he was checking something out.

He apprehensively opened the door and called out.

"Come out! I can hear you!"

He flexed his fingers around the hilt of his sword as his breath formed in the cold air around him. He waited. The bush rustled again.

"Show yourself!"

The rustle grew louder, and he steeled himself.

"It's me, Marshall Vent, please don't hurt me!" The voice was young and female. The small figure of Yanna stepped into view. She stared up at him, her grimy face appearing even more dirtier than normal. She had obviously been crying and she had rubbed the tears, smearing grime over her cheeks.

"I'm sorry. I didn't know where else to go. And Tikar said that if I ever got into trouble, I should come to you – he said you are a good man."

"He did, did he?"

The girl sobbed again, nodding.

"I'm sorry. I shouldn't have come."

The Hawk ushered her in, shaking his head.

"Don't be silly, girl. Come on in, forgive my manners. My granddaughter Marcy is downstairs, it will be good for her to have someone her age to speak to."

He looked out to the garden again, as if to check for more waifs and strays, or invaders, he didn't know which. He turned to the young girl.

"The Phantom sent you here? Where is he?"

Yanna shrugged.

"I told you, he left the city, after the King died. He said he was going to get the bad guys."

Turning to shut the door, he looked out one last time and what he saw made his heart sink and bile rise to his throat.

48

The Ghosts had stumbled along for about an hour as the fog became heavier and heavier. It seemed to cling to them as they rushed through it, as if they had been running through giant webs instead of tendrils of water. The grass underneath their feet had given way, and they were now starting to splash through the beginnings of a marsh. Several times Bex had heard the heavy splash and oaths that accompanied a trip or a fall into the puddles. She skipped along, holding hands with Ingren. Garlen carried Moren, somewhere ahead of her, whilst Iga and Radnak ran with the young goblin lords.

They had left behind the sounds of battle some time ago, but Bex had no time to shed any more tears for Mathor and the others. She couldn't imagine that they were still fighting and was sure the small defensive line had been overrun. That meant only one thing. The cavalry would now be fanning out, searching the fog for signs of the escapees. They had to find cover.

Suddenly a black shape flashed past Bex.

'*What was that?*'

'*I didn't see, but it was fast.*' Bex answered the Qoi.

Another two sped past on either side and she heard the thud of horse hooves. She called out a warning, as loud as she could.

"Garlen! Ghosts! We have company, they are here!"

Then came the clash of steel accompanied by the screams of men cut down. A shape loomed out of the fog in front of Bex and Ingren. A horseman raised his sword as his horse reared up on back legs. A Ghost flung up a block with his own sword as the rider crashed his blade down. Bex drew her greck, letting go of Ingren's hand to vault onto the back of the horse. The rider died quickly but the Ghost also struck out, cutting the horse down as well. The great black horse fell to one side and Bex dived away, striking the ground with a vicious thump.

Groggily, she clambered to her feet, helped by the Ghost and Ingren.

"We've got to keep moving." The soldier hissed at her. They turned and ran, Ingren in between them. Another horse and rider brushed past them, slashing backwards as he passed. The ghost fell, clutching his face with a terrible wail of anguish. Ingren screamed aloud and Bex pulled her to one side as she veered off in another direction.

She ran on, then skidded to a halt. Iga was on the ground, Janis standing guard over her with a dagger in each hand as a cavalryman bore down on them. Bex charged forward, sword in hand. Once again, Ingren was pushed to one side. Ishtara burst into life, the fiery demon igniting the dark fog in flames. The warhorse reared with its hooves striking air above the terrifying visage of Ishtara. For a moment, it seemed paralysed in fear and then the hooves came crashing down as Ishtara lunged past them with her sword. Both struck as one, the blade sliding into the rider's stomach and the iron shod hooves smashing down on Ishtara, glancing the side of her head and her shoulder.

The horse snorted in anger and fear as its rider sagged in

his saddle. The Cassalian's arm flopped about by his side uselessly, his sword hanging from its wrist cord. The destrier seemed to be about to attack again, trampling Ishtara who now lay prone on the ground. The damp clumps of grass around her were starting to steam from the heat of her body, which was even now starting to return to Bex's form.

The huge bulk of Bryn Kar jumped forward from out of the fog, screaming loudly and jabbing his sword at the horse's face. It turned away and planted its front feet, lashing out with both back feet. They connected with air only, as Bryn leapt to one side and swung out with his blade again. It caught the horse on its unprotected rump, and it shot off into the fog leaving them alone.

Bryn turned to see Iga, Janis and Ingren fussing about Bex. The crumpled form of the tall thief laid ragdoll-like in Iga's arms. Ishtara had reverted to Bex's true form apart from a reddish tinge to her skin.

"We have to get moving. Janis, take her sword." The Jacarnan bent down and pick her up, unceremoniously throwing her over his shoulder. Iga grabbed Ingren's hand and ran, as the young goblin picked up her greck and darted after them. The dark shape of a soldier loomed ahead, and Bryn cursed that Bex was encumbering him. He clumsily prepared to attack before realising who it was.

"Bolam's balls! Radnak, you almost got yourself killed!"

"Have you seen Iga and Janis?"

"We are here, Radnak," Iga called out as she appeared out of the fog. "Have you seen Igant?"

"Yes, he's with the others ahead. I think we have accounted for all the cavalry. There's a light ahead, Kardanth thinks it is a building. We need to regroup and lay up until morning."

"Which way?" panted Bryn. The half-orc pointed.

"Garlen is still out here somewhere. Five others are still unaccounted for."

At the mention of her brother's name, Ingren started.

"And Mori as well? You must find them! Please, you have to find them!" she implored, her voice on the verge of cracking. The gruff *sverd* nodded.

"I'll do my best, princess. Now you must get to safety."

49

K archek pushed his way into the throne room through the throng of soldiers baying at the doorway. The whole chamber was empty apart from the two thrones set at the far end facing him. On one sat, he presumed, Queen Sarsi. On the other sat a great figure in armour. His right hand held the hilt of a great two-handed sword, the tip of the blade rested against the cold, stone flagstone of the floor. About the floor were laying the corpses of the beastmen that had been sent ahead. Occasionally, Karchek could see one or another twitch as the life ebbed from them.

As immense as the figure sitting on the throne next to Sarsi was, he was not as great as Karchek. He towered over the other Cassalians and their conscripted troops. Shoving his own men out of the way, he walked forward. His own two-handed sword pointing menacingly at Sarsi and Anjoan.

Sarsi sat expressionless. The simple gown she wore displayed the cruel marks upon her arms. Her hands were completely black, and little of her own pale skin colour showed on her forearms and upper arms. The long tendril-like marks now wound their way over her throat and jawline. Her eyes shone with anger and hatred.

Anjoan Barstt stood and slowly shouldered his cold steel. He reached to his neck and unclasped his cloak, and it fell to the floor. He descended the steps from the dais to face the invaders.

Karchek stared at the armoured warrior and waved his troops forward. Thirty men entered the chamber, all from the subservient races to the Cassalians. For some reason, the blotchy bruised skin of the soldier who faced him, made Karchek slightly apprehensive.

"Once my men have finished with your champion, you and I will dance, bitch-queen. My only regret is not having your offspring here to watch your demise." The invaders spread out, starting to form a semi-circle around the single warrior.

"He is not just my champion, Karchek. You don't recognize the man you had killed, do you? Understandable as you had never met my husband. Aren't you dying to get acquainted?"

"But he's dead?" Karchek countered, a little confidence seeped away.

"Death has no meaning to a follower of Nyx, Karchek."

Anjoan faced the soldiers against him and slowly raised his left hand to point at the Cassalian on the far left. He seemed to count them off until he pointed to one dead centre. He slowly and deliberately closed his fist and, unbeknownst to Karchek's men, so did Sarsi. She murmured the ancient words of power under her breath and a look of terror came over Anjoan's opponent. He tremored and dropped his sword, falling dead to the ground as his heart burst.

Several of the Cassalians dropped their guards, some in sheer horror. One threw his sword to the floor and turned to flee. Karchek snarled and swung his sword viciously, decapitating the man.

"Cowards! It is but one man. Cut him down!" To emphasise

the point his lashed out with his sword again, in a onehanded swing and grabbed the nearest soldier to him with his free hand and shoved him towards Anjoan. The dead king cut him down instantly and then the throne room erupted into chaos. Karchek paced back and forth, howling and enthusing his men to attack.

Each attack was met without success as Anjoan struck men down to his left and right. Every now and again, a sword would slice past his defence and he would give an incredulous look as his arm or leg was cut by the errant blade. He would then snarl and double his efforts, his own blade hacking and slicing.

"I don't think your men are a match for my champion, Karchek. Maybe you would be a worthier opponent?" Sarsi had not moved since the invaders had entered her throne room. But as Anjoan fought on, the blackness was encroaching further. Her forearms were complete now and two or three black veins started to creep across her cheeks. Her right hand clasped the arm of the throne tightly whilst her left hand sat clenched in her lap.

Karchek strode forward, compelled to attack Anjoan. Not because Sarsi had decreed it, he thought to himself, but because he wanted to get this done. He wanted to feel her suffer as Remoh had suffered. His blows were more powerful than Anjoan's and he was faster than the animated corpse. Soon Anjoan was staggering backward, throwing his blade up across his head to block the mighty blows that crashed down from the giant Cassalian general.

More of Karchek's men flooded into the throne room, drawn by the sounds of battle. They watched as their general battled, shouting and hollering whilst each blow was landed upon the blocking blade. Some circled around the two and started to creep towards Sarsi. Karchek bellowed at them, his voice hoarse with the exertion. They nodded and moved back, leaving the queen alone. The message was clear; the queen is mine.

As Karchek's attention was on Sarsi, Anjoan stabbed forward quickly, catching the giant in his upper arm. He pulled the sword back and went to strike again, just as Karchek swung his mighty sword, knocking the blade from Anjoan's hands. The cassalian war general pulled his arm back and stabbed forward onehanded, the mighty sword catching Anjoan's armour and cutting through it with ease. The sword tip slipped into Anjoan's stomach and then almost through his back armour. The giant swore and cursed as he raised his boot and pushed Anjoan from his blade.

The dead king fell, twisting to fall on his front. He looked up at his wife and started to crawl towards her. She jumped from the throne and swept down to meet him. There was almost a hint of love and sorrow in the long dead eyes as she caressed his cheek with her hand, her left hand still clenched tight. Whatever spirit was present in the zombie left, causing Anjoan's corpse to fall still.

Karchek advanced menacingly, his sword tip almost on the ground as he went to grab her.

"Your champion is dead. Your husband dies for the second time. I killed him twice! And before your time is over, you will wish that you could die once. Your efforts to withstand the might of the Emperor are puny and pathetic. You wasted your strength." He reached down and grabbed her hair, pulling her up in front of him. Her feet kicked a full foot above the floor.

"Fool." Sarsi laughed as she was suspended by her hair. "My strength and efforts weren't wasted. My husband's efforts weren't in vain. He can now rest as he gave me time to pour my energy into this." She raised her left hand in front of Karchek's face. The blackness was now crossing her face in a hideous pattern, interlacing and interlocking as she spoke.

"You won't have this land, Fool. Your Emperor will suffer

the same fate if he comes as well. This is my revenge for my husband and my daughters."

A light started to glow between her fingers and Karchek felt his gaze drawn towards it, unable to comprehend or to act otherwise. The light increased in brightness, sending beams from the gaps between her fingers to crash against the walls of the room. It shone so brightly that Karchek stared as her finger bones became visible as the less dense skin and muscle allowed the light to pass through.

Sarsi's skin itched with fire as the pain intensified, at first in her hand and then throughout her body. Her skin was now completely black, the small rivers of blackness now extending to crisscross her eyeballs. And then the crystal she held in her hand started to draw everyone in the throne room towards it, sucking them into its very heart. Karchek screamed as he felt his very being pulled apart, atom by atom. The crystal shone brighter and brighter, until, like a sun at the end of its existence, it exploded, obliterating the throne room and the whole palace.

50

K oopler stared out of the tower, looking across the cityscape. Ships still circled the city like vultures over a dying calf. The sounds of battle still raged and the smell of burning rose through the night air. It was hard to see what was happening, but the defenders had been hideously outnumbered at the outset. The vaunted walls of Tannaheim had done little to protect one of the richest cities on Maingard.

"It's all gone to pot, Morga!"

"I know, there's nothing that we can do from up here. They aren't taking the walls, not when they have the city to plunder."

"We need to get down there."

"Down there?" Morga pointed down to the destruction. Even from one of the tallest points on the wall, they could still see the chaos milling in the streets and alleys.

"Way I see it, Morga, we can scoot, but where are we going to go? Once they finish here, they will find us. Or we go down there," he nodded towards the streets, "and see if we can make a difference."

"Just the two of us? Big difference!" The older soldier

protested but was picking his spear and shield up. He knew that the younger man had it right.

"Look at all those guard towers on the walls, Morga. There's over a hundred towers. That's a hundred Morgas and a hundred Kooplers sitting on our hairy arses. Over two hundred men, that can make a difference."

"I know. You've got a wise head on those young shoulders, my boy. Let's try and keep it on them though."

The entrance to the stair well was on the city side of the tower, but the stairs down were clear. Ten flights and two corridors later, they were ready to make their way out on to the streets.

"Where to?"

"I thought you had all the ideas, my boy." Morga rubbed the back of his neck just under the edge of his helmet. He pondered a bit longer. "Let's head to the barracks, we can cross Cluntarf Street, then follow Black Brook."

"Okay, that's a plan."

Koopler tentatively pushed the final door open, peering out. From what he could see, the street was clear of life. Debris and bodies were scattered about. He ushered Morga out and the pair ran across the street to the corner of Cluntarf street. This used to be a busy thoroughfare with food vendors running along the centre. The merchants on either side sold anything and everything. Now it was empty, quieter than a tomb.

They made good time, jogging from one area of cover to another, and soon came to where a bridge crossed a brook that ran through a gully. They stood for a minute, looking down into the gully. The brook was shallow, maybe never more than knee deep. It was, however, pitch black.

There was a clamour behind them, and they span to see a giant approaching them. As he walked slowly toward them, he clattered the shaft of his spear against his shield, the steel bands about the haft striking the boss of the round shield.

Morga and Koopler started. It wasn't just giant but also reptilian, standing on two feet but with a long tail for balance. Its short snout protruded from its helmet as it bared some vicious looking teeth.

Koopler gulped.

"What the fuck is that?"

"Tobe's Tits, Koopler. I have no idea." The pair split apart, leaving the lizardman no option but to approach one and leave the other one's attack undefended. Still the giant figure approached, the monotonous banging of the shield and spear starting to grate upon the Danarians' nerves.

Then, it stopped. It staggered forward before catching its balance, and then sank to one knee. It pushed out the haft of the spear to arrest its fall forward. A thin trickle of dark red blood appeared at the side of its mouth, and then it fell forward face down in the ground. Two arrows were protruding from his back. Koopler crouched behind his shield, his own spear pointing down the street.

"Who's there?"

A woman appeared out of the darkness, a bow in hand and wearing leather armour. She had dark hair and answered nervously.

"Friend! I've been tracking that one since the market on Lowergate."

"What is it?" Morga asked, prodding the dead lizard man with the point of his spear.

"I have no idea. But it's not the weirdest thing I have seen." The woman spoke. She thrust out her right hand. "I'm Mon, Mon Baxt."

"Morga. The snotty kid is Koopler. Thanks for your help there, I am not sure I fancied facing that thing hand to hand. We've been on the wall since they crossed, we felt we had to do something."

"That was my pleasure, I saw that thing kill two or three

times as I was following it. To be honest; the situation looks dire. It's chaos everywhere."

"Koopler says the Queen is at the palace by herself? No guards."

"That's crazy. I saw four of those cursed skyships heading for it earlier." She turned to point at the palace, just as the whole of the palace disintegrated in a cataclysmic explosion. The shock wave reverberated outwards, vaporizing over thirty skyships still in the air. Shards of wood rained down on the unsuspecting streets below and Morga and Koopler threw their shields up instinctively to cover themselves and Mon Baxt. The entire city fell silent apart from the echo of the vast explosion rebounding off the walls and buildings.

The three Danarians stared open mouthed at where the palace had dominated the city upon its mound. A dust cloud rose from the ruins, an eerie orange cloud glowing in the fires of the city.

"Bolam's balls!" Morga muttered

"See, I told you she was a witch." Koopler crowed.

51

M agus Vent, The Hawk, stood in the doorway of his town house, surveying the same sight that Morga and Koopler had just witnessed. His reaction was similar. Open mouthed, he stared at cloud rising from the palace ruins. Dumbfoundedly, he took several steps from the doorway and stumbled into the garden, fixated on the cloud. He was shaken from his stupor by someone viciously rattling the wrought iron gates that barred entry to his garden from the street.

"Hey!" He shouted. The man stopped and looked directly at him. He was bald, his pate shaved completely bare. His cheeks and chin, however, bristled with stubble. His tunic, once white, was stained with blood and mud, with rips and rents showing his mail underneath.

"I'm after a young girl, she ran this way. Have you seen her? She's scared and it's my job to guard her." As he realised that the Hawk wasn't moving to the gate to unlock it, he started to clamber over it. Magus Vent clasped his hand to the hilt of his sword and took a step forward. As the man jumped down into the garden, a small form bundled past The Hawk, shouting as it passed him.

"Gavan, you came! You found me!" Yanna flung herself at the newcomer, her arms wrapping around his thighs.

"You know her?" The Hawk asked, his sword still half drawn.

"Yanna? Yes, we know each other."

"Tomnar!" Magus drew his sword fully. "You're one of his as well?"

"Tikar Welk? Yes."

Yanna turned to face The Hawk, standing protectively in front of Gavan.

"Don't hurt him, Marshall. You have to believe us when we say Tikar only has the interests of the city at heart."

"Then why isn't he here, bleeding to protect it?"

"I told you, Marshall. He had to go somewhere and get the bad men!"

The newcomer turned and addressed the Marshall, his arm still on the shoulder of the young girl.

"Bolam's balls! Both of you listen. We haven't got time for this. You've seen what's happened to the palace. Right now, Marshall, you are needed on the streets – leading the men bleeding for this city. They need a figurehead and some of the generals need a kick up their lazy arses!"

"Tell me first, why I should believe an agent of a criminal?"

Gavan looked exasperated at the Hawk.

"Because that criminal is your fucking Prince, and now," he waved his hand at the cloud of dust and ash billowing into the night sky, "probably your King!"

"What?" Yanna jumped back in astonishment and stood next to the open-mouthed Hawk. "All this time, and he's been one of them?"

"What?" The Marshall echoed the young girl.

"I fought with him, years ago. I'm one of his Ghosts. Look, I'll explain on the way. I have some extra men waiting nearby." He sensed the Marshall's trepidation.

"Don't worry about your family, I'll send a couple of men back here to guard them. You stay here as well, Yanna. It's not safe out there." The young girl nodded.

"And when you get back, Gavan, you, me and Tikar need to talk."

Gavan was as good as his word. Twenty black clad soldiers were waiting nearby, and he dispatched two back to the Marshall's house. They moved through the city to one of the defender's strongpoints. Gavan noted with admiration that the older figure of Marshall Vent could keep up with the younger, fitter men.

As they moved, Gavan explained all to Marshall Vent. From Prince Garlen's return from the war, his despondency and unwillingness to take the throne. How he and his father had planned and created Tikar Welk, The Phantom – a shadowy figure to move through and control the underclasses and the city. Petty crime was overlooked in preference to removing the real scum from the streets of Tannaheim; the slavers, murderers, rapists and traitors. How the agents of the Phantom collected information within the city and the palace that wouldn't have been volunteered willingly to the authorities. All this whilst living a double life, Tikar Welk and the Lord of the Inns.

"Did his mother know?"

"I don't think so. She always seemed so disappointed by the stories of his exploits as the wayward Prince."

Ser Gavan led The Hawk and his men to the docks area, explaining the closest general was stationed there. On route, they faced a few skirmishes, the bowmen in their small force collected a deadly toll from the invaders. By the time they stepped onto the docks, their force had swollen to nearly treble the number, with city guard and militia joining them.

They found General Krebs in a warehouse, several officers with him and a few nervous, out of shape guards. The general pored over a table that had a crude map of the area etched on in chalk. Some of hastily drawn squares, which The Hawk and Ser Gavan took as buildings, had gold coins placed on them, others had copper pennies. Magus Vent noted that there were many more pennies than gold.

"What's the situation, general?" Magus asked as he strode in.

"Dire. We're the gold, if you were wondering."

"I guessed."

"I take it, surrender is out of the question?"

"You heard the queen before they came. We either die in their slave pens or we die on the point of their swords. There is no surrender. I am not going to allow every sacrifice already made to have been in vain. Danaria and Tannaheim belong to us, and this is where we take it back!"

There were nods of agreement from round the table.

"What are your thoughts, Ser Gavan?"

The red faced general looked at the mean looking soldier as Gavan glanced over the map. He thought better of questioning why the Marshall was asking advice from a common soldier.

"What's the situation with the sewers? Do we know if they are using them?"

The officers around the table shrugged. Gavan muttered under his breath and then motioned to two of his men.

"Check them out, if they haven't thought about them then this is the plan. General, mass some of your men as a diversion against this building here, keep them interested. The Cassalians don't know that my men are here yet, so they will think that is the majority of your forces. I'll lead a party through the sewers and attack this building from within instead. The rest of the Ghosts will attack it from the front after we start from the inside. Taking this building will secure the flank against the docks. Then we move on. Building by building, street by street."

The battle for Tannaheim carried on.

B ryn Kar still half carried, half walked Bex, with Iga and
Janis next to him, the remaining Ghosts and the Flyer
loosely surrounded them, apart from the five men that
Radnak had taken to find Mori and Garlen, and any other
survivors.

Out of the fog loomed a massive stone façade of a magnifi-
cent building. It stopped them all in their tracks, despite the
urgency and danger of their flight. Centre to the façade was a
pillared entrance reached by a low set of steps. The building
stretched to each side, with squat, square wings arching slightly
to the front. The centre was three stories high, the sides two.
Lights flickered in many of the windows, each framed by ornate
carved mouldings.

"What is this place?" Iga asked as they mounted the steps.

"I have no idea. It looks like nothing I have seen before."
Bryn answered.

At the top of the steps set back under a glass panelled roof
held up by four large pillars, was an imposing pair of doors.
Wide enough for a carriage to enter and taller than two men,
the door was solid oak with gold fittings. On either side of the

door was a large statue, two huge stone carvings of armoured men, carrying an oval shield and a large axe each. Whereas the stone used to build the house was a whitish limestone, the statues were a dark, almost black, coloured stone.

Two of the Ghosts approached the door. Bex lent against one of the pillars, thankful for Bryn's help. The transformations always left her fatigued. Ingren stood on the steps, looking back out to the fog, hoping that Mori would appear, being carried by her brother.

A grating sound rent the cold still air, the sound of stone upon stone. The two Ghosts who had gone to the door leapt back as the two statues slowly stepped forward. They raised their huge axes and took a step closer to each other, as if to form a shield wall and block the door.

"Leave!" one of the giants spoke, it's voice hoarse and gravelly.

The Ghosts, despite being without both Garlen and Mathor, were still professional, well trained soldiers. They formed their own shield wall quickly, a row of a dozen or so with shields, with the archers behind. Bryn drew both his sword and readied his axe. A volley of arrows was loosed against the stone men, with predictable results. One of the giants swiped with his axe causing the Ghosts to dive aside. Ingren turned around and, seeing the giants for the first time, shouted.

The giants readied themselves for another attack, but the door opened a crack and a small figure ran out. It was a small boy, perhaps seven or eight years old. He waved his hands as he came to a stop between the two stone guardians.

"Stop! Stop! Garagg and Magarag, stop!" The stone men stood silent then looked down at him. The took a step back but kept their axes raised. The boy turned and faced the Ghosts as many of them were picking themselves up.

"Tarja, is that you?" He took a step forward, the Ghosts

melting away before him, moving to each side. They realised that small and young as he was, he could still be a threat, however, they were human enough not to threaten a young child with weapon raised.

"Tarja, I've missed you!" He ran forward, crossing the few yards in between him and Ingren in a second. He threw himself at the surprised teen, wrapping his arms around you.

"Where have you been, all this time?" He said again, his face beaming with delight. He paused for a second and took a step back, the delight on his face turning to puzzlement.

"You're not Tarja!"

Ingren knelt in front of him, her arms outstretched to him. Her voice shook as she flitted her gaze from the mousy-brown haired boy to the stone guardians who still stood silent.

"No, you are right. I am not Tarja. But I am a friend, and we would be really glad if you can help us."

Tears welled up in the young boy's eyes.

"But I thought you were my sister. I have waited so long."

"Would you believe me when I say I'm a princess?"

"You don't look like a princess." Said the boy suspiciously.

Ingren laughed, looking down at her dirty boyish clothes.

"No, I don't think I do, do I? But I am, I am Ingren, Princess Ingren."

"I'm Orme. Just Orme."

"Is there anyone else here?" Ingren asked, as Iga came to her side and took a knee next to her.

"No, it's just me. Everyone else has gone." He reached up and took Ingren's hands in his.

"You are here alone?" Iga asked, an incredulous tone in her voice. He nodded, taking in the sight of the beautiful green woman for the first time.

"Well," Ingren said. "My sister is missing out in the fog as well, so I know how worried and scared you are. Can you hold my hand and help me be brave whilst we wait for her?"

He nodded again, a bright smile appearing on his little face.
"That's great. Can we come in? We promise not to hurt you or break anything."

He nodded and Ingren stood. They walked past the Ghosts and in between the stone men.

"Garag, Magarag, let them in and look out for their friends." He looked up at the taller girl, "they help protect the house. They are my friends as well."

The guardians nodded and stood up, returning to the silent, still pose that they had been in when the Ghosts had appeared at the house. Nervously, the Ghosts put their weapons up and followed them in.

53

G arlen ran with Mori in his arms. He heard someone shout about heading for the light, but he hadn't seen anyone for several minutes. Occasionally there had been a big, black shape flash past and once or twice he had cut quickly to change direction.

Mori whimpered as he ran, he had her face pressed into the hardness of his leather clad breast to muffle the sound as much as he could. He daren't call out to any of the Ghosts as he didn't want to alert the enemy to his location. The ground became rougher under his feet and he found himself stumbling frequently. He decided to slow down a little, judging caution the better part of valour.

A pounding of hooves came to his ears and he looked over his shoulder, catching sight of the horseman emerging from the fog. The rider was more surprised to see him than Garlen was, and he tried to raise his blade to swing at the runner as he passed. Garlen flung himself to one side, gauging when to do so perfectly. He cushioned Mori from the fall and rolled to his feet. He let her slide down him until she sat on the ground next to him. He drew his sword and waited for the rider to turn again.

He didn't have to wait long, the black form looming ahead of him. The rider had put his horse into a gallop, charging forward with his sword raised. As he crossed Garlen again, he slashed down hard, only for the prince to block with a raised sword. He instinctively slashed out and caught the horse's rear legs. There was a strange, inhuman sound and he had the satisfaction to see the black horse cartwheel. The rider didn't manage to throw himself off, his feet caught in the stirrups. Garlen ran to where the horse lay, whimpering and thrashing its head. The rider coughed, a trickle of blood seeping from his mouth. He still stretched out with his hand, trying to feel for the hilt of the blade that was looped to his wrist. He looked up frantically, terror in his eyes as the struggled to find the hilt. Garlen stabbed down twice, putting the rider and horse out of their misery.

He returned to Mori and bent down to pick her up. She was muttering as he reached down to her.

"It's Garlen, Mori. I'm going to pick you up. We have to get going again." He whispered. He placed his hands under her armpits and lifted her up. He could feel her heartbeat accelerate. As he clasped her to his chest again, he could feel her start to shake.

"Bolam's balls! Not again!" He looked about, not sure what direction to go in at first, but made his mind up and started to jog. His own heart pounded, almost as much as his young sister's. How could he have come this far and be in this position. He hadn't failed at anything in his life yet, having plucked his sisters from the enemy stronghold in a daring, almost suicidal mission, he now faced losing one and not knowing where the other was.

His feet squelched into wet ground, the mud and grass turning to marsh. He stopped, absolutely terrified for perhaps the first time in years. Mori shook harder, her arms and torso completely rigid, she threw back her head and let out a long, tortured moan. The fog closed in around him and he suddenly felt alone. He called out, throwing caution to the wind.

"Gordin! Bex!"

He spun round and realised he had lost his sense of direction.

"Iga! Bryn Kar!"

Figures manifested themselves on the edge of the fog, calling out to him as they loomed in and out of his perception. Mathor was there, his bald head dripping with perspiration as he swung his heavy sword. Mathor's ghost dissipated as fast as it had appeared. His father was next, hands raised to his face and clutching his throat. And then, the most terrifying of all, was his sister. He knew in his heart that it wasn't real, he was holding her clutched to his chest as it was. But Mori stepped from the fog, blood pouring from her wounded face. The ghost stopped still and turned her face to look at him accusingly. As she started to fade away, she raised her hand to point at him. Finally, his twin, Antht stepped forward on her horse. It was her favourite horse, the big grey that she had been riding when it had thrown her, killing her all those years ago. She still appeared beautiful, her red hair reminding him of his mother. She stopped, and as the horse reared on its hind legs, she lifted her hand to him, holding it out for him to take.

"Come to me." The apparition said and then faded from sight.

"Nooooo!" He screamed once more, oblivious to the black shape that charged him from the side. The final horseman barrelled into him, the horse striking him with its chest as Garlen appeared suddenly in its path. He flew through the air, his arms flailing and failing his sister as she was catapulted from his grasp. He crashed to the ground and everything went black.

54

Orme led them through the door into a huge entrance hall, that was wider than it was long. At each end, there was a great marble staircase that swept up and around to join together on a landing that overlooked the entrance. Straight ahead was an open archway that led into a fantastic garden.

"Is that real?" Ingren asked, her mouth agape.

"Yes, come and see." Orme skipped off, pulling her with him. The Ghosts were more interested in throwing themselves down to take a rest before starting to check their weapons and armour. The several that were wounded received help from their comrades tending to the wounds. Iga and her boys followed and were amazed to see what they had thought to be a courtyard, was in fact, a massive orangery. Tall trees, pines and oaks soared to the ceiling which was made of glass panels reaching to form an octagon in the centre. Imposing statues and fountains were arranged either as focal points along a meandering path, or slightly hidden by the vibrant vegetation.

"This is so beautiful." Exclaimed Ingren, momentarily forgetting the plight of her sister and brother.

"Amazing!" Iga echoed the sentiment.

"Yes, it is," shouted Orme, leading them to a fountain in the shape of a majestic horse with a solitary horn protruding from the centre of its face. "It's really good to show someone else how special *House Beautiful* is. That's what I call this place."

"It is certainly an apt name," replied Ingren, as she splashed her face with the water from the fountain.

"And you live here alone, Orme?" questioned Iga, as Janis and Igant gained the confidence to move from her side and wander through the gardens.

"Yes, it has been such a long time now. I can't remember when the Master left. I am sure he will be back soon."

"How old are you?" Iga carried on her line of questioning. It was evident to Ingren that the noble woman felt that the whole situation was amiss.

"I'm only seven," he replied, then continued, "and this is the best time of the day to play! Can we play hide and seek, please?" He grabbed Ingren's hand and swung it backwards and forwards.

"Only for a bit, it has been a tiring day, Orme. And I hope my sister is back soon."

The four children ran off, but not before Iga gave affirmation to the two boys that they could go. Iga returned to the entrance hall and spoke with Bex and Bryn, voicing her concerns.

"This disturbs me somewhat. The House and the boy. Something is very strange about this place."

"I do agree," Bryn Kar acknowledged. "There have been times when we have entered the Hinterlands, tracking war parties or chasing down bandits. I have never come across any report of a house like this in this area."

"But it is a big area, Bryn. Could it have been missed?" countered Bex.

"I very much doubt it, on a clear day, this house would be

obvious for miles."

Before they could explore the situation further, Radnak appeared. He was carrying the body of a Ghost over his shoulder, the face hidden behind him. Bex's heart skipped a beat.

'That's not the prince, is it?' Ishtara was also in shock. Before Bex could answer her, Radnak carefully laid him down, showing that it wasn't Garlen, but Gordin. He was also breathing shallowly, and Radnak beckoned Iga over.

"He is cut deeply, through his arm. It looks very serious." The tall goblin woman knelt down to assess the wound, before calling for one of the Ghosts to collect her satchel of herbs and dressings.

"What of the Prince, or Moren?" Bryn asked, beating Bex to the question. Radnak slowly shook his head, unable to look either of them in the eye.

"I couldn't see anyone else. The fog is starting to come down even heavier now. We can only look in the morning, when it clears." All three looked at each other with the same words on the tip of their tongue, but that no one wanted to say. That is, except for Ishtara.

'If it clears.'

"I should go and tell Ingren." Radnak said, standing forlornly. Bex placed her hand on his arm and shook her head.

"I'll go, Radnak. You rest up by the fires. Thank you for looking."

"She looks tired, Radnak." Bryn whispered as the tall thief walked away, her shoulders as if she had the weight of Maingard on them. The half-orc turned and looked at the retreating Samakan.

"Aye. That she does. It can't be easy with Ishtara inside as well."

Bryn Kar nodded slowly.

"We all have our demons within, Radnak. It's how we live with them that defines us.

55

The battle for Tannaheim raged on. Marshall Vent only had admiration for the mysterious Gavan and his black clad soldiers. Gavan's acumen for strategy and tactics was second to none and outshone many of the generals that had been tasked with handling the defence of the city. His companions followed orders precisely and bravely, and were quick to encourage the regular soldiers and the militia when it was needed.

They seemed blessed by Tobes and Kani, as whilst they were always present where the action was thickest, they avoided casualties.

They worked tirelessly, driving on the other defenders to feats that didn't seem possible. Their effect on the morale of the ordinary rank and file seemed to be the equivalent of several regiments of cavalry. To the largely untrained militia, relying on gambesons for armour and second-rate weapons, they appeared to be the very incarnation of Kani.

Time and time again, they isolated blocks of invaders, surrounding them in the buildings they had taken cover in, and then proceeded to eliminate them.

It came to a point that some of the client forces within the Cassalian army surrendered in small pockets. This was only when any true Cassalian fighting with them had been dispatched. This drove the defenders on, knowing that it was sometimes possible to overrun a small force of the invaders if they focused on the Cassalian officers first. However, when it came to the 'beasts' of the enemy, the men that were once men, they were put down viciously.

The force of defenders that stood side by side with Gavan and his Ghosts soon grew and grew, numbering hundreds. He took a chance and divided his forces, as the sheer numbers were starting to affect his manoeuvrability. One battalion anchored their right flank upon the shattered remains of the palace, the ruins of the wall and the great cleft that separated Gruenwild's Rock from the city, forming a natural barrier. Gavan's troops were formed up to the left flank, and the two forces moved in unison, careful not to let any invaders outflank them. He also formed reserve platoons, sitting just behind each formation, ready to plunge forward and plug any gaps that were created.

The end of Gavan's line arrived at the barracks just outside Black Brook at the same time as Koopler, Morga and Mon. The barracks consisted of a square building with a tower at each corner. The walls protected an inner courtyard along with ancillary buildings and stables. Mon and the two guards fell into line with the approaching troops as Gavan called to the soldier at the gates to open them.

"Who are you?" The guard called back. The Hawk stepped forward, his figure and visage well known throughout the palace and city guards.

"You know me. Do as my captain says and open up."

Gavan looked sideways at the Hawk and smiled.

"Promotion, eh? Does that make it my round back at the mess?"

"When this is over, Gavan, I'm handing you the keys to my wine cellar. You and your men have earnt it."

The wooden gates cracked open with an almighty squealing and the platoon that Gavan commanded moved in. The thirty men flooded into the courtyard, as a middle-aged general strode out of the barracks, his adjutant struggling to keep up.

"General, what's the current situation here?" Gavan started, as he had done with every officer he had met. The General ignored his question.

"What is the meaning of this?"

"I asked..." Gavan was interrupted as the general saw Magus Vent walking with Mon.

"Marshall Vent? I thought Sarsi had you pensioned off."

"General Farn, circumstances dictate that I am needed here. My Queen only removed me from the position at the palace."

"And that did her a world of good, didn't it? Now the bitch is dead, I take it you have come to negotiate a surrender with the invaders."

Gavan's fist crashed forward, striking the general in the face. Several of his officers, stepped up, swords half drawn and indignant at the afront dealt to their commander.

The Hawk spoke, in the tone that every guardsman in the city knew all too well.

"My Captain asked you a question. He needs an answer."

"He nearly broke my nose!" Farn coughed and spluttered.

"Do not speak of your Queen like that again!" Gavan growled, glaring at the general.

The adjutant jumped forward, snapping to attention and raising his fist in salute.

"We have 41 men present, Captain. All regulars though 14 are injured to some extent. We have enemy forces across Caleb Street in the coach house and the houses nearby."

"Do you know how many?"

The adjutant shrugged apologetically.

"Marshall! I urge you to arrest this barbarian!" General Farn protested to Marshall Vent, still holding his nose.

"You do not know when to cease, General. Please shut up!" The Hawk retorted.

"He does not deserve the rank of Captain, Marshall!" It was obvious that the General didn't know when to cease.

"Have you taken the fight to the enemy, General? I don't see any evidence of it, and if that is the case then I don't see that you deserve your rank."

The general was flustered at being addressed in this manner by someone of a lower rank. Gavan gave him no quarter.

"Your Queen has paid the ultimate sacrifice in order to protect and defend this city, and I expect every man, woman and child in this city to do the same. This group of men with me now, has fought house by house, street by street from the docks. All the way here to save your sorry arse. So, I think it is time to see what you have available to sacrifice."

He turned to the adjutant and addressed him, whilst the General went redder and redder.

"Get prepared to assault the coach house opposite, some of my men will accompany you. Your General will take the lead. If you would be so kind as to lend him a sword, he seems to have lost his."

It was at that moment that a great cheer went up from some of the men on the walls and also from the streets to either side. The men on the barrack's ramparts pointed to the sky and cheered again.

"They're going! We've fucking won!" One of the guardsmen called down.

The Hawk looked up and saw one of the skyships rise up over the city and slowly turn to face Jacarna, before moving off. He could see more men pointing and hollering in different directions as more and more ships took to the skies.

"Well, General. This must be your lucky day!"

General Farn looked relieved. He had not relished the thought of combat, and now that the Cassalians were leaving, realised he was safe again.

"Yes, your lucky day indeed, now you get to lead the victory charge against the enemy. Who knows, you might even take the Cassalian surrender." Gavan hefted his sword, calling for his men to ready themselves for more fighting.

The experienced soldier knew that the battle wasn't over and that there were still plenty of enemy in the city. It wasn't the end of the fighting, but it was the beginning of the end. Tannaheim still stood, battered but proud, and the Cassalians were in disarray. He knew that the battle for Tannaheim was drawing to a close, but the battle for Maingard was yet to come.

56

Jerone Witchguardian awoke. The boat was still and apart from the odd cough, the prison below decks was quiet. He could hear talking outside; and this time, it wan't Risas-Tu talking to his quiet boatman. Jerone could hear the response the other man gave. The voice had a heavy accent but with Jerone's limited knowledge of the outside world, it's owner could have been from anywhere.

This was it. They had reached the end of the route and his journey with Risas-Tu was over. Another would begin with someone else, if he didn't act whenever he had a chance. He looked at his neighbour. The travel and confinement had not been kind to him. He looked older and more haggard than when Jerone had been taken captive, a matter of days ago. The cover above was pulled back and the familiar grin of Risas-tu looked down. He seemed a little happier this morning. Jerone turned his head slightly and smiled. He wouldn't be that happy soon.

The slaver swung down over the edge of the large hatchway and started to descend the narrow steps. Soon the big booted feet of Risas-tu splashed down into the bilge. As he moved along the line, he kicked out to rouse his captives. Groans and moans escaped the normally mute mouths of the prisoners and the red-bearded giant chuckled.

"Change of plan. Your new owners are here. Someone had made me an offer I can't refuse!"

He took a large key from his belt pouch and unlocked the padlock holding the long chains in place. Turning to the huddling captives, he shouted loudly.

"Up! Up ye lazy bastards!" To empathize the point, he grabbed the nearest slave, hauling the skinny man to his feet. More groans and wails entailed as they pulled themselves to their feet. Jerone realised now that they were confined by one long chain and not one per row. Risas-tu pushed the far end forward, directing the end slave to the steps. Jerone, at the other end of the chain, would be last to climb out of the hulk.

It was a slow process. Many of the slaves didn't have the strength to stand but Risas-tu treated them no differently, pushing and hitting as they passed him.

Finally, Jerone's neighbour in chains started to stagger up the stairs. The big slaver turned his gaze from the young man for a second and Jerone's hand slowly strayed towards his boot. Then a voice in his head told him to stay his hand. He hesitated and the moment was gone. Risas-tu turned and grabbed his arm, shoving him up the stairway.

As his head broke the parapet of the hold, he blinked as the morning sun stabbed his eyes. He raised his hands to shield them as he stepped out onto the deck for the first time in several days. He swallowed fresh air, glad to be away from the stench and he thanked Herne, the Forest God that he had only been confined in that black hole for a few days and not as long as his companions had.

The chain of slaves was disembarking from the barge, negotiating a gangplank taking them to shore. A warrior in black armour stood at the top of the plank, ushering them past. Jerone surveyed the scene, slighting seething inside at having missed the opportunity to attack Risas-tu. What he saw made him glad he hadn't.

The shoreline was devoid of vegetation, an immense expanse of mud. A number of other craft were docked at the shoreline and several tents had been erected upon the bank. About a dozen short queues of people were dotted about the mud, all chained together with another black garbed soldier guarding each one. It wasn't the fact that several of these weren't exactly human that made Jerone gasp.

It was the two giant ships that wallowed in the mud, a good hundred yards from the shoreline. The bow of each were carved and shaped like a dragon's head. Massive jaws strutted forward, ready to pounce on prey. Two short, stubby masts sat upright from each ship's back. Jerone had seen one of these before, flying over the forest. He realised at that point that Janda had been right. It hadn't been a real dragon but one of these ships. The thought of his old mentor and protector stopped his breath for a second.

A shove in his back propelled him forward, causing him to stumble into the slave in front. Luckily, he had reached the lower part of the ramp and fell onto the muddy shore.

Several of the slaves started wailing, terrified by the ships ahead and the number of soldiers milling about. A blue-skinned guard slapped several of them in the face, causing them to quieten. Risas-tu stepped past Jerone and the forest man was annoyed to see the slaver holding the warhammer that had once been his.

A giant of a man stepped out of one of the tents and approached Risas-tu. He stood a full head taller than Jerone and his skin was deathly pale. His dull, steel breastplate had a crude skull etched upon it. Two short swords were in scabbards at his belt, and hanging next to one was a bleached skull, a bolt driven through the top with a leather thong attaching it to the belt above. He grinned at the slaver and held out a bag of coins.

"A good haul. We will be here for another twelve days. You can earn the same again with more." He indicated the line of slaves. In the other groups, Jerone could see the guards separating the slaves from each other and driving them towards a single line embarking on one of the grounded ships.

"That I will do. You have given a better price than what would await me in Jacarna."

The grim armoured warrior laughed.

"We have no need of this coin. It is of no consequence to us."

Risas-tu bounced the bag of coins in his hand and then lashed it to his belt. He turned to head back to his barge and saw Jerone glaring at him.

Jerone spat at his feet, and the red-bearded brute snarled at the chained man, stepping up into his face. Jerone could feel the spittle splash him as Risas-tu spat obscenities at him.

Jerone smiled, then like a snake pouncing on prey, he smashed his head forward, his forehead connecting with the slightly taller man's nose. Risas-tu staggered back, his hand held towards his nose catching the blood that erupted from it. He looked wide-eyed and shocked, but only momentarily. He dropped the warhammer to the ground and drew his broad-bladed sword in one motion. Jerone stood his ground, hands clenched tight in front of him as the slaver raised his sword.

"Stop!" the grey-skinned warrior commanded, his voice cutting the brisk morning air. He motioned to one of his own men, who stepped forward and unlocked Jerone's chains.

"What the fuck are you doing?" Risas-tu demanded.

"You have your coins, that makes him mine. If you want to

harm my property, then at least you can do so in a fair fight and give us a little sport and spectacle." There was now some interest in the proceedings from the soldiers who sat by the tents, warming themselves by the fires. Soon Risas-tu and Jerone were surrounded by a loose circle of men. Some of the slaves looked on, other looked away, betraying what they thought of the young man's chances. The soldier who had unlocked Jerone's chains stood back, drawing his own short sword and threw it down to the ground, so the point dug into the soft mud.

"I should have gutted you in that hold," snarled Risas-tu as he circled menacingly. The sun glinted of his sword blade and the silver rings in his ears.

"Aye, you should have." Jerone hefted the sword, feeling its weight. He hadn't had much experience with a sword before and knew he had to learn quick.

The soldiers around bayed loudly, glad for some entertainment, no matter how long it would last.

Risas-tu swung hard and Jerone could do little except dance out of the way. He bounced on his feet as his slaver circled him slowly. Risas-tu swung again, a heavy blow coming down towards Jerone's head. He threw his own sword arm up and winced with shock as steel hit steel. The sword was nearly jarred from his hand. The next few heart beats were more of the same. The red bearded slaver throwing huge blows at the younger lad, who danced and dodged out of range. When Jerone managed to get an attack in, it was weak and easily parried.

His speed and litheness were a near balance to the immense strength of the bare-chested giant. It wasn't long though, before Jerone's luck wore out. Risas-tu connected twice, Jerone barely raising the sword in time to block each blow. The third strike knocked the sword from his hand and dropped him to his knee.

"Now I'm going to gut ye, you tree-hugging shit!" He swung the big sword back to bring it down upon the hapless youth.

Jerone darted forward, his left forearm rising to meet the sword arm of the slaver. He grunted as the muscle of Risas-tu's forearm met his, nearly snapping his bone. His right hand had slipped to his boot and drew the short blade.

Too late, Risas-tu saw Jerone's hand stab upwards. There was nothing he could do to avoid it as he was already committed. Jerone drove the knife upwards, through the beard and into the softness under Risas-tu's jaw and then on into the slaver's brain. He dropped immediately to his knees, his eyes glazing over.

Jerone pulled the knife out and wiped it on the dead slaver's carmine trousers. The guard stepped forward, but the forest man held one hand out to stop him. He raised the blade to his cheek and in a deliberate motion, pierced the skin and drew the tip towards his ear. He bent down over the body and cut his small satchel from the dead man's belt, then dropped the knife.

The grey skinned commander snatched the leather purse from his hand and opened it. He pulled out the gold necklace with the gold and silver locket and held it up to glint in the sun. Satisfied there was nothing else of help or that could be used as a weapon, he dropped the chain back in and threw the purse back to Jerone. The youth strapped it to his belt and was then grabbed by one of the guards and manacled again, this time separately from his one-time companions. He held his head high as he was led past them, blood streaming from the cut on his cheek.

The guard led him towards the ship where he joined the end of the line of the slaves embarking. They were led up a wide ramp set at the rear of the ship, through a hatchway that was set a quarter way up the hull.

The guards standing near them wore leather masks that hid the lower half of their face. When Jerone got to the top of the ramp, he realised why. The stench from within turned his stomach. It was far worse than the hulk of the barge. It was a smell of fear, death and despair that washed over the slaves as they were forced on board. The slough of depression that flowed from with the darkness made it difficult for him to place one foot in front of the other.

The interior was dark, and he could make out cages down each side of the ship. At least, he thought, he wouldn't be chained up again. From the flickering light of the torches that struggled to light the hull, he could make out the pathetic figures confined within. They sat on their haunches or stood stock still. Their faces were gaunt, and their eyes were lifeless as if they were already dead. The smell of urine and excrement was everywhere, but the stench of death and despair seemed to overpower it.

A cage was opened, and he was pushed in, along with half a dozen others. The denizens of the cages didn't even seem to notice the new arrivals. He felt others being pushed in behind and, when the original occupants didn't move, he pushed through them as best he could. He could sense a clear space towards the back of the cage, where it became the hull wall of the ship. He made his way through to it and stopped. A young child was sitting with their back to the hull. It was dirty and dishevelled, and its wayward hair was muddy and stuck up in different directions. Its hands picked at several patches on their wet clothes, and then it looked up at him.

He noticed that it was a young girl, perhaps aged ten or eleven, dressed in what was once, fine clothing. Her dark hair framed her face that was covered in grime. As the young girl raised her face to him, he realised that she was terribly disfigured, her face scarred and her eyes missing. Having never been to Tannaheim, he obviously never recognized the youngest daughter of King Anjoan Barstt. But when Princess Moren spoke, although the voice was different, he recognised her at once.

"Come here, boy. I have been expecting you, Jerone Witch-guardian. Now you have found Janda once more, we have work to do."

EPILOGUE

Within the House Beautiful, Bex holds the young princess and tries to console the sobbing child. Ishtara alternates between sobbing herself and seething at the crimes and destruction that have been levied on this world and on her own. As Ingren drifts into an uneasy sleep, the tall Samakan woman disentangles herself from the teen and slowly creeps from the room. In the corridor beyond, she rests her hand on the arm of Bryn Kar and her heart skips a beat. Inside her mind, Ishtara smiles for the first time in ages.

ON THE FLOOR BELOW, the noblewoman Iga stands at the side of Radnak, as the pair stare at her two children as they sleep.

"I should return to Moond." The half orc breaks the silence. Iga nods, knowing he is right but also knowing him so well and what he will say next.

"Igant should accompany me."

. . .

BACK IN TANNAHEIM, Mon Baxt sits exhausted, with her back against what had once been the wall of a warehouse. The city is still alive to the sounds of battle – the clash of steel rings out between the groans of injured and terrified people. She is almost too tired to smile as the young soldier, Koopler, hands her a flagon of hot ale.

A young boy darts past, pausing only to leave a pile of arrows at her feet as he spies the bow laid across her lap. She groans as the call to arms rises once more and she readies herself for more combat.

DEEP within the cellar of the Hawk's house, his family sit quietly as a lantern struggles bravely against the dark. The young urchin, Yanna, sits apart from the rest, wide-eyed and frightened, feeling alone; a stranger in a strange land. Magus Vent's granddaughter who, despite being of similar age to Yanna, looks naïve and innocent in comparison, stands and makes her way to Yanna's side. She carries a doll under one arm and a small cake in her other hand. Sitting herself down next to Yanna, she offers both to the young girl, bridging the gap between rich and poor.

JERONE WITCHGUARDIAN SITS with his back against the hull of the casallian ship. He stares warily at the other denizens of the cage, snarling every now and again to warn them away from the young girl he sits next to. His mind is a mix of emotions. Releif at finding Janda but also determination not to lose her again.

FINALLY, the soldier comes to on the plains of the Borderlands, his head groggy A dull ache permeated his chest making his breath laboured. His armour was soaked, not surprisingly as he was laying for the most part, in a marsh. That much, he knew. What he didn't know was almost everything else.

He had no idea where he was or how he had got there. Why he hurt, wasn't clear either, but hurt he was. He gingerly raised his hand to his temple to find it wet with blood.

He looked about him, the day was chilly, the leather jerkin that sat over his white shirt did little to block the cold out. In every direction, the countryside stretched for miles. The marsh surrounded him, clumps of vegetation and mounds of grass sat protruding from the wetlands.

He paused once more, his mind working hard to answer the questions he had asked himself already. All the puzzles were unanswered and were also dwarfed by the major question he now asked himself.

"Who am I?"

He raised his hand and ran it through his blond hair. Unsure of everything and anything, he started to walk.

UNTITLED

Maingard Chronicles Book 3

Book 3 of the series is nearing completion and is not far away!
Here is part of the first chapter to whet your appetite.

CHAPTER 1

Marshall Magus Vent stood on the seawall staring out to the horizon, watching the approach of the fleet. This wall, along with its twin, stretched from either edge of the city to almost meeting in the middle, a warm and welcome embrace for any seaman on a cold and stormy night. He stood a few feet away from one of the vaunted Twins of Tannaheim, towers that stood at the end of each arm of the seawall, each housing a beacon to aid in navigation. He shivered as he looked across at the ruins of the second tower on the other wall, a visible reminder of the assault by the Cassalian forces.

In the distance, the red sails on the galleys were unfurled, aiding the rowers as the north-westerly wind heralded the onset of winter. The Marshall was well aware that the oncoming bleakness of winter brought more problems and issues to his city. The storms that usually lashed the coast of Danaria would only bring about more death and hardship to those that huddled at night within the fabled walls of the strongest city on Maingard.

He was about to correct himself to 'what used to be the strongest city' but then remembered the route from his townhouse to his where he now stood on the sea wall. For centuries, the high walls and towers of Tannaheim had proven not only stoic in the defence of the realm, but also foremost in the growth of Danaria as a major kingdom on Maingard. But less than a week ago, those same fabled walls had been breached by an enemy the like of which had never been seen before. Magical ships that navigated the skies as easily as if they had been on the calm waters of an inland lake, had crossed those walls. Some had pummeled the defences of Danaria from the air, with weapons powered by sorcery, others had landed within the confines of the city and had spewed forth a multitude of troops, all intent on the destruction of his beloved city. It had not been the walls that had saved them and repelled the invaders but the people themselves. It was the Gavans, the Mon Baxts and the Yannas of the city that had proven stronger than any wall, along with countless more.

The same people of his city that he had seen this morning. The survivors clearing the roads of debris and building shelters and barricades, more still dressing the wounds of the injured. The hastily raised militia now drilling in the concourses of the city under the watchful eyes of Gavan and his Ghosts. Smiths and fletchers labouring away, stockpiling weapons of war, whilst the young children of the city darted this way and that, lost in their make-believe world of play. All he saw heartened him in the knowledge that the spirit of Danaria would live on, long after the walls of Tannaheim came tumbling down.

A memory though, broke his reverie. The ghosts of his King and Queen seemed to catch the corner of his eye. He shuddered as he remembered the tall, warlike figure of King Anjoan cruelly murdered by the traitorous Eglebon Dutte, his corpse raised again by the dark powers of his wife, Queen Sarsi. As he turned, the wraith like figure of Sarsi stood next to the ghostly king. Sarsi's sacrifice had been the turning point, her dark power channelled to a shattering explosion that had devastated a major part of the enemy fleet, including the warlord General Karchek. He turned, the figures disappearing as easily as the had appeared, and he watched the oncoming fleet. The red sails were bigger now and he could count them. Ten sails, ten ships. He was glad that Sarsi had dispatched the fast ship to call for her brother's immediate return. The combined squadrons of Visney and Shales; in addition to the crews and the rowers of the great galleys were another 600 marines who would be greatly needed if another attack came from the Cassalians. And deep in Magus Vent's gut, he had a feeling that a second assault would be coming soon.

At the current speed, the galleys should be docked within the hour. That meant sixty minutes of peace before the shit-show started. Lord Shales, commander of the Third Squadron, was also the Queen's brother. A wild bull, too unpredictable to keep at court, Anjoan had despised his brother-in-law, afraid of him upsetting court with any of his machinations. To keep him in check, and to reduce his reputation at court, the King had dispatched him to every trouble spot the Kingdom encoun-tered. There at least, Shales's skills could be put to good use, aiding Anjoan and the throne. Perversely, this increased Shales's standing amongst the nobles more than if he was in court in person.

"Bolam's Balls!" he swore and spat on the ground in front of him at the mere thought of the returning Lord. If it had been just Visney returning, or any other Lord for that matter, they would have transferred their command to the fast ship to return quickly. That wasn't for Shales though. No, the arrogant bastard would keep everyone waiting and return at the bow of his flagship, like the saviour of the city. The pompous arse!

"Marshall?" His equerry asked and he realised that he had spoken aloud.

"Nothing, Sumtor. Just a thought, nothing more." Sumtor had been the adjutant to General Farn during the Battle of

Tannaheim, and now had been transferred to the Marshall's staff. The General had fallen in a glorious charge against the enemy that night, or rather he had been forced out of his fortified position by The Hawk's uncompromising captain, Gavan. Placed in the vanguard of a charge, Farn had at least died the way a soldier and a general should, sword in hand and engaging the enemy. Sumtor shuddered as he remembered the grim visage of Gavan, and the rumours that he had personally executed several commanders who had refused to take the fight to the invaders.

"Come, let us return to dry land properly and gather our thoughts before the Queens brother arrives." With that, Magus Vent, known to many in the city as the Hawk due to his raptor like nose and piercing eyes, turned and marched back towards the docks. As the pair left the sea wall, they passed sailors and craftsmen alike, swarming over the ships that lay at rest in the harbour. Many of them were badly damaged, and the ant-like hordes that covered them were either repairing those that could be repaired or stripping good wood and parts from others. The Hawk frowned grimly as he passed, aware that there were more ships that were beyond repair than not. He would be meeting with Duncarn, the Admiral of the navy later that day for a progress report.

A rider on a black horse appeared from one of the many warehouse streets that led to the dockside, and as she spied the pair, she urged the black mare into a slow trot and angled their way. It wasn't just Vent's appearance that leant to his soubriquet, his eyes picked out the details necessary to recognise the short figure of Mon Baxt, despite the hood of her cloak covering most of her face. Mon had been, or still was, the landlord of the Black Dragon Inn but in a previous life had had her fair share of adventure and glory in the wilds of Maingard. With the gold she had earnt as a sword for hire, or in the plunder of long-lost ruins, she had managed to retire and buy the Inn, known throughout the city as Ol' One Eye, on account of the carved dragon over the doorway having lost one of its jeweled eyes.

The black-haired woman reined the small plains pony in a few yards away from the Marshall and Sumtor. She pushed the hood away from her head to reveal dark hair and the striking features that could have passed for one half her age. A short sword hung from her waist and a bow was strapped to her saddle.

'A fine morning, Marshall. Forgive me if I don't get down, the main struggle of my day is getting back on.' She smiled, her dark eyes alight. Vent knew that to be a lie. Mon had been instrumental in the defence of the city and had worked tirelessly since in organising supplies and equipment.

'Another patrol?' Magus Vent asked. Mon nodded in acknowledgement.

'Yes, Marshall. I'm taking a squad to sweep the edges of the borderlands. Will collect any stragglers and supplies and send them your way.' A number of villages, farms and homesteads stretched across the plains and fields of Danaria, and also into the hinterlands or borderlands. These semi-wild plains, with their rolling hills and small woods made up the northern border of Danaria and stretched beyond the arm of protection and justice that the Red Throne had previously offered. Vent knew that Mon would need her wits about her there, and made a silent prayer to Kani, the warrior and hunters god, that her arrows would fly true if they were needed. As well as any Cassalian invaders, Mon and her squad would have the possibilities of outlaws and bandit gangs to deal with.

'Good hunting. Kani be with you.' She flashed a smile at the Marshall's words and pulled her hood up, wheeled her horse around and broke into a trot back the way she had come. Whilst her little sorties had brought a large number of refugees to the city, desperate for protection, but also bringing much needed tools and food, Magus Vent knew the real reason for Mon to have donned her armour and strung her bow again. Her friend, Bex, was out there somewhere. The tall samakan woman had been part of Prince Garlen's rescue party for his sisters, but nothing had been heard from them since Garlen had activated the magic charm that had notified his mother that the rescue had been successful. Whilst he understood Mon's desire to find Bex and her worries about her safety, he had no doubt that the sword for hire and her symbiotic 'demon' would be safe. Bex had found Ishtara, an escapee from another world who had travelled to Maingard to warn of the impending Cassalian doom. In order to save both their lives, Ishtara had fused with Bex, and they now shared the same body, able to transform from one form to another. He had been witness to a part transition, when Bex and Ishtara had warned the court. He winced as he realised that had been moments before the assassination of King Anjoan, and as the King's Marshall, that had been his first failure.

He busied himself with reports and messages whilst he waited for the galleys to arrive. As he had estimated, it wasn't long and he soon found himself striding back along the seawall, Sumtor in tow along with a platoon of guards. He nodded with grim satisfaction as he noticed the dark form of Ser Gavan tag along afterwards. He had the same tunic on that he had worn from the battle, a good washing or two had done little to remove any of the blood. He had shaved as well, his face now as clean shaven as his head.

The first galley had docked, further up the seawall due to the work clearing wreckage in the harbour. The oarsmen on either side had pulled their large oars in. These rowers were known as thals, men who owed money or had been sentenced to imprisonment. These men signed on to serve in this role to cover the sentence that the city had imposed. Their debts were covered by the crown, or their sentences reduced accordingly.

Dockers and sailors moored the large bireme and the gangplank was lowered.

Shales emerged on deck and the marines he had led for the last year snapped to attention, the sailors and thals on his flagship giving a cheer as well. The Hawk smirked as the cheer from the seawall was rather subdued in comparison.

Shales was a big man, almost as tall as his brother-in-law had been. His red hair was tied back behind his head, the long locks flowing over the immense wolf skin that he wore as a mantle. His beard was neatly trimmed to the length of a dagger and braided with gold wire. Beneath the mantle he wore the hardened leather cuirass of the marines, and a mail skirt hung from his waist to cover his immense thighs.

He stepped of the plank followed by his lieutenants and staff. Magus Vent steeled himself, aware that this first meeting between the two in several years would set their future relationship. Since the battle for Tannaheim, Vent had assumed the command of the city, taking on the role mainly from honour and a need to redeem himself from the failure of his own role as the King's Marshall. There had been moments, hours even, when he had looked forward to Shales returning, longing to pass on the mantle to the Queen's brother, and eager to retire back to his family. But he knew he couldn't walk away and do that. His entire life had been for the King and Danaria, and he was still sure Garlen was not only out there somewhere, but would return, ready to be crowned and lead his people to victory. Until that day, despite the lure of his family, he would do anything to avenge his King and Queen's death, even if it meant kowtowing to Shales.

Shales puffed his chest out and approached the Marshall. He was a head taller than the older man and a good twenty-five years younger. Behind him stood the four members of his close staff, including the youngest son of the traitor Dutte, Albron Dutte.

'You have been busy, Magus.' Shales half turned towards the city and seemed to indicate the hive of activity taking place. The Hawk frowned slightly. Was the man an idiot? Did he expect him to sit on his arse after the repelling of the invaders and do nothing?

'Of course, Lord Shales. The plight of the citizens come first, ensuring shelter and food, all the time making sure that we pose an adequate threat to the invaders, ready to take the fight to them. I thought that evident.'

Shales laughed, a booming laugh made all the more unpleasant in the Hawk's eyes because it was forced, artificial and full of contempt. He turned to his staff and they joined his merriment. That's right, thought Magus Vent, laugh you little shit - and you, Albron Dutte, because if I find that you even share any of your father's traits and thoughts about the Red Throne, your head will be sitting on a pike next to his.

'No, Marshall. I don't mean this,' he waved his hands in the direction of the workers. 'You managed to let my brother-in-law, our King, get murdered in your very presence, lose his daughters and that drunkard of a whoreson, Garlen.' He reached out to clasp Vent by the shoulder. 'Oh yes, and managed to let my bitch of a sister destroy half the city and herself. Remarkable! I can't believe you let the Lord of the Inns leave the city, or why he went. Were the taverns running dry?

'I can only imagine what I would have returned to if your messenger ship hadn't reached me for another month. At least you have left me half a city to rule.'

ABOUT THE AUTHOR

If you are reading this in 2032, Carl F Northwood is a driving force in Epic Fantasy, and the name behind many Hollywood and Netflix blockbusters.

If, however, you are reading this before then, Carl F Northwood was inspired by a misspent youth playing Dungeons and Dragons and reading illustrious tomes detailing the deeds of heroes such as Fafhrd, the Grey Mouser, Conan and many others. Now he creates his own heroes and heroines, all eager to wield swords or mutter mysterious incantations at sinister villains.

He lives in a leafy, coastal village in East Yorkshire.

Lightning Source UK Ltd.
Milton Keynes UK
UKHW021814240322
400545UK00005B/35